INNOVERA YAKOV

INNOVERA YAKOV

The Journey of a Thousand Eyes

To the Forest
Book Shop
thank you
Love
Kia

KIA GARRIQUES

First published in Great Britain in 2013 by Story Star Publishing Ltd

A CIP catalogue record for this book is available in The British Library.

ISBN 978 0 9575314 0 6

Cover design by Milly Mackenzie

Book typesetting by Wordzworth Limited

Story Star Publishing Ltd
86-90 Paul St,
3rd Floor,
London, EC2A 4NE,
www.storystarpublishing.com

To Miss Dart

for your strength and caring and above all,
for your inspiration.

ACKNOWLEDGMENTS

My thanks and gratitude to my mother and sister for helping to make this book a reality; my brother-in law Dean Straker for his friendship and support and Jacob Ross – mentor, agent and advisor for his unfailing belief in my work.

Heartfelt thanks also to the amazing team at Story Star Publishing: Rochelle Sampy, Jane Haynes and Elinor Rees. Yours have been a valuable contribution to the successful outcome of this whole process.

To Cedric Freppel, Milly Mackenzie, Kevin Par, Sarah Robertson, Taylor Parr, Lee-Anne Van Pelt and Louise Pierre thank you for your assistance. And to all of my readers and the beautiful people that I have had the pleasure of meeting and engaging with, I feel deeply indebted to you.

CHAPTER ONE

ALL THE students had rushed out from the Learning Dome. They were standing in tight, excited groups in front of the crystal structure, at a safe distance from the highest Golkan tree in Innovera Yakov.

Part mineral, part flesh, the branches of the great Golkan were thick and dark and dripping rivulets of acid. The topmost branches pierced the clouds and the shadows of its lower branches stretched several miles beyond. No one had ever attempted to climb to the top of even the smallest Golkan tree without being poisoned by its fluids. If that did not kill them, the purple sail-like leaves would wrap around their bodies and digest them. Or they would simply die from the effort. Now there they were - Krave and his crazy friend, Skylar - preparing to race to the top of the most formidable Golkan in Innovera Yakov.

Ayana hugged herself and shivered. She stood slightly apart from the others staring at the boys. Skylar was thick and broad as a boulder. The muscles of his arms and legs stood out in lumps. He was still grinning triumphantly at the gathering of students after he threw down the challenge; and Krave, to save face in front of their companions, reluctantly accepted.

These two Students were so different, it was almost impossible to imagine them as friends. Krave was tall and upright as a brightly polished spear with a beautiful crop of golden hair that cascaded down his back in waves. Even from the distance that she was standing, Ayana sensed his nervousness.

She projected her thoughts at them, hoping that she could stop their recklessness by turning their minds to something else: perhaps an air-sprint towards the distant blue peaks of the Ishu Mountains, and back; or a bout of Sky-Roll where they would pit their speed and strength against each other in the air without endangering their lives so stupidly. They might break a limb or two while working up the other students to a frenzy of excitement, but at least they would recover and mend - with her help of course — and Innovera Yakov would settle back to its routine of rest and study.

Ayana closed her eyes and concentrated. *Ignore him, Krave, its suicide.* But suddenly she found she could not reach Krave. Something was blocking her thought-flow.

She looked up quickly. Her eyes fell on the two tallest, most striking girls amongst the crowd of milling students — Gamma and Blu Tara. The twins were side by side. Gamma's hands were covering her face and she was about to cry. Blu Tara's mane of hair which ran down her back like a silken waterfall had become bright red and animated. The mineral lens that protected everyone from those terrible eyes of hers was bright pulsating cobalt.

A chill ran through Ayana. *Blu Tara. She's blocking me. I can't believe she's doing this. Why?'*

Gamma, who could have stopped Blu Tara, was obviously too distressed to notice.

Ayana turned her attention back towards the boys under the tree. Again she sensed the reluctance in Krave. He looked even less sure about the challenge now, although Skylar's voice was louder and more boastful.

'The winner — and that will certainly be me — the winner gets whatever he asks of the other, anytime he asks for it. You big enough for this, Krave? Are you big enough?'

Ayana could see the spittle around Skylar's cavernous mouth. The massive muscles of his shoulders were twitching as he goaded Krave. The skin of his arms was just as rough as the bark of the Golkan tree. Ayana wondered what Krave *liked* about this dangerous lump of mouth and muscle. She did not know a single student who got on with him. Skylar did not just bring them all trouble. Skylar *was* trouble. He thought nothing of forcing the weaker students to do things that put their lives in danger. And yet the bond between Skylar and Krave seemed unbreakable. In fact they called each other 'Brother.'

Ayana kept her eyes on Krave's face. She loved ...looking... at him. His skin seemed to gather all the light of their Innoveran sun and change it to a golden glow. *And when he smiles....* Ayana took a long, deep breath and tried to calm her heart.

Blu Tara was still blocking her thoughts. Hard as she tried, Ayana could not get through to Krave and Skylar. Blu Tara's thought-words crept into her mind and echoed in her head, *Save your energy, Scarface. Let the two fools die. Let the Golkan suck their bodies dry and feed on them.*

The tree had sensed the intentions of the boys. From deep within its core, the soft drumming of its heartbeat had begun to rise.

Krave and Skylar suddenly appeared to change their minds. Ayana felt sure of it. Even Skylar was quiet now. They stood a little way from the great Golkan looking up to where its massive branches seemed to brush the burning Innoveran sun. Surely they could see for themselves that there was no safe way up the tree – not with those bristling spikes, the poison and those life-sucking leaves.

Krave and Skylar turned around as if to tell the crowd that they had changed their minds. But then, they all heard it at the same time – even if it was no louder than a whisper: Blu Tara's soft, musical chuckle followed by her deep, caressing voice.

'You call yourselves Innoverans? Surely you are not! You make us drop our lessons, drag us out here with the racket you were making - for what? Just to show everyone how scared you are? Just to prove that you don't have the courage of an Earthbound?'

Blu Tara turned to face the students. 'Look at them! Even the great Odors Apeno must be ashamed of little Krave and Skylar.'

Blu Tara's voice imitated Skylar's, 'I will race you up the Golkan Tree and then you'll be forever mine.'

A wave of laughter filled the air.

'Tara, stop it! Stop it now!' Gamma's skin was pulsing with outrage; the lens over her eyes had darkened.

'Ah!' Blu Tara chuckled. 'I agree, let's leave the cowards to themselves. Because that tree was sure to get them and not even Scarface here...Oh, sorry I mean Ayana our little healer, would have been able to save them.'

'Can't you see what she is doing?' Gamma shouted. 'Can't you see she's...?'

But it was too late. A roar of anger came from Skylar. 'Stardog,' he snarled. Blu Tara smiled at the insult.

'Let's go!' Krave shouted back and the two leapt onto the lower branches. They began racing up the tree, criss-crossing the poisonous bark and the dripping branches with such speed it drew gasps of admiration from the crowd.

With every leap, the snapping blue leaves swung back to close over them. The Golkan's heart was thundering as Krave's and Skylar's feet struck against the bark like metal rods. Ayana felt its pain.

Soon they were no more than dots in the distance and yet Ayana, like all the others, could hear every breath they took as they hurtled towards the top.

Just before the halfway point, when Krave was about to overtake his friend, Skylar pushed him hard. Krave hollered out in panic, desperately wrapping his arms around a branch. But he regained his balance instantly and pushed on, narrowing the gap between himself and Skylar. A buzz of excitement rose up from the crowd. Krave was fast – a golden streak against the black body of the tree.

The Golkan's heart was pounding so furiously now even the grass on which the students stood vibrated. The throbbing was unbearable. And Ayana felt her own heart rate rising. She knew that it could not go on like this much longer. All her senses told her that something terrible was about to happen.

'You're hurting it,' Ayana yelled, but when she looked up both boys were out of sight. *Krave*, she whispered, trying to block out the pain she felt from the tree. Ayana closed her eyes and waited for the worst.

Suddenly she heard screams. All the students, except Gamma and Blu Tara, were rushing towards the Dome in a wave of scrambling bodies. Ayana looked up. Then she joined the screaming.

Two shapes were plummeting towards the ground. No doubt the poison had penetrated their skin and rendered them unconscious.

Anticipating the fall, the rest of the Students had scrambled from the area. The bodies came crashing to the ground. The tree stopped whipping and flailing. Its heartbeat immediately died down.

Everything had suddenly gone quiet. Gamma leapt forward towards Krave, but just as she moved Blu Tara appeared in front of her. Her eyes were now a crimson red. 'Too late,' she said. 'They asked for it.'

Gamma shrank back and dropped onto the grass at Blu Tara's feet.

Ayana stirred. Her heart was so filled up with Gamma's sadness, there was no room left for her own feelings. Gamma was as different from her twin sister as a warm breeze from a firestorm. She was full of love for everyone – and wouldn't hurt a Starfly.

'Save him!' Gamma begged. She rose to her feet but Blu Tara pushed her down and stood over her. And still Ayana heard Gamma's inner plea, 'Please Ayana, save him.'

Ayana walked towards the broken bodies on the grass. She knew that every student's eye was on her now. They had seen her heal the wings of damaged flame-birds, or the strained ligaments of reckless students when they collided during race-games, especially the dangerous Sky-Rolls that Skylar loved to challenge the other boys to. But she'd never been faced with two broken bodies with barely any life in them. And Ayana knew that once she went to help them she could not afford to fail. For, as they'd all been told by the Voice in the Learning Dome,

When you use your gifts for anything, all responsibility shifts to you. It is the way of Innovera.

'Help him, Ayana. Please.' Somehow Gamma had broken away from Blu Tara and was standing beside Ayana.

Ayana knelt beside Krave and turned her face up towards the five moons of Innovera. As she did so, Blu Tara's thoughts slipped through her head like a tiny blade of ice. *No use, Scarface. They've already left us. Let them disappear.* Ayana blocked her out.

'Odors Apeno,' she whispered, 'hear me now. Fill me with the cold life of your moons.'

Ayana bowed her head and waited. Everything was still. The distant howling of the winds that beat against the Eshu Mountains reached them. Now she rested her hand on Krave's throat and every broken limb, every bit of tissue that held his beautiful body together became clearly mapped out in her mind. And - yes - deep inside of him she felt the tiny, weakening flame of life.

Only she - Ayana - could feel the cold shower of light that fell on her and seeped though her body. She whispered the words again, and something like a cool wind began to stir in her. She moved her fingers up towards Krave's face. His body bucked, a choked cough erupted from his chest and Krave sat up.

Gamma flung herself at him. 'Krave – Are you all right?' She pressed her face against his neck and stood there shaking.

Krave eased himself out of Gamma's arms, his eyes searching frantically around him. Finally his gaze fell on the broken shape of Skylar sprawled face down the ground. Krave stumbled toward his friend.

'What – what happened to him?' He shouted.

'Same thing that happened to you, Skyworm!' One of the students shouted back. 'Leave that one there, Ayana. He's better off gone. Disappeared! Done with! Nothing but trouble!'

Ayana barely heard him. She was renewing her powers. Krave had taken every bit of energy from her. Now there was hardly any time. But she had to finish what she set out to do. Much as she disliked Skylar, her role was to heal. Odors Apeno's words came back to her.

Every Innoveran has a reason for being here; even the ones you believe are bad. Your purpose is to heal and not to judge.

It would be too late for Skylar unless she tried to save him now. And that meant only one thing: together with the little energy she had already gathered from the moons, she had to use her own life force. And she knew that it might kill her.

Once again, Ayana closed her eyes focusing her mind until she felt her body sink into a pool of blue, throbbing light. She knelt over his body. She placed her palms over his face, braced herself and summoned all of her remaining strength into her hands. Slowly a wind gathered around her as a rush of dizziness began racing to consume her.

So that he may live, I give him of my own life. May the moons of Innovera save us.

A wall of darkness closed in on her vision like a collapsing tunnel. She blacked out.

CHAPTER TWO

AYANA AWOKE to the gentle humming of her Bubble-Pod. She was stretched out on her cot and a protective sheet - thin and light as Innovera air - was covering her. She felt grateful for the comforting energy it was seeping through her body.

Soft hands touched her face. She swung her head away, then realised that it was Vinton, her friend and guardian who always turned up from nowhere whenever she was in distress. He was there beside her and yet she could see straight through his little compact body to the curved crystalline walls of her room.

Sometimes she wondered if Vinton was real, or whether she invented him with her powerful mind. He always knew what she was thinking and she couldn't block him from her thoughts. Yet he had a voice that was all his own which sounded like a child's and she knew that Vinton adored every bit of her.

Vinton was the only one who liked her whole face. Sometimes when she was asleep, he would part the white curtain of hair that hid the right side of her face and she woke to find him staring at her with admiration in his eyes.

'Ever look at them proper, Myana? Such lovely pattern.'

Ayana touched the peeling scars that ran from her right ear

all the way down to her cheeks and glared at Vinton. 'Why would I want to look at scars that spoil my face, Vinton? You know anyone who likes being ugly?'

'Ugly! Not ugly, Ayana. I telling you always — it's beautiful. Ab-a-sol-loot-ly lovely. A map maybe? Maybe secret map that Odors Apeno put on face?'

Ayana smiled bitterly at Vinton. 'A map that scares everyone away from me?'

A thought suddenly occurred to her. 'Vinton! Who brought me home? How did they get inside my Pod?'

'Well, funny thing that was. Vinton threw a sly smile at the ceiling. 'Pod won't open to no one else, not even to me, Vinton. And you unconscious. And...'

'Tell me, Vinton!'

'Well, not Skylar. Pod will never open for him. Skylar very lucky boy. Saved him you did. He recover now in Healing Dome.'

'Vinton!'

'Lifted you like his very own beloved, The Golden One did. He was almost weeping with gratitude. And you know what? He kissed you, very tenderly I must say, on your left ear.'

Ayana felt her heart flip over. 'Krave? Did he see, did he….' she could not finish the question.

'No,' Vinton wagged a finger at her. 'He did not look scar-side, Ayana. The Golden One did not. But,' Vinton wagged another finger, 'Pod open up to him. And that only happen if...'

'Don't say it, Vinton.' Ayana covered her face with her hands.

Vinton said it anyway. 'Only if you really want him come inside with you.'

'But I was unconscious!'

'Not the point, Ayana. Point is, everybody see Ayana Pod-home open door for Golden One – no problem!'

While Vinton chattered on, Ayana's mind drifted back to the incident by the Golkan tree: the boys falling out of the sky and hitting the ground with such terrible force and the energy it took from her to bring Krave out of his coma and mend his limbs.

She vaguely remembered kneeling beside Skylar and reaching out to touch his face. After that — well — after that, there was nothing until she woke up in her Pod with Vinton hovering over her.

There was something about it all that frightened her. Not only did Gamma reveal her feelings for Krave to everyone, it was obvious that she was connected to him in a powerful and surprising way. It was clear to Ayana that Krave and Gamma were like that for some time and they had been keeping it secret. How did Gamma manage to cloak so much of her thoughts and feelings from them all? How could her twin, Blu Tara, not known of it? What if they decided to... she could not bring herself to think the word.

And why was the powerful Blu Tara so afraid of this? When Blu invaded Ayana's thoughts, Ayana had also been able to access hers. It was linked to her gift of healing and should never be used to harm another Being. She was different from all the other Innoverans in that way. No one could enter her mind without her knowing what was also in theirs.

Ayana lifted herself from her cot and stared out at the Ishu mountains, past whose peaks they were all forbidden to travel — that was until the day came when they would all be forced to take to the air and face the terrible dangers in the world of darkness just beyond, that they called Verheer. Ayana hugged herself and shivered.

'Vinton, why is Blu Tara so afraid? Why's she so desperate to see Krave die?'

'Krave and Gamma — e-very-body know their secret now. Blu Tara — jealous maybe? Big jealous, I think.'

'It's not jealousy, Vinton; it's fear.'

'They twins; they come together; they die together. Me, Vinton, say it's jealousy.'

'Then why does Gamma want to separate from her?'

'You read what Gamma thinking?'

'No. We all saw it. She couldn't keep away from Krave. If Gamma has to choose, I believe...'

'That answer your question then. That's why Tara want Krave dead. Now, too much question, Myana. You dizzy me with them.'

'Well, like I said, I accessed Blu Tara's thoughts. She's prepared to destroy her own twin sister if it comes to that. Why? That's what I want to know. And if Blu Tara knows I know this what do you think she'll do? What would happen if — Vinton?'

Ayana looked up, Vinton was no longer there.

CHAPTER THREE

'BETTER NOW?' Ryder asked. Ryder was a quiet, handsome Male - as tall and slim as an Innoveran willow.

'I'm fine now, thanks.' Ayana continued walking towards the Learning Dome.

'Glad to hear that,' Ryder smiled. 'Can I, erm, walk you over?'

'Won't be necessary, thank you.' Ayana smiled at him and hurried on.

Unhappy is the male who satisfies the eyes and not the heart. Those were Vinton's words. She remembered them every time Ryder reached out to her.

His manner with her was always gentle but he barely looked her in the face. During their time of Rest he would go to the furthest end of the playing grounds and practise with his spear. It was a long crystal pole that flew from his hand like a bolt of lightning.

As the seasons passed, he picked out objects that were further away and smaller. Sometimes his target was so small it was barely visible in the distance: a red dot, a pinprick of colour. He never missed.

There was a trick he did that Ayana found unnerving. Ryder would ask a volunteer to stand close to him. Then without looking up Ryder shot the spear directly above their heads. They would watch it sail into the air and then curve downwards. Very few of them had the nerve to follow the whistling descent of the weapon. It landed with a sharp *thwack* in the small gap between Ryder and his volunteer.

He did these things to impress her. He would glance at her as if asking for her approval. She always pretended she was not watching.

He irritated her; made her feel guilty and self-conscious, especially when he went out to the foothills of the Ishu Mountains and returned with a cluster of crystals that looked like a Golkan Lily. Once it was a scent-stone that filled their heads with wonderful waking dreams. He never put them in her hands. He laid them at the entrance of her Pod so that she could not miss them when she left or entered.

She never took them. Accepting Ryder's gifts would be opening his heart for hurt. She did not want to leave him hanging on to false hope.

How could she bring herself to tell young Ryder that the only Innoveran - the very thought of whom made her breathless - was Krave Solan?

Anyway, if she told him he would probably laugh. Who was she to even dare to want the most desired male in Innovera Yakov? Krave Solan - desperately loved by the most formidable and striking female amongst them all: Gamma the gentle Fire-Queen herself.

That was why she did not thank him for his presents or take them from where he left them. That was why she pretended she did not notice him.

What does he see in me anyway? What does he really want?

CHAPTER FOUR

BLU TARA was raging. Her hair had gone fiery red and her skin had turned sizzling amber. The grass around her feet was smouldering. She switched her head to one of the high peaks of the Ishu Mountains and lifted her lens. A bright streak erupted from her eyes. The top of the mountain exploded in a haze of smoke and fire.

Moments later they all heard the distant boom of collapsing rocks. A short while later the vibrations reached them.

The students were gathered at the entrance of the Learning Dome. Many of them rushed back inside and were now staring out at Blu Tara with apprehensive eyes.

She had been at it from the time she left her Pod. Even the Voice in the Learning Dome fell silent. Gamma walked into the fire that swirled around Blu Tara and grabbed her sister's shoulder.

A panicked voice rose up from the students at the entrance of the Dome, 'Quick! They are going to merge! They will destroy everything.'

There was a stampede for the safety of the building.

Now only Blu Tara and Gamma were left in the open space outside. That was what they all thought until Blu Tara turned and saw Krave leaning against the smooth walls of a nearby Pod. He was looking calmly in her direction. His bright blue crystalline eyes were glittering and the fingers of his right hand were curled in slightly towards his palm.

'Krave!' Gamma shouted. She tried to run towards him. Blu Tara grabbed her arm and pulled her back. Gamma's panicked gaze did not leave Krave's right hand. Only she knew what would happen once he straightened out those amazingly long fingers in self-defence or anger. During one of their many secret meetings he astonished her with the power he possessed in them. He pulverised rocks and melted metals to impress her. And when he finished his display, he smiled and told her that it was nothing compared to what he could really do.

Blu Tara turned to face Krave. Her face was twisted in a wicked smile.

Krave moved further out into the open, his glittering eyes never leaving Blu Tara's face.

Blu Tara released Gamma. She lifted her chin at Krave and grinned. 'Got you now. That little show was all for you, Cutie. And it's gonna be your last.'

'Blu, you can't!' Gamma threw herself at her sister.

'Stop me!' Blu Tara cried.

'You do not understand,' Gamma screamed. 'All three of us will!'

Krave was now well away from the colony. His golden hue had been replaced by a pale metallic shimmer.

'Let's merge,' Blu Tara whispered. 'Let's supernova him.'

'No! You stupid girl, I won't!'

'Then I'll do it on my own.'

'Stop it,' Gamma raged. 'He's not just what you see. He's a Sol...' Gamma covered her mouth with her hands.

'Look at him,' Blu Tara jeered. 'Gone white with fear. He really thinks he can take me on!'

'He can,' Gamma snapped. Her skin had darkened and her eyes were now a smouldering sapphire. 'I'm telling you he can.'

Blu Tara raised her hand towards her lens.

Krave's right hand instantly turned a coruscating silver.

It was then that Gamma moved - so swiftly it took both of them off-guard.

In a flash, she moved in the middle of the field between them. Her hair was spread out in a flaming fan. Legs apart and drawing herself to full height, Gamma looked every bit as formidable as Blu Tara.

'You'll strike me first,' she said to both of them. 'Go on! Go on! Then neither of you will have me.'

Blu Tara flew to the right of Gamma; Gamma followed instantly. Blu Tara swung away – fast as a blur – but Gamma moved with her, remaining always in her sister's line of fire.

'Get out of the way,' Blu Tara screamed.

'No!'

'Get away, Gamma.'

'Make me!'

'Then I'll...' Blu Tara took to the air. As if she'd read her mind, Gamma rose with Blu blocking every move her sister made.

Gamma's voice rang through the Innoveran air. 'He will destroy you too, Blu. He's a Solar just like us.'

By then they had travelled a great distance from the Dome. The students came out to follow the drama between the quarrelling sisters.

Krave had moved further out too, so that if Blu Tara managed to get past Gamma, the students or the buildings of the colony would not be affected. After a while, he turned his back on them although his hand remained a burning white.

No one would know how the battle might have turned out in the end. Many of the students blamed Blu Tara for what happened next. They claimed that it was the mixture of fire and dust and ice that Blu Tara stirred up in the mountains that triggered the solar wave. Others said that it was Odors Apeno's way of showing disapproval.

It happened suddenly. The bright hues of the sky paled as if a light had been switched off. A wave of choking heat and gases sent them scurrying for the shelter of their Pods and the Learning Dome. Great waves of fiery wind and dust rolled in on them. The screams of the students who had been furthest out filled the air.

Ayana knew nothing of the trouble outside. She had been in her Pod searching for answers to the many questions that plagued her constantly:

Who am I, Vinton? Why aren't I as lovely as the others? How do I really feel about Krave? Is it love? If it is not love, why did my Pod welcome him without my permission? If it is love, why am I so attracted to the strange male in Verheer? Can I love two males at the same time? Is it possible? And if it is possible; is it right? How can I make Krave love me? Where did the scars on my face come from? Why can all the others fly and I have to use my Sylva to move through air?

Vinton did not answer her.

When she left her Pod, Ayana was so lost in thought she did not notice the fiery sky; nor did she see the panicked gesturing of the students from behind the transparent walls of the Learning Dome.

It was only when she smelt the burning in the air and looked at the grass beneath her feet that she realised the danger.

The world around her was blindingly lit up. She heard howling in the distance as if all the demons of the underworld of Verheer were let loose on Innovera Yakov.

The horns of all the crystal domes in Innovera Yakov were blaring.

Soon the acid rains would come. They would eat into her skin and leave her even more deeply scarred – that was if she managed to survive it. Ayana knew of no one who had ever survived a Solar wave.

The first few drops hit the trees, withering their delicate leaves immediately. Ayana was halfway between the Learning Dome and her Pod. The Dome was safer and she had no time.

She pulled the protective membrane over her face that Innoverans carried with them all the time. She could not make it to the shelter in time but still she released her Sylva, lodged against her left breastbone, and dropped it at her feet. The Sylva spread bright and shimmering in front of her, like the wings of an Innoveran Sailbird. Ayana stepped on it. She was about to shoot off, when the first heat wave struck her. The Sylva shrank, and she dropped onto the grass at the foot of a Golkan tree.

All around her she could hear the screaming of those who had been too far out in the open, as the fire ate their flesh and reduced them to nothing. There came the awful groan of Golkan trees as they hit the ground, followed by the heave of the earth as it sucked everything that had fallen, back into itself. *If the tree she was sheltering under fell....*

Ayana looked up from beneath her tree to see Gamma and Blu-Tara high in the air, just ahead of the first storm-wave. She watched them merge and became a single body with two bright heads. Fused like that Ayana knew that the twins were now indestructible. Then she saw Krave moving like a golden arc of light towards the sanctuary of the Learning Dome. She called out to him, but before she could catch her breath to raise her voice again he was inside the edifice.

Then the rest were all in – at least those who had escaped. The Golkan tree thrashed and heaved above her head fighting to hold its ground as the air began to burn and the heat intensified.

Ayana saw the heavy crystal door of the Dome slide shut, while shimmering wing-like sheets rose up from all sides and completely masked the building.

It's not my time, it's not my time to go, she whispered – angrily, defiantly. *It cannot be, for I am the only healer here. Innovera needs me.*

She remembered the words of the voice:

It is only in times of desperation and defeat that your full powers will come forth. But you must believe this. To believe is to survive.

I will, she shouted, *I will!*

She was sweating and breathing heavily. Ayana lifted her eyes at the moons of Innovera. *All my life I've done your bidding; now do mine. Save me!*

The earth convulsed beneath her. The Golkan tree came crashing down. Its great roots hung high above her head, dripping its poisons. Gradually, the heat became more bearable. She found she was surrounded by a transparent dome that looked so fragile she felt she could poke a finger through it and break it like a bubble. Ayana searched for the source of the apparition and realised with some amazement that it was emanating out of her.

Locked inside her personal fortress, sweat poured from her body. She glanced over at the Dome in which so many of her student friends found refuge. Had they forgotten her? Couldn't someone have thought-messaged her and warned her?

'They fools, Myana, who fly away when trouble. You no fly but you fight fire with bubble.'

'Not now, Vinton,' Ayana snapped. She had to keep her thoughts focused. She only needed to hold out a little while longer and then everything would be back to normal. She was still exhausted from healing Krave and Skylar. Now, with having to hold this protective shield over herself she felt like collapsing.

'They jealous you, perhaps? They...'

'Go away or I will banish you forever. It's not even like you're real. Else, you would get me out of this.'

'I did. We did.' Vinton said indignantly.

'We? Who's "we", Vinton – who's...'

'You safe, Myana. Vinton must go now.'

Vinton was right. Just as suddenly as it appeared, the cloud vanished. The heat wave melted away as though it had never happened. The air slowly returned to normal. The sky changed to a glossy green. A heavy breeze appeared from nowhere and instantly cooled the area. Where the fallen trees crumbled into the earth, infant plants emerged in their place, covering the ground in new growth. They grew quickly, their leaves flapping in the air as if they were applauding Apeno's destructive performance.

Ayana waited until she heard the students emerging from the Dome. With a swift wave of her hands, the bubble around her folded and disappeared into her chest.

'One of these days you're going to get roasted.' Blu Tara chuckled.

The twins' appearance made her jump. Their sudden arrival filled the air with a hot breezy residue.

Blu Tara flicked her jet-black hair. 'What would we do if you went—Poof—along with the other losers?'

Gamma reached for Ayana's hands and squeezed them gently. 'When we realised you were missing it was too late. Can you find it in your heart to forgive us?'

Ayana glanced around her. The students were scattered all over the open field now filled with grass and flowers. Laughter and conversation filled the air. It was almost as if they had forgotten what had just happened.

'I wonder if they would forget me too, like they have forgotten those who have just been taken.' It was one of the great mysteries of their world. When an Innoveran perished or passed away, memories of them were as brief as a passing breeze. Not long after it was as if they'd never been there.

Blu Tara came and stood in front of Ayana. She walked as though she was floating on air. There was not a hair out of place, or a wrinkle on her garment. *And*, Ayana thought, *she doesn't have a horrific scar on the left side of her face like me.*

The lens over Blu Tara's eyes was shifting between green and amber. Ayana felt Blu Tara trying to probe her thoughts. She quickly cloaked her mind and turned her back on her.

'Who are you?' Blu Tara queried.

'You know who I am.' Ayana spun round to face her.

'How did you survive the storm? You are the only one who survived – how come? What did you do?'

I survived and that's what matters. If you'd been looking out for your fellow Students more might have survived.'

'Are you suggesting that I'm selfish?' Blu Tara moved closer to her. Even when she was angry she was beautiful. 'What did you do to save yourself? I want to know.'

'You don't scare me, Blu.'

'What are you hiding, Scarface? Nobody knows exactly where you've come from.'

'Same with you,' Ayana shot back, same with all of us. Do *you* know where you're from?'

'But you're almost like an Earthbound.' Blu Tara pointed at Ayana's face. 'Flesh that burns and never heals. You can't fly without that thing,' Blu Tara pointed a sizzling finger at the Sylva. 'And you sweat. Only Earthbounds sweat.'

'Let Ayana be, Blu Tara,' Gamma cut in. 'She's our only healer. Won't that make anyone special?'

Blu Tara pulled away. 'There's more to you and I'll find out. I always find out. And one more thing,' Blu Tara threw a wicked smile at her. 'While you were out there frying I heard you calling Krave. Krave was the only one you called to. Why?'

Ayana's heart leapt with surprise. 'You heard me?'

Ayana's response was a mistake. Now Gamma was looking at her - very, very closely - and her lens had darkened to a throbbing purple.

'Really?' Gamma said.

Ayana recovered quickly. 'Krave owes me. I saved his life. Besides who else could I have called to? You said you heard me call for help. Why didn't you two do something?'

Her words seemed to put Gamma at ease. 'Sorry, Ayana, I honestly didn't hear you.'

'I'm not finished yet Scarface,' Blu Tara hissed. 'Here's another question: what were you doing in your Pod while you were meant to be out here? Everyone else was.'

'I was resting. I forgot. That's all.'

'Leave her alone!' Gamma grabbed Blu Tara's hand. 'We have to talk; I haven't forgiven you.'

Ayana watched nervously as the twins disappeared into their Pod.

CHAPTER FIVE

THE STUDENTS stood in the Grounds of the Learning Dome and watched Gamma and Blu Tara take to the air together. The twin left two burning trails of fire behind them — one gemstone pink, the other a blazing amethyst as they headed for the stratosphere of Innovera Yakov.

Up there the freezing atmosphere cooled their skins.

Innovera Yakov was spread out below them in all its glory. In the east the shimmering green peaks of the Ishu Mountains penetrated the clouds. Directly below, they could see the colony of Pods in which they and the other Students lived. They glistened like bright drops of water in the multi-coloured sunlight. Off to the other side was the twinkling roof of the Learning Dome at the very edges of the Golkan Forest.

The larger of their two amber suns was directly above the other. And the mysterious blue moon of Dotan was at its very brightest. All this meant that it was the Time of Rest.

While Gamma and Blu Tara climbed the air, the other Students would be returning to their Pods to sink into the wide yellow cot that floated above the floor. Before they closed their eyes, a soft transparent membrane would detach itself from the curved ceiling and settle over them. When they woke up, their energies would be replenished.

'We shouldn't be up here,' Blu Tara said, throwing a quick glance at her sister. 'We should be resting and replenishing ourselves.'

Gamma did not respond.

They were up here, way above their world for the privacy and the quiet. It was Gamma who insisted on this meeting.

When their colony was no more than a smudge of colour beneath them, Gamma swung around.

'What's your problem, Blu! Why do you want to kill Krave? And it's as if you were prepared to fight me too? What's Krave Solan done to you?'

'Done or doing,' Blu Tara flared. 'Listen Gamma!' Blu Tara's hand reached out to touch her sister.

'Don't touch me. I'm not sure I want you near me after what you did today. I'm asking you again, what's your problem with Krave Solan?'

'You know what the problem is so don't talk as if you're dumb. You did a very silly thing blocking me like that. I would have crushed that Stardog before he could wink.'

'That's what you think. I was trying to tell you something.'

'That he has some kind of hidden power? I heard you Gamma. I would have crushed him anyway. He was asking for it.'

'Edict A, Blu Tara — the very first thing we learned when we got here. You forget the teachings of The Voice. To seek to destroy your own is to turn against yourself and all of Eden Gobad,'

'Unless you're certain they'll destroy you.' Blu Tara cut in fiercely. 'I'm fighting for my life here, Gamma — your life and mine. Do I have to tell you what you already know?'

'They say we're twins; we're not just that. Twins are what you get in the ancient world of Earthbounds where males and females merge in a brief and clumsy frenzy. Two new Beings incubate inside a little Pod the female carries in her body. And in the end two smaller Beings just like them emerge.

We — me, you — are not like that. We come from the same flame. We share a single core. We are complete only when we fuse.'

'So!' Blu Tara threw an angry glance at Gamma. 'What happens when you run off with Krave Solan? I'll tell you what: you go somewhere secret and you merge, or try your hardest to; and if he's not for you, as I believe, you're both destroyed. On the slim chance that it happens, you become something else. Either way, where does it leave me?'

'If that Stardog manages to merge with you I lose half of what I am. You become something different. Well, I tell you now Gamma, I'm not going to be sitting doing nothing while that happens. And yes, that frightens the hell out of me — you leaving me or dying with that, that *Male*. Because either way I lose.'

'Get used to it, Blu Tara. My life is mine.'

'No, it's not; it's ours. To lose you to him is to lose too much...'

Gamma was silent for a long while, her eyes fixed on the darkness that hung like a great black curtain pulled around the edges of their world. Blu Tara followed her gaze, and was as distracted as Gamma was by it. The Voice in the Learning Dome spoke many times about that darkness. That great dark boundary that encircled Innovera Yakov was where their world ended and the Underplace, Verheer, began.

When Gamma finally spoke, her tone was gentler.

'I understand all this, Blu. I know the risk. I fight myself about it all the time. I try to break away from him. But I can't. I give up when I see him. It's like something in him is calling me. Dragging me towards him. It's like Krave's carrying another world inside of him and it holds the key to who I really am.'

'You need a Male to tell you who you are?'

'A time may come when you too will love...'

Blu Tara's laugh was sharp and short.

'Love! She's telling *me* about love. You think you know all about it; don't you? You, who, even while you look like me, talk like me, merge with me, access my thoughts still have everything come to you *before me* without even trying - you think you know what love is?'

Blu Tara stared her sister in the face. 'Let me tell you what you don't know about love, Gamma. It is a curse. You will scoop out your core and abandon it just to have the Being that you love. You will steal another person's life force if it makes it easier to get it. You will abandon the world you have been cradled in, betray everything and everyone you care for. You'll give up your name for it.'

Blu Tara's voice went soft and dreamy. 'You will gladly close your eyes and embrace the world of darkness. You will kill or die for it. And you will hate yourself for the weakness that it brings on you. So don't talk to me about love.'

Gamma shook her head. 'You're not making sense,' Blu Tara. 'You talk as if... I'm the one who should be upset about all this.'

Blu Tara lifted her hand dismissively. She pointed a hot finger at Gamma. 'Anyway don't forget what we are.'

'And what are we?' Gamma glared at her.

'Different. Strange. Something to be frightened of. Two Beings that can fuse and burn everything to ashes. That's the way they all see us down there. That's what the Stardog wants from you - the powers you possess.

I hate them all. With their suspicious, shiny faces and their empty games. I hate that Voice which drones on and on at us in the Learning Dome as soon as we've finished resting.

Innoverans! All those perfect, pretty Beings; they remember nothing — it's the curse of this shallow, shining world. Tell me, Gamma - what do you remember of the world we come from before your Odors Apeno dumped us here?'

Gamma swung around to face her sister fully. 'Blu Tara! What's got into you? Where's all that coming from? I've never heard you speak like that before. This is about Krave and I- not you!'

Krave and you - don't make me laugh. And, oh! Here's a big difference — between you and I this time, Twin Sister. It's the answer to your question that you brought me up here to ask.' Blu Tara mimicked Gamma's soft and musical voice, *Why do you want to kill Krave?*

Here's the answer, Gamma. I will do whatever I have to do to save myself. I'm the half of you that's not like you. I don't have a weeping heart. Now I'm out of here. I need my Rest.

CHAPTER SIX

WHEN BLU Tara returned to Innovera Yakov, she did not go to their Pod. Instead she alighted on the roof of the Learning Dome and stared down at the Pods glittering like polished quartz in the near distance. Theirs was the largest in the colony. It stood a little way off from the others – a glowing purple that always remained the same colour regardless of the changing light outside.

She was surprised at how much she revealed to Gamma up there in the stratosphere. Gamma was right. She was becoming a danger not only to the others, but also to herself. She had to control her moods. She came too close to exposing the one thing that Gamma should never be aware of. And the consequences...Blu Tara didn't dare think of that. What if her words had awakened Gamma's memories? What if they made Gamma realise who they both were? Till now fragments of their past life surfaced only in her sister's dreams which she, Blu Tara, did everything to persuade her were silly, empty nightmares.

What if Gamma really knew that she too had a weeping heart? In fact, a bleeding one!

Blu Tara closed her eyes and projected her thoughts beyond the boundaries of their world.

Sometimes you hear me calling. Sometimes I think you don't want to see me anymore.

You hardly ever listen. You hardly come now when I call.

What have I done? What have I not done for you! What won't I do?

For you!

Blu Tara's lens darkened to a deep pulsating black as her thoughts returned to Gamma and Krave Solan. Up there above Innovera Yakov, in the stratosphere, Gamma's words ran like a cold white blade across her heart. *It's like Krave's carrying another world inside of him and it holds the key to who I really am.*

She, Blu Tara, was prepared to face every danger Innovera Yakov threw at them: the Solarwaves that appeared from nowhere and consumed the land, the terrible rising floods from the River of a Thousand Eyes and that final deadly quest at the end of their exile in this world that Innoverans called The Journey; but Gamma threatening her existence by giving herself over to Krave was something she could not allow.

One day soon, her sister and Krave Solan will not be able to hold themselves back.

They will bring their bodies together and breathe in each other's energy. They will try to merge. If they are wrong for each other, they will die and disappear.

If they succeed they will become powerful new beings, separate but connected, like I am now with my sister, each adding the powers of the other to their own.

Blu Tara closed her eyes and projected her mind once more.

Yours is the edict I will live by. Yours are the words that live in me.

What I want, I have. What I can't have, I destroy.

CHAPTER SEVEN

ALONE IN her Pod, Ayana thought about the tall, dark-haired Being who lived in Verheer. This was what she was doing before she left her Pod and wandered – almost fatally into the Solarwave. She'd been trying to enter the forbidden world of the Verheerans with her mind.

Earlier, Blu Tara's questions frightened her: *what were you doing in your Pod while you were meant to be out here?*

At first she wondered if Blu Tara found a way to invade her thoughts undetected. But Ayana soon realised that it was Blu's suspicious mind at work. And yet, how close she came to guessing!

Ayana picked up her wide-toothed comb. She smiled at her little friend, stroked it and carefully ran it through her thick curls. The crystal comb purred contentedly as it settled in her hair.

It was her way of preparing herself for another forbidden mind-journey. There were so many terrifying stories about Verheer.

The people on the other side of their world were classified as savages. She could only imagine the many horrors that were hiding in the darkness past the borders of Innovera Yakov. Living in Innovera Yakov was not all that great, especially with

Blu Tara and Skylar always stirring up trouble. But at least in their world of twin suns and crystals they never had darkness.

For a very long time she simply could not understand why a place would be dark at all. Not until the Voice at the Learning Dome explained to them that Innovera Yakov did not revolve around its sun. It did not share light and darkness equally like the planet of the Earthbounds. Their sun always remained above them, and Innovera Yakov spun and basked forever under it. This meant that half of the world beneath them never received light.

Down there, it was said that Beings moved in a permanent watery darkness. The powers they evolved were frightening. They fed on the life forces of other Beings and craved the brightness of Innovera Yakov. They could enter other worlds through the minds of those who tried to reach them with theirs. That was why it was forbidden for any Innoveran to even think of doing so.

Once, many lifetimes ago, an army of Verheerans surfaced from their world in great numbers to take over Innovera Yakov, the Voice said. They almost succeeded. But there was one thing that drove them back into their ocean-darkness.

'And what is that one thing?' Every student chorused at the same time.

'*You will all find out on the Journey,*' came the answer. '*But that knowledge alone will not be enough to save you.*' Then the Voice went silent.

Ayana knew all this and yet she felt she could not help it. She almost felt sorry for the handsome, pale-faced young Male who lived there.

Drawn at first by the stories of this strange world that existed under theirs, she secretly visited Verheer through the portal of her Sylva. No one else in Innovera Yakov knew the true powers of her Sylva. Not only did it transport her body; its shimmering surface could take her mind to other worlds.

Over time she grew fond of the dark figure in her mirror. She'd been secretly following him for a few moon-circles. His face was mostly concealed in darkness, as though a shadow hung over him all the time. He looked stranger than any Male she had ever seen in Innovera Yakov. He was certainly taller than any of them and was always dressed in dark clothing that covered him from head to toe. She did not mean to fall in love, but she realised the stranger had won her heart.

She had seen a few of his companions and they too were dressed in dark clothing. Against the gloom, it was very hard for her to make him out sometimes. Yet she was fascinated at how easily he seemed to navigate through the dim landscape.

What kind of eyes did he have that allowed him to see through darkness so easily? No Innoveran could do that. Once in class, the students took turns at being locked away in a sealed room and the exercise had stirred up a deep fear in all of them. Even now she felt the fear squeezing her body. She, like the others, could have escaped with her mind but the point of the exercise was to experience the darkness of Verheer and remain completely in it. Could the inhabitants of Verheer see in the light? Or did they have some other way of navigating?

She had never seen him talking. He was silent and beautiful. She imagined him with black curly hair and eyes as dark as the ocean that surrounded him. He couldn't see her and that was fine, because she was good at loving him from a distance. When Ayana watched him intimately and anonymously, she pretended that he was her true love. From the safety of her mirror-shield, she could not be rejected. She would never be judged. She was different and so was he.

She would get into an unfathomable amount of trouble if anyone found out about her plans. That was what had so terrified her when Blu Tara began to pry.

Those creatures that live in Verheer are Consumers and Possessors, they had been told. *Protect your shadow. If they walk on it they will slip into your skin and consume you from the inside.*

They will wipe away all trace of your existence. Stay away from the dark side. We are protected by the twilight border that separates our world from theirs. Stay away from Verheer. Two different sides; two different species; two completely opposite worlds.

Breathing deeply, Ayana placed her right palm on her Sylva and whispered:

Follow the pathway of my heart and let me in. He, who lives on the other side, show me him.

The surface of her Sylva became a cold glow in her hand. She slipped a finger through as though it was made of water. She made gentle circular motions in the middle with a finger. Ayana watched the watery surface warp and change until it revealed the silhouette of a figure surrounded by darkness.

'There you are,' she smiled.

The particles on the surface of her Sylva moved in ever widening circles. Ayana blew softly on the shimmering surface. She could see him more clearly although darkness still enveloped him and his face remained hidden.

'Ice,' she breathed softly. Something told her that was his name.

There was also something in the way Ice carried himself and the ease with which he moved, that made Ayana think he was someone important in Verheer.

There was a limit to how much she could spy on him though. Already she was there too long. The longer she stayed, the greater the chances he would pick up her vibrations.

She had heard about a Verheeran — perhaps the healer she replaced - who used his powers to access a Verheeran portal.

He got so absorbed staring into that world that it finally sucked him through to the other side. Nobody had heard from him, or about him since.

Ayana removed her fingers. Ice was travelling from the depths of the cold dark waters to what looked like a new world filled with colours and structures of glass and metal that rose into the air. It was as if he was searching for something. His energy was low. She could feel him weakening. His shadow staggered behind him.

'What's wrong with you?' Ayana whispered.

He stopped and leaned his back against a wall. For a while he stood against it then disappeared into it.

'I wish you could see me,' she murmured.

'Ice!' What a strange name.

Now he was walking briskly with his head covered. He stopped and stood still for what seemed like forever. He turned around and looked straight at her. Panic rocked her body. *He knew she was there.* He stared into her for a second. His eyes were bright as stars. The light from them almost blinded her. Ayana covered her face. The light slowly dissipated.

When she looked up, he was striding briskly towards the distance.

So his eyes are like stars! That's why they are able to see in the dark! They are made for darkness. Maybe he didn't spot her? Or perhaps he did and... She throbbed with excitement. She had learned something new. She had discovered one of their secrets.

Ayana couldn't see him anymore. It was as though he had once again become part of the darkness. This always happened. She would follow him and then just like that, he would disappear into the void. Sometimes she waited a while but he didn't show himself again. She was about to close the portal of her Sylva when she felt a rush of thought-words in her head.

'You okay, Scarface?' It was Blu Tara.

Ayana hastily covered her Sylva and turned it over. 'What's on your mind, Blu Tara?' Ayana dragged the words out. 'What's bothering you? I can feel it.'

'Me worried? Nothing worries me.' Blu Tara said. She sounded irritated.

'Nothing like what?' Ayana threw back.

'What do you know about Krave?'

'Nothing you don't already know.'

'I want to know how this Stardog managed to get to my sister. I want to know his weakness.'

'Does he have a weakness?' Ayana asked.

'Everybody has a weakness.'

'Really? What's yours then?' Ayana narrowed her eyes and smiled.

There was a long silence before Blu Tara answered. 'Listen Scarface, I know you want him. Do you want Gamma to know this? I can tell her if you make me.'

Ayana forced a laugh. 'What makes you think I know his weakness?'

'You healed him and that − that annoying friend of his,' she purred. 'That gave you access to his life force, didn't it? I know you know. Be a friend ... erm,...Ayana.'

'Say it, Blu. Say it! Call me Scarface like you almost did again. Go on! Why don't you ask Odors Apeno?'

There was another long silence. When Blu Tara's voice came again soft and almost pleading. 'Sorry, Ayana. Look I promise you; give me what I want and I'll make Krave come to you. You'll have him for yourself. Isn't that what you want?'

'Even if I could, I wouldn't.' Ayana told her.

She suddenly remembered that she hadn't closed her portal in the Sylva and flipped it over. Ayana gasped. Ice was back.

This never happened before. She had never seen him disappear only to return a little later. She stared at his shadow. He was in a strange place again. It didn't look anything like the darkness he usually inhabited. In fact it seemed as though he was sitting in a building. People were feeding themselves and they seemed to be talking to each other the way she heard that Earthbounds did.

'I have to go,' Ayana said abruptly, and blocked out Blu Tara before she could protest.

The place Ice was in looked vaguely familiar. It didn't resemble the bleak landscapes of Verheer.

Then the realisation dawned on her. *He's an Escapeet! He travels freely to other worlds without the need to exploit the minds of others.*

Escapeets were meant to be a fantasy; even the Voice had said so. But these Beings that blended into other worlds and were said to be impossible to detect were not a myth. Ayana leaned in closer. She was sure he was on Earth. The Beings amidst whom he stood looked like Earthbounds. What was he doing there? Earthbounds were full of imperfections. They suffered many ills in their very brief lives. The laws that governed them were different from other, more advanced, worlds. Yet Odors Apeno said the world of the Earthbounds was important. Earth, he said, was The Planet of Beginnings.

The Earthbounds walked straight through Ice. They seemed oblivious to the fact he was standing amongst them. His gaze rested on an empty seat. He sat down.

Two young girls walked over to where Ice was sitting. They plopped down into the seats, so that the larger of the two was sitting on him.

She could not keep her eyes off this lonely voyeur. This tall, dark mysterious figure with eyes that shone like the stars and who seemed so full of mystery, yet so consumed by sadness.

Her feelings had taken on a life of their own; they almost made her afraid of herself and the softness that she felt for this creature.

Suddenly a thought hit her. What good is it if I can see him but he can't see me?

Ayana caressed the Sylva.

'Every time the wind blows, the world stops for a moment, the stars and the moons of Innovera glow more brightly. Let my words reach your ears and capture your heart,' she whispered. 'Just this once.'

Ayana brought the mirror up close to her face with shaking hands.

'When I say, "I see you", you will see me too,' she whispered.

'I-I see you.' Her words echoed back at her and for a while nothing happened. Ayana let out a breath of relief.

It didn't work!

Then slowly she saw him appearing - a shimmering reflection from within the female Earthbound. Ice's image faded in and out of the Earthbound like a flickering candle. He was locked within her and now he was rising out of her, and while he did the Earthbound began to disintegrate, melting away like bubbles in the wind. It happened so quickly, Ayana barely realised it until the Earthbound had almost disappeared. Ice came to his feet. He seemed more upright and stronger now.

Ayana could feel the heavy thudding of her heart. In Innovera Yakov they had heard so many stories about Earthbounds who disappeared in thin air never to be found. The Beings of that world believed that their friends or family had either died mysteriously or had been abducted. Now she knew better. From time to time Escapeets renewed themselves by feeding on the Earthbounds.

Ice looked up suddenly and stared into Ayana's eyes. A stiffness came over her body. A terrible coldness began to fill her up. She found she could not move.

A furious voice filled her Pod. 'Why are you watching me?' Who are you?' The voice demanded. 'Why do you follow me? Answer me!'

Something yanked her stomach. What felt like a giant hand was grabbing her lower abdomen, and was about to pull out her insides. Ayana tried to scream but her mouth wouldn't open. The words were locked within her throat and forced back to the depths of her, threatening to strangle her.

'Where are you from? Which world!' The grip inside her tightened. The luminous eyes bored into her. 'Who sent you?'

She struggled to break his gaze. Waves of coldness were spreading though her body.

'You are from Innovera Yakov,' he said finally.

She could feel him draining her of her life force. He was trying to enter her. Ayana fought to control her thoughts and turn them against this intruder but the pain was too much. She gave up fighting. She felt herself go limp. *This is it,* she thought. *This is...* Then suddenly he loosened his grip and she tumbled to the floor.

The world around her darkened, and in the darkness she heard Vinton's voice – no longer a child's but full and thundering. 'Finish!'

She heard something smash against the wall of her Pod.

Vinton's voice filled the room again. 'Finish, Myana. Now you safe!'

CHAPTER EIGHT

WHEN AYANA came to, everything was back to normal. She felt as if she'd just survived a drowning. She was sure she blacked out. Fear and disappointment shook her body. Ice wasn't what she expected. Before, she imagined him as a mysterious figure, desperate for a companion. But he turned out to be cold and dangerous. In all that horrid time that he had her in his grip, she didn't feel his heart at all. It was as if he didn't have one.

And he tried to kill me!

Now that Ice knew that she had been following him, and that she lived in Innovera Yakov what might he come and do to her? He was an Escapeet after all. He could find her anywhere, at any time.

Stupid! Stupid! This was the last time ever that she would do such a thing.

Although she had a strange feeling of satisfaction too. She was probably the only one in all of Innovera Yakov who crossed paths with a Verheeran – an Escapeet to boot - and survived.

A destroyer! She shook her head with disbelief.

Could everything she heard about those Dwellers of the Dark be true?

Maybe he's a survivor, she told herself. *He's just trying to survive.*

Vinton popped up in front of her.

'Don't fool yourself, Myana. You fool yourself too easy. You bring big danger to Innovera Yakov. He Escapeet. He rob you of all life.'

'He's only a young Male,' she said. 'Lonely. I feel it here.' Ayana touched her breastbone. 'Same age as me; perhaps little older.'

'Big-boy, yes. But very bad big-boy. You no take care, he come for you. He come for me, Vinton too. He see me save you so he come for me too.'

Ayana straightened up. 'I have to stop him,' she said.

'No! You leave alone. Next time he consume you.'

'He released me, didn't he?' She insisted. 'Why did he release me when he could have taken me?'

'Because, me, Vinton save you.' Her little friend became agitated. 'You fool yourself. Loving make you foolish. You leave Escapeet alone now. You leave alone forever. Ice no good for nobody.'

'He's lonely Vinton. I felt his loneliness. He's searching for something that means a lot to him. I felt it. Maybe I scared him.'

'Ice no scared. You scare yourself. He killer Being.'

Vinton rested her Sylva beside her. 'You go again, maybe I not there next time to save you. Maybe next time you turn nice food for him.'

Vinton disappeared.

Ayana stared at her Sylva and shivered. She hoped Vinton was wrong and yet... Ice was captivating. She still felt a strong bond with this stranger that had only just tried to kill her. It was like he was sending off some strange chemical that lured her into him.

'What's wrong with me?'

Ayana tried to forget the threat in Ice's words. '*Who are you? Why are you following me?*'

She wished she had the chance to answer him and tell him that she did not know exactly who *she* was. She would have offered to help him find whatever he was searching for. She would have been his companion, and they would both be less lonely.

Ayana summoned her comb. It settled in her hair and hummed. She lifted her Sylva and turned it slowly in her hand.

'Ice.' she whispered. She was missing him already.

CHAPTER NINE

GAMMA LEANED against the walls of her Pod looking across at the Ishu Mountains. They were a wonderful purple in the Innoveran light. She saw no trace of the assault that Blu Tara had let loose on the peak to the extreme left of the tallest one. There was a halo of clouds above it – all pinks and blues and greens. She loved looking up into Eden Gobad - their universe - because it made her feel more at home in Innovera Yakov.

She was having those bewildering dreams again. Often they were violent blurry images of an old man standing beside her. But sometimes he was so vivid that she reached out to touch him only to realise that he was not real. If she closed her eyes, she could see his fiery skin and emaciated body staggering in an open desert of boiling red dust.

In the dream, he told her he was her father and by this she understood that in some way this man helped create her. His words haunted her. No one in Innovera Yakov had any experience of having had a maker. If they did, she did not know of anyone who admitted it.

Now these visions were visiting her more often. In fact they started again when she began sneaking away with Krave to the very edges of that forbidden place between Innovera Yakov and Verheer they called The Dimmer Zone.

During her rest with Blu Tara there appeared in her mind a very clear image of the man talking to her. She reached out to touch him, only to find her fingers slipping through his body as usual.

In this dream she was already a young woman. The old man took her hands and whispered, 'Always remember that your father loved you, my child. I can't watch them take you away. So let it be that I die by your hand instead.'

The image faded away and was replaced by his lifeless body sprawled among the rocks.

Gamma returned to the cot and sat shivering beside Blu Tara.

'Why are you upset?' Blu Tara's face was pale, her expression unreadable.

'Those dreams again?' Blu Tara shook her sister gently. 'The usual nonsense? Tell me what they were this time. What did you dream?'

'I saw him again,' Gamma muttered hoarsely.

'And?'

'I don't know - Tara we don't have makers, do we?'

'Earthbounds do. At least that's what I heard. We don't. Blu Tara shrugged. I'm sure it's nothing. I should be getting the same dreams too. And I'm not.'

Blu Tara stroked her sister's face.

'What if he exists, Blu? What if I really have a maker? Doesn't that mean that...that something – Innovera, me, you – everything is wrong?'

Gamma rose to her feet and stared down at her sister. 'What are we, Blu? What's the point of us? Who did this to us? Why is it that only *our* eyes are shielded? Don't you get tired of this lens over your eyes? It's like there is something in our eyes with a life of its own.'

Blu Tara flung back her hair and grimaced. 'Ever crossed your mind that those visions might be warnings? That they're telling you something about this Male you lost your head to? Maybe,' Blu Tara sat beside Gamma and hugged her. 'Maybe it's telling you Krave Solan is not for you. In fact I'm pretty sure...'

'Been having them before I met Krave. Thought you always knew that.' Gamma cut in impatiently. 'You blaming that on him too?' She hugged herself and lifted her face dreamily at Blu Tara. 'Imagine that – a maker.'

Blu Tara stood up. 'Lucky Male. Scarface wants him too. Her Pod opened to him that last time she blacked out.'

Gamma shrugged. 'Yes, I know. Krave said. She's not the first.'

'Want to talk? Want to go up there a while?' Through the transparent walls of their Pod, Blu Tara pointed at the sky.

'I can't.'

'Can't or won't?'

Gamma did not answer.

But Tara's skin flushed an angry, glowing red. 'What are you hiding Gamma? How come I can't follow you anymore? How come I can't contact you when you're out there and I want to? What's he done to you?'

Gamma crossed her arms and looked at her. 'I keep telling you about that temper Blu. You can't always have your way.'

Blu Tara flung back her hair and glared at her. 'Watch me,' she sneered and left the Pod.

Gamma unclipped her hair and let it drop to the small of her back.

Recently, she sensed Blu Tara's secretive attempts to invade her thoughts, especially when her sister thought she was asleep or resting. They had vowed over a bloodstone never to do so unless they absolutely had to in order to protect each other. Now she could barely let her guard down before she felt her sister's probing thought-waves trying to enter her head.

Gamma tossed back her hair and stared at herself in the mirror. If only Krave could see her eyes. If only she could see her own eyes for that matter. Krave wanted this more than anything. But he would be reduced to cinders if she took off her lens. Yet she could not imagine a future without him being there all the time. He said the same to her and she knew that he meant it.

Gamma made a thick smouldering rope of her hair and curled it round her shoulders. She stepped out of the Pod looked around her quickly and took to the air. In an instant she was high above Innovera Yakov, heading northeast towards the Ishu Mountains. She immediately felt Blu Tara's presence. Gamma kept climbing until Innovera Yakov was no more than a sparkling green globe circling beneath her. The presence of her sister was becoming stronger. Gamma speeded up, and sure enough Blu Tara's pace quickened after her.

She was in the shadow of Ayana's blue moon when she made a curving westward path and did the trick that Krave had taught her. Gamma blanked her mind completely and cooled her core until she was barely conscious of the world around her. She allowed herself to fall like a cold comet down towards the Dimmer Zone. She'd calculated carefully. The slightest error and she would be lost forever in Verheer, on the other side of the Dimmer Zone.

Soon she felt the thick and strangely acidic air at the other side of the Ishu Mountains. She revived her life force, heated up and followed the long dark valley that led her to the foot of a black rock-tower beyond which there was only darkness.

There was no sign of her sister anywhere.

Gamma followed the sound of thrashing water until down below her on a ledge that jutted out from the face of the rocks she saw Krave.

Here in the Dimmer Zone, where the rays of the Innoveran sun merged with the darkness of Verheer they were no longer connected to anything but each other. Krave said he discovered this part of the Dimmer Zone out of desperation to be alone with her and away from her interfering sister. One day he'd taken to the air, determined not to return until he found somewhere. And then it occurred to him that the most convenient of all places would be where no one else would dare to go or where they were forbidden.

It was in this twilight world of whirling winds and thundering water that Krave revealed many of his secrets to her, especially the hidden power in his hands.

The first time that she heard the beating water just behind the tall rocks, Krave told her that it was where the world of Verheer began and Innovera Yakov ended.

Gamma alighted in Krave's arms and buried her face in his neck. He held her close. Gamma shivered with the electricity that oozed from his skin. He whispered her name and his voice bounced around her body like an echo chamber.

Krave rubbed his nose against her forehead.

'Flight, my beloved,' he whispered. 'Are you ready?'

Gamma held on to him for what she knew was about to come. Krave tightened his grip in the small of her back and Gamma steadied herself. She closed her eyes and smiled. Then the lift! With his powerful arms he threw her so high and so fast into the air he soon became a tiny golden sparkle a great distance below her. Catapulted by his energy, Gamma flew past the minor moon of Dotan in a rush of joy, her body, tingling with the sensation of Krave's fingers on her skin. It felt as if he was still holding her, still lifting her with invisible hands towards the stars of Eden Gobad. It was a long time before Gamma began to descend in a frightening rush towards the rocks.

But she was not worried. She trusted Krave completely. Gamma allowed herself to fall and when it felt as if it was too late, that she was certain to hit the waiting rocks, Krave raised his arms towards her. White light fanned out from his fingers and surrounded her. It was as if she'd been caught up in a rain of tiny stars. It slowed her down and somehow cushioned her; leaving her with a feeling of such warmth and lightness Gamma felt that in that moment, she herself was made of Innoveran air.

She landed in Krave's arms.

'Krave, I-I'm...' she could not speak. She did not need to anyway.

Krave cupped her face in his hands and blew warm air along her cheeks and down her neck. 'I know, he said. I am for you too, Gamma. All of me. Now my turn, my Fire Queen.'

He released her and stepped back several paces.

Gamma sucked in air and held it in. Pressing against the lens on her eyes, she felt the temperature rise inside her until all of her became a red and pulsing glow.

'I'm hot,' she laughed.

'I know,' Krave said, his voice rolling from his chest in a soft sweet wave.

'Look out!' she cried. And then her breath exploded near his feet.

Krave shot into the air like a yellow comet. He did not rise as high as he had thrown her but he made the most of it while he was in the air. He created intricate fiery patterns as his body looped and spun: the shape of a Golkan leaf, an exploding Starfly. Finally he traced her name in a fiery golden weave against the sky. He came down in a rush and landed directly in front of her.

'Phew! That was hot,' he laughed. Then he took her hand. 'All of this – you and me – all of this is so perfect and yet you are afraid to merge your energies with mine. To partake of each other's power and become something better, more fine-looking and stronger.'

'Not afraid. Krave. I want this too. All of it. Even if it might kill us when we try. I would take the chance if Blu…'

'Your sister is a thug. She's controlling you through fear. And you're allowing her to scare you.'

'How many times must I tell you this, Krave: she's my twin? If – if we do this. If we merge, even if it worked, she is sure to suffer terribly. We've been together all our lives. We've slept and fought and fused; we've experienced the same things for as long as I can remember. You could hardly separate our thoughts. We've believed we were never going to separate. A sudden break will be too hard.' Gamma laid her head against Krave's chest. 'Apart from that I'm yours.'

'You're not,' he told her calmly. 'We cannot be until it happens.'

'I wish we were born in another world,' she said. 'Sometimes I wish we were both Earthbounds. However short their lives are, at least the rules of love are different.'

Gamma disengaged herself from Krave. He leant against the rocks, his bright eyes fixed on her.

'I haven't told you about my dreams, Krave. I have feelings of being in another place and another time, as though I'm missing someone important. There's always a little girl in my dreams. Something tells me that little girl was me. But it can't be because in those dreams I am not a twin. There's no Blu Tara with me. I need to understand these things before it happens. Before we give over ourselves completely to each other. Next time we come...'

'There will be no next time, Gamma.'

Gamma swung around to face Krave. 'What do you mean?'

'When you're ready for me, I'll know.'

'Krave! If you loved me you would not say a thing like that.'

'I say that because I love you - maybe too much; it's stealing my strength. It's weakening me here. Krave tapped his chest.

'I'm sorry, but can't we...just...wait? Then I promise you next time I come to you we'll give ourselves.'

Krave began walking towards her, 'You promise?'

'Krave. I...'

They heard thundering in the near distance, just behind the rocks. The Verheer ocean-tide was rolling in and rising. Soon there would be water at the foot of the rocks below them and whatever creatures it might bring with it.

'Home,' Krave whispered urgently. He took her hand and pulled her close to him.

They leapt together, rising like a gold and silver streak of light into the air. From the rising waters on the other side of the rock steady eyes looked up at them. They followed their trail until Krave and Gamma disappeared through the clouds of Innovera Yakov.

CHAPTER TEN

SOMETHING ABOUT Skylar changed while he was in the Healing Dome. Intricate patterns of lines and circles decorated his skin now. His hair was not the same straight black mass that fell straight down to his shoulders. It had turned an iridescent greenish hue, and hung like strips of glossy fabric from his head. His eyes were now a deep turquoise and his voice had also changed. It rolled out from the pit of his stomach when he spoke and they could hardly hear him breathing.

When Skylar was not with Krave, he was out amongst the animals in the damp grasslands near the Swamps of Innovera. Somehow the new Skylar looked more handsome and mysterious.

There were many rumours about him: *That's Odors Apeno's punishment for the nasty person he was. He's probably possessed by the demons of Verheer. Stay clear of him.*

If Skylar heard the gossiping, he did not care. He left the students when he wanted to, and disappeared. And when he did, it was impossible to find him.

One thing that never changed was Skylar's closeness to his brother, Krave. In fact, Krave was the only person that he listened to or spoke with.

Soon enough, they all got accustomed to Skylar's new look and silent ways. And the closer they got to the Innoveran Games, the less preoccupied they were with him because their preparations concentrated all their energies.

The Innoveran Games took place just before The Alignment. At the end of every ten thousand orbits, the five moons of Innovera Yakov aligned with the sun. The light was different: a tungsten yellow that settled like a shimmering sheet on everything. The air was coolest then; the winds were soft and caressing. And there was no threat of unexpected Solarwaves. Sounds travelled great distances. If they concentrated hard enough they could hear the great dark ocean of Verheer thrashing against the wall of rocks that separated both worlds. Some Innoverans claimed that they could even smell the ocean — a faint odour of rotting things and cordite.

Every student had to take part in the games. It was meant to test their powers and resourcefulness and for them to discover how much they had developed. There were no rules. If there were, The Voice did not explain them. Yet everyone seemed to understand in which order the three events came, and how long each one was meant to last.

The events happened in the order of the danger they presented: first the Skyrolls that tested their powers of concentration and control. Crystals thin and delicate as flakes were laid in a small circle on a large flat gemstone at the edges of which a jagged crown of mineral spikes protruded. The students would take to the air in pairs and rise until they were barely visible against the clouds. Then at the sound of the horn from the dome, they allowed themselves to freefall like dead bodies. They were not allowed to use their powers in the terrible plummet downwards until the horn blasted again. Once they heard the sound, they used whatever powers they possessed to guide them onto the tiny spread of crystals. If they fell outside the circle they failed. If they landed too heavily, the crystals were crushed into powdery fragments and that also meant they failed. Sometimes they hit the mineral spikes and needed to be rescued.

The Game of Blades came after. It tested their reflexes to the extreme. They divided into two opposing teams – males and females equally – and stood six paces from each other. Each Innoveran chose a dagger or a spear. There was no prompting horn from the dome. They had to be attuned to the smallest movement of the other side as the blades darted from the hands of their foes, straight at their bodies. Amongst each group there were the truly gifted throwers. Blu Tara and Gamma were known for their speed and quick reflexes. They caught the blade by the tips and returned it instantly with such deadly accuracy that their rivals dared not even blink. Krave and Skylar were celebrated champions. Their weapons of choice were the Silverstone daggers they made themselves to fit their hands exactly. Shay, the strange girl who observed everything and hardly ever talked, was fought over by both sides because she seemed to know exactly what was coming just before it happened. And then there was Ryder - the good-looking blue boy with extra long limbs whose gemstone spear returned to his hands however far and hard he threw it. Ryder was never known to miss his target.

Many of the younger students stood slightly behind these great Throwers for protection, but they still got hit, crumpling onto the grass as the flying blades sunk into their exquisite bodies.

Ayana was the only one not allowed to participate. Her job was to use her gift of healing. She rescued the fallen students every time. She stood well out of their range, legs apart, arms outstretched, her palms pressed flat against each other, head slightly bent in concentration. When a student fell, she directed her energies at them. Soon they were on their feet again and facing the other side. Because she was there some of them became reckless. Over and over again she revived them knowing that she would be so exhausted at the end of it, it would take her a full cycle of her moon to recharge herself. But now she loved the sensation of the energy coursing through her body. She felt as though she could live forever; that she - Ayana - would never die. Now, in this raging Game of Blades she had a full sense of her worth to Innovera Yakov.

They were nearing the end of the Game of Blades when Skylar shocked them all. Blu Tara threw her dagger at him full force. Skylar heard Shay's warning cry. Skylar must have seen the blade coming but he did not try to catch it. The weapon buried itself in his chest. Ayana turned her energies towards him, but she pulled back, holding her hands in front of her in confusion. She'd felt no energy or life from Skylar. She hadn't been able to reach him.

Yet Skylar was still standing. He was carefully closing his large hands around the handle of the blade. Even Blu Tara looked worried. Then in one swift movement Skylar pulled out the dagger and dropped it on the grass. He parted the fabric of his garment and gazed down at his chest. He looked up at the others, smiling. There was no trace of a wound; not even a dent on his smooth, patterned skin where the knife entered.

A burst of applause rose up from the students. Skylar lifted his head at them and shrugged his massive shoulders. This uncharacteristic modesty and the little smile that crossed his lips brought another round of applause from them.

Shay who was standing slightly apart from the group walked up to Gamma and tapped her shoulder. Gamma turned to her and Shay whispered something in her ear. Gamma looked at her twin sister then quickly back at Shay as if to speak to her. But Shay was already pushing her way through to Skylar.

The girl did something strange. She stopped in front of Skylar and looked into his face and then she rested her palm against his face. She held his eyes with her own. No one had ever seen such tenderness from her. Skylar shook his head and looked across at Krave. Krave turned his face up to the sky pretending he did not see his friend trying to get his attention.

Ayana looked on dumbfounded. *She's offering herself to him. She's telling him that she's for him.*

Shay took Skylar's hand. Skylar did not resist her, nor did he seem to welcome her..

He turned away from them and headed for the open fields beyond. Shay followed close behind.

The games were almost over - or at least this part of it. Sometime after they had rested and renewed their energies, they would begin The Game of Minds. And one thing Ayana was certain of, there was not a student amongst them who would not be dreading the Finals of that game.

Ayana was distracted by Ryder. He was watching the backs of Shay and Skylar disappearing in the distance and toying with his spear. She had to admit to herself that she admired his quietness and his magnificent form especially when he threw his spear. Ryder was so swift in his movements that he was no more than a blur. Most times when he saw her, he nodded politely or smiled. *Perhaps I should...*

Ayana did not complete the thought. She sensed Ryder's intention the instant he balanced the glittering weapon in his hand. He spun round in a dizzying whirl and hurled it straight at her.

Ayana had no time to think. She dropped to the grass the instant that Ryder leant back and raised his hand. Even as she was dropping to the grass she was pressing her index finger against her breastbone. The spear struck the shield that sprung up before her. It stayed there in the air as if it was embedded in something solid. Ayana rose to her feet, pushed a finger through the bubble and rested it against the tip of the hanging spear. Her bubble disappeared and still the weapon hung in the air with her outstretched finger pressed against the tip.

There was nothing but silence around her. She lifted her head and looked ahead to where Ryder was standing. He was a tall blue shape against the Innoveran skyline. His two hands were cupped around his mouth and his eyes were wide.

'Why?' Ayana projected her thoughts at him. She was surprised by her own calmness. 'Why, Ryder?'

Ryder's thought words came back, frantic and apologetic. 'I-I don't know, Ayana. My hand — something made me do it. In the name of Odors Apeno, I swear I couldn't help it.'

Ryder was staring at his hands as if they did not belong to him.

With the spear still hanging on the air, the students formed an excited group around Ayana.

Gamma scattered them. Her body ignited into a ball of living flames. 'Leave her alone,' she snapped. 'Enough excitement in this place! You all right, Ayana?'

Ayana relaxed her finger and the weapon dropped onto the grass.

'I'm- I'm... I'll live,' she said. She could not keep back the trembling in her voice.

'Come, I'll take you to your Pod. I'll deal with Ryder later.'

'He said it wasn't him. He said...'

'Let him tell me that when I go to see him!'

Gamma cooled off quickly. She reached out and pulled Ayana close to her.

'You bleed, Ayana. Don't let anyone see that finger. Then they'll all believe that you're an Earthbound now....'

Ayana looked at the red stripe of blood trickling down her finger.

She felt Gamma's arm tighten around her shoulders. 'Only Earthbounds bleed. That's what everyone is told. But...' There was a new respect in Gamma's voice. 'Those powers, Ayana - where...How...?'

Gamma pulled her close again, communicating now in thought-words. 'Your secret; your weakness. I-I think I know it now, Ayana. It is safe with me.'

Ayana brought her lips close to Gamma's ears. 'Leave Ryder alone. I believe him. It was a test. Everyone here was tested except me. It was my turn. I think Apeno used him. What Shay told you, be careful, Gamma.'

Gamma relaxed her arms. 'You heard what Shay told me?'

Ayana eased herself from Gamma's arms. 'Yes, I was tuned in to everyone. I had to be to heal. Your sister heard her too.'

'You're sure?'

'Yes, Blu heard it. That's partly why Shay's gone with Skylar. She wants him to protect her. Gamma, I have to go. Ryder – leave him alone. Please.'

'As you wish Little Healer. I'll let off Ryder this time.' Gamma blew warm air in Ayana's face and took to the air.

Once inside her Pod, Ayana could not rest. Her mind kept returning to the Game of Blades and her discovery of her own powers which she had believed were possible. Till then, Ayana had always known that her powers did not match those of her peers. She didn't have their speed or strength. All she had was the ability to protect herself.

Ryder's flying spear was as unexpected as the new powers she experienced when he launched the weapon. He was as shocked as she was. She saw that by the fright on his face after the spear left his hand. He looked even more alarmed when it did not return to him, realising perhaps that she Ayana, had in fact disarmed him. She invaded his thoughts immediately and aggressively the moment she asked him, 'Why?'

His answer had been truthful.

So what happened to her out there? Was it the same thing that happened to Skylar? What she experienced was an enhancement of her powers. Skylar's change was more mysterious. It was almost as if, after he fell from the Golkan tree, he became a completely different being. Everything about him was different. He'd grown almost three times the height he was before he fell. The most puzzling things of all was the fact that when she moved to heal him, she could not feel his life-pulse, yet he was alive.

Her mind went back to Shay's shameless adoration of his strength. Shay was frightened enough of Blu Tara to want to merge with Skylar. But it was clear to Ayana that Shay felt something stronger and more tender for him, even if Shay's offer had no effect on Skylar.

In the Game of Blades the Voice told them of only two types of participants: Dodgers and Deflectors. Dodgers were the swift ones. They could duck or dive or swing away from an oncoming weapon in an instant. Deflectors used their inner energies to change the path of the blade away from them. She – Ayana, was naturally a Deflector. Skylar was none of these. He had become an Absorber. Whatever happened to him after he fell from the Golkan Tree, gave Skylar the powers of a Verheeran.

Look at the way he healed himself. Ayana thought. *Who or what is Skylar now?*

A vision of Ice appeared in her mind. Ayana hugged herself and shivered.

CHAPTER ELEVEN

GAMMA RETURNED to her Pod with Blu Tara following close behind. Gamma was careful to cloak her thoughts. She sat on the cot, ignoring her sister completely while she slowly unwound her hair.

'Ayana,' Blu Tara started. 'Did you see that? Scarface was...'

'Amazing,' Gamma cut in sharply.

Blu Tara raised an eyebrow, 'Well...'

'Well what, Blu? As far as I know there's never been one like her. A healer with those powers. And she's getting stronger all the time.'

'That's the problem,' Blu Tara frowned at her.

'Why's that, Blu? As far as I'm concerned the girl's a gift. You saw the way she healed the others during the games. Your problem is, Blu...' Gamma began re-coiling her hair into a thick rope. 'You don't like anyone. Nothing pleases you. That's why you have no friends.'

'I have all the friends I want.'

'And that friend I suppose is me?' Gamma cast a cynical glance at Blu.

'Of course!'

'I've begun to wonder about that, Blu Tara. We're meant

to be the same, aren't we? So why do you feel so much like a stranger sometimes'

'Gamma! What's got into you? What's the problem? Why are you pulling yourself away like this? I can't talk to you; I don't even know what you are thinking. From the moment you left the games you're cloaking your thoughts.'

'How do you know I'm cloaking if you weren't trying to intrude? You're trying to access my thoughts and feelings at every turn. I feel you like a needle just outside my head. This was not just a shallow promise that we made; it was a vow, never to access each other's thoughts unless we agree to. We swore on a bloodstone and yet you break it. Why?'

Blu Tara clenched her fists and turned away. When she turned around to face Gamma, the red of her lens had softened to a gentle yellow.

'I'll tell you why Gamma: I can't help it. That's why.'

Blu Tara knelt before her sister.

'I don't know if you remember this - something that the Voice said. It is perhaps the only thing I really remember. The only really interesting thing it said. The subject was the Earthbounds. And it was I who asked the question: what was it that made those beings so destructive? Why were they always warring and killing each other? Do you remember the answer, Gamma?'

Gamma shrugged.

'Well,' Blu Tara said, 'It was because they do not have the one thing that all Innoverans have - a seventh sense. The most important one: knowing what the other thinks or feels. So they guess, and they always assume the worst. That's why they turn on each other all the time.'

Blu Tara knelt in front of her sister. 'I am worried Gamma. I am really worried. I-I don't want to misunderstand you.'

Blu Tara's thought-voice sounded far away and faint.

'How can it be that you really want to break from me? I who've been with you from our very beginning? How can you choose another Being over me? What choice is there when there's no choice? And already I feel I'm dying.'

Gamma reached down and cupped her face. 'You're not dying,' Gamma said. 'I will know it the same time as you do. Isn't that how it's meant to happen?'

'You complain that you can't access me anymore. Well, Blu Tara, it is to spare you this.' Gamma rested her forehead against Blu Tara's and uncloaked her mind.

'Feel my pain, Sister. Feel my fear and my confusion. Feel the love I have for you and Krave. And understand me once and for all!'

Gamma pressed her forehead harder and blew in Blu Tara's face.

Blu Tara shuddered violently and a terrible groan escaped her. She wrenched her face from Gamma's grasp and backed away from her.

'In the name of..of - Gamma! It's, it's...' Blu Tara struggled to find the words and finally gave up. She lay down on the floor of the Pod and stared up at the ceiling, her whole body quivering.

Gamma rose, and with a gesture made the walls of the Pod transparent.

Gamma had drawn herself up to full height. Her voice filled up the space.

'Now you see, Blu, why it's impossible for me to choose. But there has to be a choice and I cannot make it on my own. And there's no way that you can help me. When I see Krave next, I will take him to the Place of Knowing.'

'No!' Blu Tara sat up abruptly. 'After that, you cannot change your mind. It's a curse. It's too...too final.'

'Whatever the decision is Blu Tara, I will go with it.'

CHAPTER TWELVE

WHEN KRAVE rose from resting, he saw the Silverstone tablet on his Podseat. Its colour was Gamma's gemstone pink. He spread his palms and the tablet lifted itself and settled in his hand.

Gamma's stylish script appeared on the surface.

If it is the will of Odors Apeno, I will be for you. I will no longer meet you in the Dimmer Zone. Next time we see, it will be at the Circle of Knowing.

There was a bright red flourish that was Gamma's signature which also told him what mood she was in when she wrote the note.

Krave stood staring at it for a long time, then as if awakened from a trance, he breathed on the the tablet and Gamma's writing sank beneath the bright surface.

He brushed the Silverstone lightly with his thumb. He concentrated briefly and his reply appeared in a dense and shimmering golden script on its surface.

Then the Circle Of Knowing it will be.
Everlasting Love
Krave Solan.

'Go,' he said, turning away from the stone. The tablet shimmered and disappeared through the walls of the Pod.

Blu Tara sensed her sister's thoughts. In her distress Gamma had revealed her intention. She was going to communicate with Krave. Of course she could have sent him thought-words but thought-words between lovers were considered unromantic. Messages on encrypted Silverstones were all the rage in Innovera Yakov.

Blu Tara mumbled an excuse and left Gamma to herself. Now she stood waiting outside in the shade of a blossoming Redwave tree and sure enough she saw Gamma's Silverstone emerge from the Pod, rising high into the quiet air, heading for Krave's Pod in the near distance.

She narrowed her eyes and followed its trajectory, saw it slip into the walls of Krave Solan's Pod and nodded with satisfaction.

Now that she knew the true strength of Gamma's feelings, Blu Tara was more determined than ever to stop her sister. Besides, Gamma was suspicious of her now. Gamma's new untrusting attitude was just as dangerous to Blu Tara's existence as Krave's intrusion in her sister's heart. The emotions she felt in Gamma were truly terrifying: Confusion, doubt and a kind of lovesick desperation that weakened her sister in a puzzling way. Was that what Innoveran love was like? And if it were so, was Innoveran love good for anything?

When the silver tablet re-emerged from Krave's Pod, Blu Tara brought her hands together sharply, pressed a finger against her forehead and concentrated. She had never done this before. She had never had a reason to do this. And if Gamma found out, it might push her sister to break away from her completely. But these were desperate times and sometime in the future Gamma would understand. Blu Tara was counting on the fact that she was so much like Gamma that the tablet would not sense the difference. After all, they were split-core twins. The Silverstone hesitated in the air. It was a bright glass bubble high above her. The slowly it began descending. The tablet hesitated for a while then it settled in Blu Tara's hand.

Blu Tara scanned Krave's lovely script and curled up contemptuous lips at his words. *Everlasting Love, my...*She blew on the Silverstone until Krave's writing disappeared.

She did not try to imitate Krave's golden script. But she had to be careful to disguise hers. She chose the plain Roma writing that most Innoverans used. Between lovers it was an insult, since it meant that no effort had been put into it. That suited her just fine.

Be confused no more, Gamma. I've made the choice for you. I've decided that I will no longer see you.

Blu Tara concentrated. She needed something that would leave no doubt in Gamma's mind that this message was from Krave. She remembered the times she tried to follow Gamma and the mysterious way she lost all contact with her just as she entered the shadow of the minor moon of Dotan.

How I used to love to watch you come to me beyond the moon of Dotan. I find no more joy in that. All I ask from you now is to stay away from me.

Krave Solan.

'Go!' Blu Tara said releasing the Silverstone. She cast a final look at the tablet as it rose above her head. Then she took to the air.

Blu Tara followed the same path that Gamma took when she sneaked off to meet Krave Solan. Ever since that first time that her sister lost her, she'd been trying to work out what Gamma did to disappear so suddenly and mysteriously.

Yes, it was always at the same place, just after she melted in the shadow of the Dotan Moon. Whatever the trick her sister used it always worked. There was no sense of her presence anywhere. Not a single pulse from her. Not a trace of Gamma's inner heat-force.

It was as if her sister ceased to exist. She wondered if it was some new and unexpected power that Gamma discovered and was hiding from her.

From where she was now, high up in the Innoveran stratosphere she could see the purple plains of Anov spread out all the way up to the foot of the Ishu Mountains.

Beyond the mountains she studied the darker skies where Verheer began.

Even in her state of mind she could not help but notice the wonder of the world below her and what she would be losing if Gamma's foolishness got the better of her. All that talk about hating Innovera Yakov was only partly true. It was the waiting that got her down. It was the feeling of being abandoned here. It was the frustration of feeling like a ghost to the one Being that she cherished above all else.

Blu Tara found herself doing this more and more - climbing high into the freezing zone above their world and remaining there until she needed to return to the Pod she shared with Gamma to renew her energy.

Never before had she craved this sub-zero cold. Now it felt worse than thirst. She couldn't remember when it started, when she began to be aware of the furnace inside her body that she and Gamma were 'born' with. The fire was their weapon and their life force, like that magic fluid which the Voice told them, flowed inside all Earthbounds and the creatures that they lived with. It was what kept them alive.

Now for some strange reason she began to feel the heat inside her body. At first it was no more than a few small twinges. A sudden rise in the temperature of her skin or breath that she had no control of.

In the beginning she ignored the signs. She did not want to think about what this might mean. But as time passed she could not ignore it. The sensation and discomfort were getting stronger. Her own fire was consuming her from inside.

She had no doubt that it was because of Gamma's obsession over Krave. Their love is killing me, she thought. I'm burning with my sister's love for someone else.

She wanted to destroy Golden Boy - if only for this. She wanted him out of their lives. Out of *her* life. But that was becoming more and more difficult.

Blu Tara rolled up the fabric of her garment and stared at her arms. A web of grey lines ran all the way down from her elbow to her wrist. 'I'm dying,' she whispered angrily. 'They're murdering me with their love.'

CHAPTER THIRTEEN

AYANA ENVIED the Innoverans who - like Gamma and Blu Tara - could fly. They simply took to the air and were off to wherever they wanted to be. They only used these powers to the full when they competed, or when they had to protect themselves from danger. Even the lowly Flitters could stay in the air as long as they wished. These pretty Beings were the fetchers and carriers of their world. They cleaned and polished the Pods, tidied the Learning Dome and were attracted to anything that shone. The explosive Izus — small and tough as rocks — were defenders of the sacred crystals in the Garden of Knowing. They stuck to themselves and were friends with no one. Like Gamma ad Blu Tara, they had no trouble flying.

Krave and Skylar could fly but not in the same way that the twins did. Blu Tara and Gamma remained in the air as long as they wished. Krave and most of the other students were Leapers. They rocketed into the sky, travelling great distances, but eventually their momentum slowed and the gravity of Eden Gobad brought them back to land. Ayana could do none of these. She depended on her Sylva to carry her. She would step on it and it would instantly spread out under her feet. Silver straps weaved themselves around her feet and calves;

then she took to the air and guided the Sylva with her thoughts.

She did not know how she came by it. Sometimes it seemed to have a mind of its own. In times of danger it would override her wishes and take her away from trouble.

What Ayana had above all else was the power of Projection. Her body remained in the same spot while her mind reached into places far beyond her. The others who had similar abilities were not half as powerful as she was.

Still, she felt it was not enough. In her mind, her powers were not nearly as valuable as the gift of speed, which most of the others had. Besides, they had no scars on their faces. They were almost perfect in every way.

'You are who you are,' Odors Apeno told her once. 'Fulfillment lies in purpose and your purpose is to heal. Who are we to question it?'

The games that demanded so much of her healing powers were still on her mind. She discovered some wonderful new things about herself, especially the quickness with which she could now heal. Even Blu Tara could not hide her admiration. And Krave - he looked at her as if she were a new and different Being. He really looked at her now. She often felt his eyes on her, as if he were seeing her for the first time. She was happy that she impressed him.

What a shock when Ryder flung his spear at her! Her reaction was even more surprising. Ayana remembered the calmness that came over her the instant she saw the weapon coming. It was as if Odors Apeno himself was standing over her. He'd taken a seat inside her very heart and gave her a tiny portion of his power.

'His' power - Ayana wondered why Apeno was a 'He' for females in her world, and a 'She' for all the males. It just felt that way to each of them. For those like Blu Tara who did not feel Him, Apeno simply did not exist.

The Voice told them that Earthbounds could not hear their Odors Apeno anymore because, over time, they stopped listening. At first, many Earthbounds thought their Apeno had abandoned them, or died and disappeared. As time passed, they forgot that they ever had one. The generations that followed did not even know that, once, they too had a voice to guide them.

Ayana tried to clear her mind of all these thoughts. So many things were bothering her. The most worrying of them all was discovering that she - unlike anyone she knew - bled like a lowly Earthbound. Worse still, Gamma knew her secret and she realised immediately that this was Ayana's greatest weakness.

As if that were not enough, the sight of the red trickle on her finger started something strange inside Ayana. She began having a series of bewildering dreams.

During her Rest, immediately after she returned from The Games, the image of a woman appeared in her mind. She was dressed in a flowing purple robe. In her left hand, she was carrying a staff and her right hand was resting on the shoulders of a girl. There was a bundle strapped to the woman's back. From that bundle, the head of a crying child protruded. The child was a boy.

Ayana dragged herself from the cot. She walked around her Pod wondering what it meant. Exhausted, she returned to lie down and tried to force herself to rest.

The dream returned. This time the woman was standing on the shoreline of some vast twilight world. Behind her were the sounds of battle. The woman's voice rode high on the wind urging a multitude of Earthbounds onwards.

They were surrounded by terrible sounds: the screams of beings the likes of which Ayana had never before imagined. A mass of fallen Earthbounds were strewn all over the dark land. The magic red liquid that was their blood was flowing from their bodies.

Ayana woke up shouting for Vinton but her friend remained silent.

Afraid to return to her cot, she sat in her Podseat feeling feverish and dizzy. Flashes of the great battle replayed in her mind. They were always with the same woman, shouting in the wind, waving the long staff in her hand with two children in her care.

Were these dreams or memories? If they were not dreams when and where did all this happen? If it really happened, where were the woman and the boy? Ayana could not remember ever being a young girl. She could not recall a woman or a brother either. Their origins were one of the great puzzles that they all lived with, in Innovera Yakov. Were these visions a clue to her beginnings? Why was she so certain that she knew that woman and the child? What made her feel so sure that she was that little girl?

Ayana tried to reach out to Odors Apeno, but He too was silent.

She could ask the Voice at the Learning Dome for answers but the students would certainly turn on her with suspicion on their faces. It would prove to them that she was an outsider – a stranger to their world. Perhaps even a Verheeran spy.

Ayana fingered the scars on the right side of her face. They were always there – like purple lines that ran all the way down from her temple to the line of her jaw. However often her skin renewed itself – and it did so after every Rest – the scars were always there. How did she get them? Did it have something to do with the grey tormented world that appeared in her dreams?

That place was strange and yet it felt familiar, especially the atmosphere in which there was neither sunlight nor complete darkness. Maybe it was not another world, she thought. Maybe it was somewhere here in Innovera Yakov. The more Ayana thought about it the more convinced she became.

Where in all of Innovera Yakov does such a place exist?

There was just one answer: *The Dimmer Zone.*

With a click of her fingers, she made the walls of her Pod transparent. Although it was still the time of Rest, there were students out in the fields pitting their skills against each other. Every one of them was preparing for The Journey. They were getting themselves ready for every possible danger because none of them knew what to expect after they took to the air and headed for the darkness beyond the Ishu Mountains. The Great Journey would be the end of their lives as they knew it. That was what the Voice said.

In these times at the end of every lesson it reminded them of The Journey.

When you set off, it may mark the beginning of your end, or the start of a new and more powerful existence.

Many of them, it said, would not make it to the other side. The number that survived depended entirely on them. And it was not necessarily the fastest or the strongest that will be victorious.

Ayana looked again at the deep grey curtain beyond the Ishu Mountains and her heart tripped over. Their time was getting nearer. At the next Alignment, they would all be sent off to the darkness over there.

Ayana stepped outside and summoned her Sylva.

Vinton appeared in front of her. 'Where you go now, Myana?'

'You say you know my mind, so you should know.'

'Yes, I know. But me, Vinton, polite. That is why I ask. Where you go Myana?'

'Go away, Vinton. I called for you earlier. You refused to come. Why now?' Ayana stepped on her Sylva.

'You go, you make more trouble. Odors Apeno, She no like it.'

'Then why does He fill my head with so many questions?' Ayana jabbed a finger at her temple. 'I ask for answers. Nothing! All I get from both of you is silence. If he doesn't want me to go, then let him tell me so himself. Let Him stop me!'

'He no stop you. You got free will. All Eden Gobad got free will.' Vinton dusted his hands. 'Your choice, your problem. You go to Dimmer place, maybe you no come back.'

'And if I don't?'

Vinton looked alarmed. His little transparent body dimmed. 'No talk like that, Myana.' Vinton glared defiantly at her. 'You go right now; I not go with you.'

'Did I ask you to?' Ayana threw back and signalled her Sylva to rise.

Once in the air she felt better. She could feel the wind tugging at her garments and her hair as she floated higher. She could even expose her whole face to the skies because there was no one around to stare at her scars and whisper.

She gazed down at Innovera Yakov. It was wonderful beneath her - all shimmering blue grass and great Golkan trees with their mysterious blue leaves and beating hearts. Starbirds flew past her like bright daggers, heading for the high air of the Ishu Mountains. The great River of a Thousand Eyes flowed quietly beneath, reflecting the glorious multi-tinted sky.

She headed west towards the great swathe of darkness. Soon she would be over the Swampland just before the great river disappeared into the dimming light, on its way to Verheer.

Her Sylva slowed down.

'Come on,' she coaxed. 'Where's your courage O Silver One? How else would you know the forbidden parts this world?'

She knew that her Sylva was reflecting her own uncertainty. The truth was she did not know exactly where she was going. The Dimmer Zone was vast. It ringed their world. She could have headed in any direction and ended up in some part of it.

The journey was long and tiring. As Ayana left the sunny heat of Innovera Yakov and soared through a dense forest towards Verheer, she could feel her pounding heart. She tried to block out the fear that was gathering in the bottom of her stomach. The forest was not like those in Innovera. The trees were tall but there were no blue leaves on the branches. As she got closer to them she could hear piercing cries rising up from them, and could just make out yellow roving eyes peering up at her.

'Maybe I should turn back?' She muttered as she glided deeper into the forest. She glanced down again at the vast wasteland below her. Each tree was so intertwined with its neighbour she wondered what strange creatures there might be under the wretched canopy.

She looked around uncertainly knowing that if she slipped and fell Vinton's fears would be fulfilled. And that could easily happen if the Sylva sensed her nervousness.

Ahead of her she saw the Dimmer Zone approaching and despite herself she became more and more apprehensive.

'Vinton,' she whispered. 'Are you here with me?'

No answer came.

On her right Ayana glimpsed a wide clearing. She decided to head for it. She would rest there a little and try to gather her thoughts before going on. She swung the Sylva sharply - too sharply, because it tilted violently and she felt herself falling. From the moment she began to topple, the Sylva released the straps around her feet.

Ayana hit the ground hard. She was partly cushioned by her protective shield, but she had dropped from a great height and the impact left her dazed and gasping on the ground.

From the edges of her vision she saw movement. She forced herself to sit up. The trees around the the clearing had become agitated. Their naked branches were untangling themselves from each other and clawing at the air. Then she felt the ground vibrating under her. It took a while before she realised what was happening. The trees were pushing out their roots towards her.

She looked around and could not find her Sylva.

She scrambled to her feet and began to back away but the roots - now partly emerged from the soil - were approaching from all directions. She realised her inner shield was useless. It protected her from the dangers that came from above and around her, not from what rose from underneath.

She kept backing away. She summoned her Sylva again; felt its presence nearby but it did not respond.

Ayana covered her face cursing herself for her stupidity; for not listening to Vinton's words of warning. Odors Apeno would not help her now because she had openly defied Him. She thought she heard voices — or perhaps it was a growl. She heard the growl again, much louder this time and suddenly the shivering earth under her subsided.

Heavy footsteps were approaching. Trembling, she removed her hand from her face and looked up.

A large upright man-shape was walking towards her.

'Skylar!' She gasped.

Skylar was walking towards her from the very depths of the threatening forest. And he was not alone. Shay walked behind him. She looked pale and fragile against Skylar's massive, muscular body.

How could Shay and Skylar walk so confidently through a deadly Living Forest?

Even now as Skylar approached her, with the Sylva tucked under his arm, Ayana could not feel his life-force.

What are they doing here? What has he become?

Skylar dropped the Sylva at her feet and looked down at her from his great height.

'Crazy Innoveran Female,' he said in his booming voice. 'You tired of living?'

Ayana looked into his face, at the patterns on his skin and his flowing greenish hair. 'Who - what are you, Skylar? What brings you here? How come I cannot feel you?'

Skylar lifted his heavy shoulders and dropped them. He did not answer her.

Shay brought her face close to Ayana's. It was all Ayana could do to block the girl from invading her thoughts.

Shay was the one person that Ayana suspected had been on The Journey before. She knew more about it than anyone else. Shay acted strangely and sometimes it seemed as if she could see through anyone that she looked at. Because of this, no one trusted her.

Now seeing her beside Skylar with her pale yellow hair fluttering in the wind and her eyes so green and sparkling they reminded her of gemstones, Ayana could well believe the rumours about her. *A Witloc* - descendent of the first beings on Innovera Yakov who inhabited the caves of the Ishu Mountains.

Ayana remembered the words Shay whispered to Gamma, which she was sure Blu Tara overheard. *Your sister has a dark secret. There is another force controlling her and some day it will force her to choose between you and itself.*

'What are you doing here Little Healer?'

Ayana pretended she did not hear Shay.

'Ah!' Shay smiled and wagged a finger in her face. 'I don't need to read your mind. Did you know that your body also thinks? Don't forget I'm an Intuit. All I have to do is look at you.'

Shay straightened up and grinned. 'I know for a fact you're searching for someone, but that person is not here. A whole universe away perhaps, but definitely not here.'

Ayana looked at Shay and then at Skylar. Skylar barely seemed to notice the girl beside him. If there was anything he loved at all, it was his brother, Krave. Surely Shay would know this, wouldn't she? And yet Ayana felt the girl's desperation to be with him. Her desire to merge.

Shay believed that she could make Skylar want her just by tying herself to him and by following him to any wilderness he chose to roam. Being an Intuit would not help her know the truth. Whatever it was that changed Skylar, made him into a Being that was impossible to read.

Skylar appeared to have forgotten them. He was examining the Sylva. He held it up to the sky then pressed it against his chest - all the while passing his hands along the surface.

She suspects he does not care and she's afraid, Ayana thought. *She's afraid of Blu. She's following him for protection. Is that all? Skylar of all beings, why not another.'*

'I don't want anyone else,' Shay shot back. 'Careful what you think, Scarface, I'm reading you.'

'Only if I let you,' Ayana glared at her and looked away. 'What makes you think Blu Tara is so bad for Innovera Yakov?'

'What makes you think I think that?' Shay threw back.

'I heard what you said to Gamma.'

Shay laughed. 'You couldn't have. You were too busy patching up the others.'

'Blu Tara heard you too. And I know you realise that. Is that really why you stick to Skylar? You really think he will protect you?'

'That's where you're wrong.' Shay looked Ayana in the eyes. 'Tell me Ayana Maya: why do you think that almost every life form has the urge to merge?'

Ayana shrugged.

Shay narrowed her eyes at her. 'You've never asked yourself that question? Why this terrible urge to merge even if we know that it might kill us? Look at Gamma Girl and Sunny Krave. Look at you and...no! I will spare you the embarrassment.'

'I'll tell you why, Ayana: because deep down in our selves we're all alone. We're lonely. It doesn't matter how much we pretend otherwise, we're lonely and it frightens us. When you merge with someone else it's different. It is the best thing that any Being can ever ask for - knowing that when you can't carry yourself any more, there's another there to carry you or simply to remind you that they are there.'

Ayana shook her head, 'Even if he doesn't want...'

'Don't say that!' Shay turned blazing eyes on her and pointed at her own face. 'These two eyes - you do not know what they have seen. You do not know what they can see above and beyond the rest of you. And believe me, Scarface, I see what's coming. Not all of it; just glimpses. That's why...' Shay did not finish.

They were both so engrossed in their argument they did not notice Skylar wandering off.

He was in the far distance and disappearing fast.

Shay's face paled. 'Get out of here,' she snapped. 'If you know what's good for you.' Shay ran off at great speed.

Ayana watched Shay's pale yellow hair streaming behind her as she half-flew, half sprinted after Skylar.

From the distance, Shay's parting thought-words reached Ayana, 'You asked him what he is but you already know. You just don't realise you know it. Look at him with different eyes, Little Healer. Remember what he did to save you. Remember everything and then you'll know.'

Ayana summoned her Sylva. The Dimmer World was darkening. She stepped hurriedly onto it and ordered it to rise. The Sylva obeyed her, turning in a tight circle for the distant skies of Innovera Yakov.

Remember everything...remember what he did to save you.

It was only when Ayana looked down again at the tangled branches below her that she realised what Skylar had become. Not only that – Ayana's heart flipped with excitement - Skylar was the first sign of the Blossoming, the great Changes that were to come upon them in preparation for the Journey.

CHAPTER FOURTEEN

BLU TARA climbed to the upper window in the Learning Dome. She scrutinised the shadowy figure watching her from the shade of a Golkan tree. Despite the brightness outside the figure still seemed cloaked in darkness. She knew he was aware of her watching him.

It was clear that he was not worried about being seen. *And why should he be?* Not only was he from another world, he was also an Escapeet.

The figure remained still and silent as a Volcan statue. Blu Tara fought the urge to go to him.

She let her hair ripple slowly. He made a slight movement with his hands in response.

She desired him so much and yet she was forbidden to go near him. *If Gamma finds out,* she thought.

Blu Tara tried not to think about it.

Fighting Gamma would only end in them destroying each other. That was a risk that she, Blu Tara, had been prepared to take from the very beginning. And she'd already done many things for that silent figure out there. *Ice.* Ice was her greatest weakness.

If Gamma finds out... how can I handle her? What can I do to keep her in her ignorance?

It was becoming more and more difficult because the closer Gamma got to unravelling her dreams, the nearer she came to realising exactly what kind of sisters she and Blu Tara really were.

Ice's thought-voice reached Blu Tara. *My domain awaits me now. There are pressing things that I must do. It will be some time before I come again.*

Ice sounded faint and distant. He was preparing to leave her.

'Don't go,' she said. 'Stay with me a little longer. Please!'

She asked this every time he was about to leave her; but he never complied. Still, she felt better knowing that Ice would come again. And if he didn't she could wait. As long as it took. She would. But it would not be for too long again. She was sure to meet him on The Journey.

Blu Tara turned away. She knew that when she looked again, Ice would not be there.

She was glad for one thing: in Innovera Yakov, Beings had no memory of the exact time they arrived in this bright world of minerals and crystals. Beings in most other worlds she heard of — including Earthbounds and Verheerans - were different. Earthbounds remembered their childhood and even their makers. Verheerans, Ice said, could recall the moment of their birth.

But, Blu Tara realised that, for a few Innoverans, the things they were meant to forget in their previous life remained buried in their core. Sometimes these memories surfaced unexpectedly in dreams.

That was the problem with Gamma. She was glad that the Journey would soon be upon them and they would have to leave Innovera Yakov. She, Blu Tara could no longer convince Gamma that the visions she was having during her Rest were just an empty fantasy.

Blu Tara remembered everything. She did not understand why, in Innovera Yakov – the planet of forgetfulness – she had not lost her memory like the others. Before Innovera Yakov, they lived in a fiery world of rocks and dust. There were many suns. The Beings that lived there loved the sizzling air. They bathed in the lava of the great volcanoes, which filled them with abundant energy and replenished their fiery core. Beings from other worlds never invaded them. The heat alone kept them at bay.

They were happy; they were powerful; they were the children of their suns. She - Blu Tara - was Gamma's best friend.

Gamma had always been striking, with eyes that twinkled like a distant galaxy and long fiery hair that ran down her back like molten lava. Because of her great beauty, her people named her, Itania - the name of the most magnificent of all their suns. Itania was also a Dreamer. She loved looking through the portals of their world into other universes.

She wanted to be a *meteon*, one of the great travellers from their planet who crossed the universe as comets and returned with news of strange worlds and even stranger Beings that inhabited them.

It was Magaeia one of the most daring and experienced of their travellers who, after many seasons of voyaging, told them of an underwater city where Beings lived and moved in watery darkness. Nothing could be more different from their own planet of heat and fire, and scorching colours.

Itania did not believe him. Magaeia was insulted. Itania insisted that it could not be true.

It was then that Magaeia, still upset with Itania, told her he would prove his words to her. He took them to his domain, and from some secret corner of his place pulled out a gleaming square of fabric and spread it before them.

He touched it and it came to life. Worlds appeared in front of them, whizzing past in a swirling parade of suns and moons and whirling galaxies.

After a while, Magaeia whispered words and everything slowed down.

The underwater world appeared.

That was how it began.

Many seasons passed and Blu Tara - always in Itania's company - visited Magaeia's place, to stare into the underwater world and follow its inhabitants. They marvelled at the magic of their bright floodlight eyes and supple, flowing bodies.

Then Itania saw him. He was taller than the rest and moved amongst his fellow Beings with such speed and grace, it made her gasp with admiration.

'In his world,' Magaeia said, 'he's royalty, just like you Itania. Look at the way the others move aside for him. And he's a traveller like me. He's an Escapeet. He can travel to other worlds with ease.'

'Can he come here?' Itania asked. 'Can we make him come to us?'

Magaeia looked at her with frightened eyes. 'No! It is forbidden. The Great One will destroy us. At best, we'll be cast out from our world. Leave him be.'

But the sight of that Being had changed something in Itania. When Magaeia left for another of his journeys Itania came to Blu. 'Magaeia is journeying with his old friend, Azman. He's left his Sylva and is sharing Azman's. Will you come with me?'

'He told us it is forbidden. He's already broken our edicts by showing us this world.'

'We will not speak of it to anyone. Not even between ourselves.'

In Magaeia's domain, with his Sylva laid out in front of them, they navigated to the stranger's world. And gradually Itania lost herself in it. Nothing gave her more pleasure than to follow that stranger as he moved about in his world. But as time passed, it was no longer enough for her.

They were bent over the Sylva when Itania looked at Blu with wide disconsolate eyes. 'I cannot rest; I find no joy in anything else. He's all I think about. Sometimes I dream he's holding me and more and more I want to make it real. Do you understand?'

Blu understood. She too had been having dreams of the stranger holding her.

By now they had lost their fear of being cast out of their world.

'I want to reach out to him,' Itania insisted. 'I need to hear him speak.'

Blu looked at her and nodded.

They held hands and sent out thought-words through Magaeia's secret portal. They waited.

He was gliding away at great speed towards some great dark edifice in the distance.

They touched the surface of the Sylva and tried again. Still the figure did not heed them.

'Come to me Dark Stranger,' Itania whispered. 'Come to me right now.'

Just when it seemed that he'd disappeared, the figure returned. A flood of light emanated from his eyes and lit up their faces. They did not blink. The brightness of their suns was far greater and they were accustomed to staring directly into them.

A resounding thought-voice filled their heads.

'Who are you?'

'I'm Itania, I carry the name of our favourite sun. Blu is my companion. We have been watching you.'

'What do you want?'

'I want what I do not yet have,' Itania answered.

'I have no time for riddles. Where are you from?'

'I am from The Red World. I am from the Zone of Flames. I've followed you for many seasons.'

The eyes of the stranger dimmed. 'You speak to me without fear. Why?'

'Fear is not what I have been feeling all this time.'

'What is it you that feel?'

'Your loneliness. Your strength.'

The eyes dimmed further. 'You are of the light and I the darkness. Is it not forbidden?'

'Why ask me this? You already know the answer. What is your name?'

'Here, they call me Ice. In other worlds I am known by other names.'

'Can you not come to our world?'

'I cannot come to your world.'

'Then I will come to yours.'

'I am of the water; you are of the air. You will not survive.'

'Then I will meet you in another world where we can both survive.'

The stranger paused and for a moment, the light in his eyes went out.

'You speak as one who does not know fear. You interest me. How would you come?'

'I will find a way. I want to see your face.'

'You do not need to see my face.'

'Then how else would I know you when I see you in that other world?'

'How did you recognise me now?'

'Look straight ahead. I will show you mine.' Itania pulled back her hair. She spread her palms on the Sylva and brought her face down close to it.

The stranger's voice went soft and deep and musical. You are.... How do you say, 'beautiful?'

'How do you say it in your world?'

'There is no word for beautiful here.'

'I want to see your face now,' Itania said.

He hesitated a long time, then his hands reached up and drew back his hood. Dark eyes in a long pale face stared back at her. It was the face of a young Male. His thick fan-like spread of hair bobbed behind him. *You too are beautiful.* The words had come from Blu who had been silent all along.

The sight of Ice's face had changed everything for Blu. He was more handsome than she'd ever imagined. And the energy that came from him, despite the unimaginable distance that separated them, filled up Magaeia's domain.

Blu did not know when she began craving Ice's attention. But for the many seasons that followed, she and Itania secretly met and spoke to him in Magaeia's domain. He was always there waiting. He did not notice Blu. Those magnificent eyes were only for Itania. And Itania never suspected that she, Blu, would also travel across every galaxy there was just to be with him. Why Itania? Why not her? Wasn't she just as deserving? Wasn't she as powerful as Itania with hair like molten copper? Wasn't she also of noble birth?

Once, she sneaked away from Itania just to be alone with him. She wanted to make him know that there was nothing that Itania would do for him, that she would not. She sat down before the Sylva and called his name. She touched it with both hands. She called many times; repeated every incantation that Magaeia taught them. Ice did not appear.

As the seasons flowed one into the other, Itania's love for the distant stranger grew. The longing in Ice's eyes was also heartbreaking.

Then a time came when Itania said, 'I want to go to him alone.'

'Why?' she asked, struggling to conceal her hurt.

'That is what he asked for,' Itania answered.

'If it is your wish,' Blu mumbled and left.

But she could not forget him. Ice was like a slow eruption in her very core. Blu Tara wanted him for herself.

That was why she told Magaeia when he returned from his travels, about Itania's assignations with the stranger from Verheer. She reminded the old traveller of the danger to his existence if the Sun Consuls found out that it was he who showed this alien world to Itania and herself. Blu reminded him of the punishment. 'Your core will be ripped out and the shell of your body discarded.'

As she expected, Magaeia was terrified. From then on it was easy. They hid Magaeia's Sylva in Itania's father's domain then reported to the Council of the Consuls.

Everything happened quickly after that.

Itania and her father were taken. Itania was to be banished and be deprived of her name. Her father would be destroyed.

The second part of Blu's plan was more dangerous. She would abandon her inner core and infuse herself with Itania's. Then they would fission. She would become another Itania. Identical in every way. After all, they were children of the sun. It had been done before.

In exchange for her abandoned core, Magaeia prepared the cooling liquids and watched over the process.

When Blu finally revived, Itania was still asleep and Blu was smiling. The old man could not believe his flaming eyes.

'Which one are you?' He said.

'I am Itania now,' Blu answered. 'I want to use your Sylva.'

'I do not have it any more.' Magaeia made to walk away.

The Council gave it back to you. I saw. Take me to your place. Or do you want me to tell them everything?

With the Sylva in front of her, Blu summoned Ice. His shape appeared and then his face.

'Itania,' he called, and his wonderful voice washed over her.

'Ice,' she said, 'I want to tell you something.'

She filled her thought-voice with as much distress as she could muster. Blu told Ice that her friend had emptied herself of her life core and fused with hers.

'What does that mean?'

'We are now the same and yet we're not. She's a shadow of myself. She shares my heart.'

'I do not understand.'

'You cannot tell the difference between us now. But the colour that I've chosen for my flame is blue.' Blu stopped and looked away. When she turned back to the Sylva she made herself sound frightened. 'She's been found out. She will be given another name and banished.'

'Why did she do it, Itania?'

'I do not know I-I think that she believes you are for her. She will do anything to have you.'

'She tried to reach me once,' Ice said. 'I did not answer her. Where will they send her, Itania?'

'Some other world - I do not know.'

'Then go with her. Find a way to do that. I will meet you there.'

'How will you find me, Ice?'

'Do not worry, Itania. Wherever you are, I'll find you.'

'There are many named Itania in my world. I will carry another name – one that I will always answer to.'

'What name?'

'Blu Tara.'

'It is not the name I want for you.'

'Then call me what you will.'

Ice nodded. The image in the Sylva faded.

They were posted to Innovera Yakov - the Planet of Forgetfulness. Itania's new name was Gamma.

It took many cycles of the Innoveran moons before Ice found her. Blu saw him standing in what came to be his usual place, under the Golkan tree a short distance from the Learning Dome. She ran to him. But she went through Ice as if he were a shadow.

Something in the Innoveran air, perhaps, made a ghost of Ice.

And yet Blu Tara could hear him clearly.

'I am what I am now. I become substance in our darkness. There is no darkness here.'

He looked her up and down with sad eyes.

'You are so close; yet I cannot see you as clearly as I did before. I do not understand. You are standing right before me; yet why do I feel so...so lonely?'

With a sob of panic Blu reached out to embrace him. Her arms went through his form.

'Tell me what to do,' she cried, 'and I will...just tell me, Ice.'

She heard his voice faint like a whisper. 'I'll come again, Itania. I'll come until I don't have to anymore.'

Ice had been coming ever since.

CHAPTER FIFTEEN

WHEN THE Silverstone tablet landed on Gamma's cot she was afraid to touch it. From the instant she sent it off to Krave she was seized by doubt. Did she do the right thing? Perhaps she'd been too hasty. Should she have chosen gentler words? Would he understand her confusion? Should she have also told him that if she had the freedom to be with him, without all the complications, then she would gladly risk everything for him?

She reached out nervously for the tablet, placed it on her knee and sat back on the cot.

She read the words. She read them again and tried to still her trembling hands. Whichever way she looked at them, however much she scanned Krave's script, the words remained the same.

Be confused no more, Gamma. I've made the choice for you... All I ask of you now is to stay away from me.

Krave Solan.

Gamma dropped the Silverstone. She felt as if all the heat in her had died.

'It was all a lie,' she muttered.' A lie. He does not love me. These are not the words of someone who feels love.' Gamma stared numbly at the tablet. 'He did not even use his script. And to think I was about to risk so much for him.'

Suddenly she was angry. She thought of a string of scorching thought-words to send him. She would deliver them with such force they would burn his brain. Then she thought better of it.

Perhaps he was worried about Skylar, or the Journey, or her. Maybe he was jealous of her connection with her sister.

Her anger flared again.

But this coldness from him, the harshness of his words, this insulting script. What have I done to deserve this?

She picked up the Silverstone, ran a brutal finger across its surface and called up the many layers of love notes, wishful thinking, funny words and promises that passed between them.

'Erase!' She snapped and shook the Silverstone. The words flowed across the face of the tablet in a dizzy scroll as they disappeared forever.

'Done,' she said. 'He took me for a fool, did he? We'll see about than Krave Solan. We'll see!'

She sank back trembling on the cot.

'What's the matter Gams?' Blu Tara appeared in front of her. Gamma did not sense her coming in.

Gamma pointed at the tablet. 'He doesn't even want to see me.'

'Who doesn't, Gamma?'

'Who else?'

'Talk to me Gamma, I don't understand what you're saying.'

'Krave dropped me. It's finished.'

Blu Tara knelt before Gamma and took her hand. 'Dropped you? How?'

Gamma shrugged off her sister. 'Well, you have what you always wanted. And to tell you the truth, it is a relief. It is better to know what he is like now.'

Blu Tara shook her head. 'And to think I was just about to tell you...'

'What?'

'It doesn't matter anymore.'

'What, Blu Tara?'

'I wanted to say I've given up. I'm sick of it - the arguments and the fighting over him. I won't ever lose my temper over him again. I wanted to prove to you that I am serious.'

Blu Tara stood up and walked to the other end of the Pod. Her back was slumped. She unknotted her hair and let it fall. It spread down her back and across her shoulders.

'I kept telling you not to trust him. Males are Swampdogs. And he's the worst type. It's our powers they are after, not us. So!' Blu Tara cast a sideways glance at Gamma. 'He wants you to stay away from him. What is his weakness, Gamma?'

Gamma did not answer.

'Gamma?'

'I cannot tell you that.'

'Why not?'

'I don't want to and I promised.'

'He didn't keep his promises to you, did he? Why should you keep yours?'

'I have to talk to him. I want to watch him in his face and hear him say it - that...that.'

'Face it Gamma.' Blu Tara swung around to face her sister. 'He's rejected you. Where's your pride? What would the others think of us when they hear about you crawling back to Krave? Do you think they'll respect us after this?'

Blu Tara walked slowly towards Gamma. 'I love you with my own life Gamma. I do. I will die for you and you already know that I'll kill for you.

You opened your mind to me last time, and let me feel your pain. It was the worst I've ever felt. The worst! Me, I would block him out completely. Block out the hurting and the wanting. Because...'Once again Blu Tara lowered herself in front of Gamma. Krave will not give up. He will change his mind and try again because he's desperate for what you - for what we have. He wants our strength. Block him out completely, Itania. That's why I want to know his weakness - so I can protect you from him.'

'Funny.' Gamma said, looking straight at Blu. 'Why did you call me "Itania"?'

'I don't know what you mean,' Blu Tara said impatiently.

Gamma slid to the floor, so that her back was pressed against the side of their cot. 'You just called me *Itania*.'

'I didn't, Gamma. Couldn't have.'

'You called me, *Itania*. It was the name the old man called me in my dreams.'

'Then you must have told me.'

'Did I? I don't remember ever....'

'We were talking about Krave. Why all this talk about foolish dreams now?'

'Because you called me, *Itania* and...'

'I did not, Gamma. It must be your mind!'

'Okay,' Gamma said. 'I'll tell you what Krave's weakness is.'

Blu Tara settled back. 'I'm listening.'

'It is the same as mine.'

'And what is yours?'

'You already know. Aren't we the same?'

'Are you playing with me?' Blu Tara's eyes suddenly ignited.

'Watch your temper, Blu. I keep warning you about that. Didn't you just say you'll never lose it again?'

Blu Tara stormed out of the Pod.

CHAPTER SIXTEEN

WHEN SHAY returned from the Swampland with Skylar, it was clear that she had changed. She walked more confidently. She smiled more easily. She no longer trailed behind Skylar. She strolled ahead of him.

Before, Ayana never noticed her pale beauty. Her blond hair had turned silver-white. She seemed much taller and slimmer, and she moved in her shimmering green robe as if her feet were skimming the ground.

'They've merged,' Ayana thought incredulously. 'They have actually done it.'

But then, she realised they couldn't have done so if what Shay herself had suggested about Skylar was true.

Remember how he saved you now. Remember everything.

Gamma popped up beside Ayana. She too was watching Shay as she left the open fields and entered the compound of the Learning Dome.

'You see that?' Gamma whispered admiringly. 'Another goddess walks amongst us.'

Leaving Shay to walk on, Skylar turned off the path and approached them smiling.

'Seems like they've both drunk from the Lake of Happiness,' Gamma chuckled.

Skylar reached down without warning and lifted Ayana high above his head. She held onto him kicking and shrieking and laughing at the same time.

He held her above his head for a while; then he put her down.

'You better now?' He asked, nudging Ayana with an elbow.

Ayana nodded, feeling suddenly flushed with happiness.

'Heh!'

Gamma doubled up with laughter. 'Heh? Is that the way you laugh now, Skylar?'

Skylar grinned at her. 'Heh!'

Another burst of laughter escaped Gamma. 'Lovely Male,' she said. 'You've finally grown up.

'And Krave?' Skylar asked.

Gamma cooled abruptly.

'He's my brother,' Skylar said. 'I never see him hurt so much. O Fire Queen please talk to him.'

'He does not want to see me.'

'I don't believe. He loves you like I love him. Perhaps more.'

Gamma raised an eyebrow at Skylar. 'Perhaps?'

'Heh!'

Despite herself Gamma broke into another fit of giggles.

She stopped because Skylar was not teasing anymore. He was quite still as if he were listening to something in the air.

Ayana looked past him and saw what must have made him go so quiet.

Shay was about to enter the Learning Dome. A group of eight students - all Males – were heckling her. They were calling her by the old name that they used to insult her with: *Slutlod*

Ayana knew straight away that they were resenting the change they noticed in Shay. The new confidence with which she carried herself now was clearly not going down well with them.

Sizler was the worst. He was good-looking and he knew it. He had a mane of rippling white hair and a body that Odors Apeno seemed to have carved with his very own hands. He was as loud and reckless as Skylar used to be. A great Sky-Roller, Sizler had a following of young fools who desperately wanted to be like him.

Shay dropped her hand from the door and began to back away from them. She moved back slowly down the path as if she had all the time in the world. Her eyes were sparkling in the light. Sizler and his companions quickened their steps and surrounded her. Shay drew herself up to full height and stopped walking. She was taller than they were.

The fact that Shay no longer bowed her head and hurried away seemed to agitate Sizler even more.

'Slutloc!' He shouted. 'Been out looking for Verheerans?'

Gamma could not bear it. She swung around, her hair a twisting coil of flames.

Ayana felt the rush of heat and moved away with quickening heartbeat. 'There will be trouble,' she mumbled to herself as she clasped her hands and went into healing mode.

Gamma lifted a quick finger to her right lens. Skylar grabbed her hand.

'No!' he said.

Gamma pulled away from him. 'It will not happen,' she hissed. 'Not while I'm standing here. It will not!'

Skylar grabbed her hand again. 'It will not, O Hot One. Please hold on!'

Gamma looked into his face and frowned. Then they heard the screams.

When they looked over, Shay was still standing amongst Sizler and his friends but they were doubled over at her feet. Their hands clawed at their heads as if something terrible was lodged in there.

Shay's fingers were pressed against her temples and she'd gone rigid. A small wind was tugging at the edges of her robe. And her eyes. *Her eyes!* Ayana shook her head in astonishment. Shay's eyes were glittering like polished crystals.

Shay dropped her hands only when the bodies of the young men crumpled at her feet.

Ayana rushed over to them, passed a hand across each body and straightened up. 'Knocked out,' she sang, a big smile on her face. 'Out cold! But they'll liiiive!'

Ayana turned to Shay and took her hands. She felt something strong and deep and pulsing within the tall girl.

'Shay,' she whispered, raising herself on the balls of her feet and kissing her. 'You...you're amazing.'

Shay lifted Ayana's hand and brought it to her lips. 'Healer,' she whispered back. 'Learn what I've learned out there.' She raised her chin and directed it at the wastelands in the distance. 'Love yourself. Believe!'

Shay floated back to the Dome.

Skylar had his hands around Gamma's shoulder. He seemed to be smiling at the world. 'O Fiery One, you see! Like you said, 'Happen it will not!' Heh!'

Skylar dropped his arm from Gamma's shoulder, winked at her and left them standing there.

Gamma was speechless. 'Wha- what happened there, Ayana - what....?'

'I think I know,' Ayana answered quietly. 'I felt it inside Shay. It is the Season of Upliftment. It is the time of change. Apeno is preparing us for the Journey. Shay is just the first.'

Gamma nodded soberly then shook her head. 'Not Shay. It was you. Remember Ryder and that spear? And then of course there's Skylar. Now it all begins to make sense.'

Ayana touched the scars along her face. 'I hope it isn't finished, Gamma. For me, I mean. I-I hope I get a different body. A new face at least.'

'It's all in your mind. You're wonderful.' Gamma seemed suddenly distracted. 'I'm thinking now that I would have liked to speak to Krave before the change happens to him and me. I would have liked to know if - if...' She threw an anguished look at Ayana. 'Sorry, Little Healer. I-I don't know how to say it. I'll see you around.'

CHAPTER SEVENTEEN

BY THE way Shay was leaning against the doorway of the Learning Dome, Gamma knew that she was waiting for her. Once again Gamma found herself marvelling at Shay's new composure.

As soon as she entered the doorway, Shay took her hand. 'Thanks Gamma.'

'For what?' Gamma looked quizzically at her.

'For helping.'

'I didn't,' Gamma said. 'You did it all yourself.'

'Thanks all the same,' Shay smiled. 'Let's just say, your attitude was encouraging.'

' Even the way you talk is different.' Gamma shook her head and grinned.

'You never heard me talk before,' Shay said, 'because nobody really listened. That's the problem with bullies, they mistake quietness for weakness.'

'But something did happen to you,' Gamma insisted. 'You're not the same.'

'I want to talk about you Gamma; not about myself.'

'What about?'

'About love… about…'

'I'm not talking about Krave.'

'Did I mention Krave? Anyway, I think you should talk to him.'

Gamma felt her temper rise. 'He should talk to me. He's the one...'

'He's been trying,' Shay cut in.

'It's done, Shay. It is.'

'No its not.' Shay rested kind eyes on her face. 'Your body tells me it isn't. I'm reading you, Gamma. I'm reading all the questions that are troubling you right now. Was it just a hoax? A charade between two magnificent Beings?

You tell yourself you hate him now. Shay imitated Gamma's voice. *But why does his image keep haunting me so much? Did he love me?*' Shay prodded Gamma with her finger and laughed. 'You should see your face now, Gamma. But, I'll tell you what, I've begun to think that maybe that's the wrong question to ask.'

'What's the right question then?'

'Well, here it is Gamma,' Shay splayed her fingers as if she were about to count. 'Can I find the strength to love without needing to have my love returned? Now that's a question because,' Shay folded a finger. 'Who says that one has to have the love they're offering returned in exactly the same way, especially when the other person didn't ask for it?'

'You're talking about yourself, Shay.'

'Maybe I am, maybe I'm not. Perhaps I'm talking about both of us. But here's the answer to the big question you are really asking because I know - and every fool around here knows - your love is alive and you are still hoping. *Was he for me and me for him? Were we meant to merge?* Watch that face of yours Gamma; I'm reading you!'

Shay leaned close and dropped her voice. 'You can still go to the Circle of Knowing and find the answer. Krave doesn't have to be there. Take something that belongs to him with you - a little gift or something. Hold it in your hands. Face the stone and ask. Then watch the colours change until they settle. If it turns red and stays....'

Shay cocked her head and stopped. 'I see your sister coming.'

She walked off quickly but her last message came in thought-words to Gamma. 'Remember what I told you. She's not good for you. Hope you get to see that before it is too late.'

CHAPTER EIGHTEEN

KRAVE SOLAN was convinced that something went wrong with his communication to Gamma. Her behaviour made no sense. Whatever it was, he saw Blu Tara's hand in it. A few words with Gamma, even an apology if she demanded one, could quickly set things right. But Gamma was blocking him out completely. However hard he tried he could not reach her.

Maybe it was his fault, maybe by coming together with Gamma the way he did angered Odors Apeno. Perhaps it was because he broke the natural laws of their world by approaching Gamma first.

He knew - like every Innoveran did - that females chose their partners.

The females of their world were the ones who picked whoever they wished to merge with. It was not only by attraction. Attraction was fine, but it rarely ever came first. Attraction was often fatal because it sometimes led to deadly combinations that ended in the destruction of each other.

What mattered was how their individual powers combined. For some reason that puzzled Krave, females were the best at choosing. They were experts at the laws of combination.

In the secrecy of their Pods they sat with numerous charts and graphs spread out on their cots. With the aid of these charts they assessed the abilities of everyone: the particular powers of their mind, the grace and speed with which they moved, their special gifts and the way they handled danger. By the time they finally made their choice, they already had a clear idea of the new powers they would both gain by combining with the Being of their choice. She would then approach her candidate, show her charts and explain what they were likely to become when they combined their forces.

The combinations were marvellous. Sometimes females preferred other Females kind for their special gifts of grace and foresight. Males often merged with other Males to boost their strength and speed. Males and females - when perfectly merged - became a formidable unit.

Those who preferred to be on their own and explore their powers to the limit fought and died alone when they were faced with danger.

He - Krave Solan - had broken the rules by approaching Gamma first. He did not give a second thought about the dangers of combining. He wanted only her. He dreamed only of this striking pink girl who was bright and gracious as a Starfly and delicate as the petals of a gemstone flower. And here he was now suffering the punishment for ignoring the rules and choosing her. He saw the difference between Gamma and Blu Tara straight away.

He could not understand why everyone else confused the two. Gamma was a spark of perfect light; her sister was an ugly Solarflare.

Krave raised himself off his cot and stared out of his Pod, hoping to catch a glimpse of Gamma. He hardly went out anymore.

He looked down at his feet and his golden eyes began to darken slowly. He was not ill. Sickness was something only Earthbounds and Verheerans experienced. And yet he could no longer fly.

He examined the purple swelling that was spreading from the side of his knees all the way down to his ankles. It felt as if there were some living things in there. At first he thought that Swamp-worms had infected both his legs. Maybe they had attached themselves to his brother, Skylar, who unknowingly brought them to his Pod. But Krave realised that it could not be because even if the swelling kept increasing, he felt no pain. It was not gnawing at his body either. But it kept him grounded in his Pod since he could not afford to have the others see how weak and useless he had become. *Unlike my brother, Skylar.*

Every time Krave watched Skylar appearing from the Swampland in the distance, with Shay trailing behind him, he wondered what had happened to his brother.

The first time Skylar went off with Shay, Krave followed them. They headed straight for the Swampland. That place was like a bit of Verheer that managed to make its way into Innovera Yakov. The trees were alive. Their roots did not feed from the soil but on the living things that strayed beneath its shade. Yet from way up in the air, he watched Shay and his brother enter it and emerge on the other side as if they were taking a stroll on the grounds of the Learning Dome.

When they returned, Krave confronted him. 'If you were not my brother, Skylar, I would say you were Verheeran.'

'Verheeran!' Skylar boomed. 'You insult me with that name.'

'Then what are you?' Krave demanded.

Skylar pulled him close and whispered the explanation in his ear. Krave stared at him with amazement.

It was then that Shay advised him about Gamma. 'She needs

to be with you, Krave. Not only out of love. It is to save herself.'

'Save herself from what?'

Shay looked Krave in his eyes. 'From the darkness. That is what I see.'

Krave shook his head. 'We've broken the rules. This is our punishment.'

'If you two didn't break the rules; the rules would have broken you. Love creates its own rules. That's what I believe. Gamma carries a great power, but it is not all hers. It might never be. I-I have not seen this clearly yet, Krave. It will come to me in time. It is not only her sister that is the problem. Find a way to stay with her. You understand?'

'She no longer wants to be with me,' Krave said.

'You don't have to be with her to stay with her. It's two different things. If what you feel for her is any good or real then not having her will not stop you caring.

Gamma still carries you inside her - so much in fact, she is seeking an answer from the Circle of Knowing. Do you know what that means?'

'I know,' Krave said.

'Then do what you should do.' Shay pointed a finger at her heart. 'You are the one who started it. Loving is not always easy.'

Krave looked at his brother and then at Shay. He saw the sadness in Shay's eyes.

'I'm sorry,' he said to her.

'Sorry for what?'

Krave looked at his brother again. 'I cannot tell you this, Shay. I cannot tell you yet. When will Gamma be there?'

'In ten thousand counts,' Shay said and left the Pod with Skylar.

Krave left his Pod early. Gamma's decision to go to the Circle of Knowing meant one thing: she had not completely abandoned him. Normally, with a single leap, he would take to the air and arrive there very quickly. Now it would take him a great deal longer.

He had only seen the Circle of Knowing from the air. It was in that valley deep in the foothills of the Ishu Mountains that they called The Dazzle. The circle was so strewn with gemstones, it looked as if all the best and brightest jewels of Innovera Yakov had been scattered there. Some students believed that the millions of glittering jewels on the ground were the eyes of Odors Apeno.

Krave knew that Students went there only when they felt they no longer had a choice. Sometimes it was to resolve a dispute that became so dangerous, it threatened the existence of the colony or when a Being was so torn between decisions they did not know what to do.

The Circle of Knowing was their last resort. Whatever it decided they could not go back on it, or have it changed.

That was the problem, Krave thought. In Innovera Yakov Beings were changing all the time.

There were those who at first were not compatible. But if they stuck together and believed, some strange chemistry between them happened. Then merging became possible.

He heard of Innoverans who were so impatient for an answer, they went to the Circle too soon. The gemstone in their hands turned green instead of red. They returned unhappy and distraught, condemned to be apart forever.

Perhaps, with Gamma, he'd been too impatient. Didn't she keep asking him for time? But no – like a fool he did not listen!

Gamma's words came back to him. 'Some things you have to wait for, Krave. Some answers only come with time.'

When Krave arrived, he climbed the foothill until he sat at the mouth of a cave directly above the Circle. He pulled back his hair and knotted it behind his head. Then he lay flat on his stomach. Even if Gamma looked up she would not be able to see him.

Gamma came down from the clouds like a beautiful pink ribbon of light and alighted in the circle. He almost called out to her.

'Apeno!' He whispered, fervently. 'She is your greatest miracle.'

From the corner of his eye another flash appeared. It was a blue twinkle that disappeared as quickly as it showed. Krave looked up quickly scanned the foothills around but saw nothing, apart from the grassy hillsides and towering mountains.

Gamma picked up the crystal and bowed her head. Krave felt his heartbeat rising. If he had to stop her, it had to be now. But he'd promised Shay that he would leave her alone.

He, like every Innoveran, knew the words Gamma was about to say by heart. It was one of the first things that they learned.

Two paths lie before me.
I do not know which I must choose.
Whatever you decide
On my life I must abide by it.
Your choice will become mine.
I will not question it. I will obey.

With her head still bowed, Gamma took another object from her garment. It was a piece of rock. Krave recognised it instantly. Once, in the Dimmer Zone after he shot her in the air, Gamma took that piece of rock and held it out to him. She asked him to infuse it with the electricity from his hand. She could hold it when she was missing him, she said, and feel his energy.

Gamma lifted both the crystal and the piece of rock high

above her head. A bright cascade of light descended around her hands. Then it became a kaleidoscope of colours.

Krave leaned over the ledge, his heart thundering so much he was afraid that she might sense him watching her.

The colour of the gemstone changed again. It became a pulsing scarlet. Then it dimmed and took on a soft green glow. Krave's heart sank. Gamma's distressed cry rose up to him.

But it wasn't over.

The crystal brightened suddenly - shifting between green and red, then pink, then....

A burst of white light seemed to come from nowhere and explode in Gamma's hand. The crystal and the rock flew from them. Krave rose to his feet, scanning the foothills with his eyes. Then he leapt.

He landed directly beside Gamma and placed himself in front of her.

'Pick it up,' he said, still scanning the mountains.

Gamma looked at him confused.

'Now!' He insisted. 'Take the crystal in your hand.'

Prompted by Krave's urgency, Gamma snatched up the crystal from the ground.

Another burst of hot, white light came from one of the peaks of the Ishu Mountains directly ahead of them. Krave's right arm shot up. A storm of writhing lightning erupted from his hand. The air around them crackled. Then it cleared.

'You all right?' He said glancing back at Gamma.

Gamma nodded. She looked pale and shaken. 'What happened?' She said.

Krave turned to her. 'Your sister, no doubt trying to burn you up. I'm quite sure it's her. That ray came from up there.' Krave pointed at the peak.

'My sister's ray is blue. That one was white.'

'Has to be her,' Krave insisted. 'Who else wants to kill us for no good reason?'

'Can't be,' Gamma dropped the crystal on the ground. 'That's the problem. Everything is Blu! As far as you're concerned she can do no good.'

'Who else shoots micro-solars apart from you and her?'

'My sister wouldn't do that.' Gamma turned her back on him. 'Besides,' she swung around to face Krave. 'What business have you got here?'

'You should be thanking me, Gamma. Not scolding me as if...'

'Answer me, Krave Solan! Did you follow me?'

'Your sister...'

'Don't talk to me about my sister. I said it couldn't be her.'

'Who else then? Who...'

Before Krave could finish speaking, Gamma shot off. She was now a streak of pink against the bright Innoveran sky.

Krave lifted his hand and sent a golden arc of electricity after her. It was meant to tickle her and remind her of their times in the Dimmer Zone.

The sky reddened around the distant shape of Gamma. Suddenly a solar flare lit up everything around him. The shockwave lifted him and threw him hard against the rocks of the mountainside.

'That's it, then! I'm done with you,' he mumbled before sinking into unconsciousness.

When Gamma stormed into their Pod. Her eyes were flaming crimson.

Blu Tara was resting on their cot, wrapping her hair around her arm.

'Where were you?' Gamma said.

'Exactly where you see me now.' Blu Tara answered quietly. 'Why?'

Gamma shot out a hand and pressed Blu Tara's temple. 'You're hot,' she said. 'Why are you so hot?'

'I'm always hot,' Blu Tara raised a curious eyebrow at her. 'And so are you. By the way you're very hot right now. What have you been up to?'

Gamma looked doubtfully at Blu, then turned away. 'I hope he's alright.'

'Who?'

Gamma swung around to face her sister. Her eyes had gone a dangerous red. 'I want a straight answer, Blu Tara. Answer yes or no. Did you follow me out there?'

'Out there, where, Gams?'

Gamma pushed her thumb against Blu Tara's temple. 'Uncloak your mind and answer me.'

'I can't do that, Gamma.'

'Why not?'

'That is - unless you do the same.'

'Did you follow me?'

'Follow you where?'

'Did you?'

'I just told you.' Blu Tara released her hair and yawned. 'I am exactly where you found me.'

Gamma sank onto the cot beside her sister. She unwrapped Krave's gift from the fabric of her dress and held it in her hand. There was no energy left in it.

It had gone stone cold.

Chapter Nineteen

It was Ryder who found Krave's body just outside the Circle of Knowing.

Ryder said he was out near the foothills practising with his new spear, riding the air on it in fact, when he saw the little golden spark way down below. He descended for a closer look and discovered it was Krave.

He'd brought the body back and laid it on the grass, just outside the Learning Dome.

Ryder stuck the tip of his spear on the ground beside his feet. It was more magnificent than the one he had before. It was a bright silver-blue and shimmering with energy. The first one disappeared he said. This new one had mysteriously replaced it.

He looked down at Krave, shook his head and moved away.

Students gathered quickly and surrounded the prostrate Krave. Everywhere Females were weeping. Many of the Males who secretly adored Krave were struggling to hide their grief.

Skylar stood above his brother like a towering Golkan tree. A constant rumble came rolling from his chest. He would not let anyone near Krave - not even Gamma, who was so weak with grief she could barely stand.

Ayana pushed her way through the crowd of students.

'This is my work,' she said to Skylar.

Skylar moved aside for her.

Ayana knelt beside Krave and passed her hands across his face. There was no breath. She pressed his chest and felt for the pulse beneath his clavicle. She felt nothing.

She closed her eyes and called upon her moons. She was weak and trembling when she looked up at the stricken faces around her.

'I feel nothing,' she said.

A terrible rumble erupted from Skylar.

Ayana leaned down and pressed her lips against Krave's ear. 'Heartbreaker, Lovetaker,' she whispered, 'You beautiful son of our suns. Too many of us here love you. You must not leave us now. I beg of you to rise.'

'Take him to the Healing Dome,' a voice suggested.

'What is already gone cannot be healed,' another voice replied. Skylar cast a wrathful glance at the speaker who shut up immediately.

Gamma was so distraught, Blu Tara had to lead her away.

Ayana knew that Gamma went off with Blu because she could not bear to witness what would come next: the melting away of Krave's body. The colour would slowly drain from him. He would become transparent before The Fading.

Within half a cycle of their moon, they would not even remember him. It was the way of Innovera.

'You're sure he's left us?' Shay asked Ayana.

Ayana stood up. Most of the other students were now leaving for the Learning Dome. They were already beginning to forget, Ayana thought. But she, she vowed she never would. And yet there was not much she could to make herself remember. It was the way of Innovera Yakov.

Ayana hesitated. 'With Skylar I feel nothing, Shay. Yet Skylar is with us. They are brothers. Maybe it is the same.'

'You feel nothing? Nothing at all?' Shay sounded shocked and frightened.

Ayana drew Shay aside and spoke into her ear.

'There is something. But it is not inside him.'

Shay clasped Ayana's hand and looked her in the face. 'Tell me Little Healer. Tell me it is good. May Apeno forgive me, but if I could pray to you I would. Tell me it is good. Not even for his sake, but for mine.'

'Why, Shay? Why for your sake?'

'Skylar lives for what he loves. He lives for his brother. I am not enough. I wish I were but I'm not. I find shelter in that love.'

Ayana felt so sad for Shay she wanted to cry.

'Shay,' she said.' What I felt was not inside Krave. Inside him was cold.' Ayana lowered her voice even further. 'What I felt was in his feet.'

'Then,' Shay smiled hopefully at her. 'Then he is not.... gone?'

'That I cannot tell you,' Ayana whispered. 'That I do not know.'

CHAPTER TWENTY

THE SADNESS that overcame Gamma was unbearable. She wanted to fade away with Krave. She wanted to die.

'I killed him,' she cried.

It was the first time she had ever done anything like that. It was meant to be a harmless blast. Krave was a Leaper, wasn't he? He could have easily avoided it.

Oddly, no one seemed to blame her. After telling Skylar what she did, he shook his head. It was impossible for his brother to die at the hands of a Female, he said, especially the one he loved above all else. Skylar did not tell her why he believed this.

It made Gamma's grieving worse.

Blu Tara tried to console her. 'It couldn't have been you, Gams. It had to be something else.'

But realising that she could do nothing to console her sister, Blu Tara threw one last look at Gamma and left the Pod.

Gamma sank back on her cot and replayed in her mind, the times she spent in the Dimmer Zone with Krave; the thrilling electricity that came from his hands which so excited her. She remembered the way he carved her name against the sky and the gentleness with which he always held her.

Exhausted with her own grief, she drifted off to sleep. Soon her head was filled with images of the strange world that she so often dreamed about: a world of boiling skies, fiery dust and molten rocks.

She saw herself sitting in a cave of some sort with a dark-haired girl. They were both staring into something. A figure floated in the distance; then gradually a face appeared before them followed by a voice that resonated in her head. It was a voice so deep and filled with longing that it stirred up something sad and soft in her.

The darkness melted into a boiling world of light and heat. The elder who said he was her Maker called her by that strange name: *Itania*. He was kneeling before her and holding up a solar blade. She took the blade from him and began to raise it.

Gamma shot out of her dream.

She did not know how long she remained on her cot but it must have been a long time. Outside the students had started a game of Sky Roll and she was still sitting in the same spot when they finished it. Now there was only silence outside and the faint throbbing of the Golan Trees.

It took a while before she realised that Blu Tara was standing in the far corner of the Pod looking quietly at her.

Gamma raised her head and flung back her hair.

'Tell me, Blu. Do you understand what it feels like to destroy the Being that you love?'

'I told you Gamma, you did nothing to Krave Solan.'

'I wasn't talking about Krave Solan,' Gamma answered quietly, 'I was talking about my Maker - my..my father.'

Blu Tara strolled over and sat down beside her. 'How many times must we go over this? You never had a Maker. We never did - apart from Odors Apeno maybe...'

'No? Or a friend named....I didn't get the name. Or it does not come to me now. Yes, sorry - I was dreaming.'

'There is a way to stop it, Gamma.'

'I know,' Gamma replied. 'I drink from the River of a Thousand Eyes. But only a fool would do that. Who wants to forget everything?'

'Not everything, just the dreams.'

'What if I don't want to do that?'

'You do. Believe me, Gamma. It distresses you too much.'

'Everybody dreams. They just won't admit it because it is said to be a weakness. At least that's what Shay said.'

'Shay! Blu Tara shot to her feet. 'What does she know? Pretending to be what she isn't. I don't like the ground she floats on!'

'Ever crossed your mind that she does not like you either?'

'Well,' Blu Tara pointed at her lens and smiled. 'We'll see about that; won't we?'

'You mess with her and you mess with Skylar.'

'She's nothing to Skylar. He doesn't give a damn about her.'

'How do you know that?'

Blu Tara shrugged. 'It's obvious. In any case what can he do?'

'Touch Shay and you'll see.'

'See what!' Blu Tara glared scornfully at Gamma. 'He's just a lump of- of mineral. What's there to see?'

'You don't know what he can do. In fact neither of us knows. He might make you fade away..'

'Then you'll disappear too.'

Gamma shrugged. 'Then so be it.'

'What's got into you Gamma. What's this all about? Do you think that you're the only one here suffering. Do you really think that this thing is not affecting me too? Look – I'll show you something.' Blu Tara rolled up her sleeves with violent motions of her hand. She exposed the web of grey lines that ran along them.

'This is what's been happening to me. I'm dying. All because of you and this stupid thing you've got with Krave. I cannot bear my own heat now. It's like I'm burning up inside. Do you know what I have to do now?'

Gamma raised an eyebrow at her. 'No, tell me, Blu.'

'I go up in the air, whenever I get a chance to cool down. I crave the cold. So why should I be grieving for Krave Sonar?'

'Foolish!' Gamma said.

'What? You're telling me I'm lying? You telling me I'm not serious?'

Gamma smiled again. 'I'm telling you, you're silly.'

Gamma calmly rolled up her sleeves and exposed her arms. 'See? I have the same lines too.'

'You - you're dying too?' Blu Tara's voice had dropped to a whisper; then it rose with indignation. 'And even though you know that you still...'

'We're not dying, Blu Tara. It is the Change. It is beginning to come upon us.'

Blu Tara paled. 'Are you – are you sure?'

'Yes, I am. Dying my eyes!' Gamma chuckled. 'Thanks for that Blu Tara. At least you lifted my mood.'

Chapter Twenty-One

AYANA TOOK her Silverstone Tablet and swiped the surface quickly. She concentrated and soon her script began to appear.

All around me I see the Changes happening to the others. I feel nothing. What will I become? When will it begin for me?

If I had a choice, I would have the golden skin of Krave, the beauty and height of Gamma and the wisdom of Shay.

I would have my shoulder blades grow out of my skin. I would have them spread so that they become wings.

I would not be a lowly healer. I would be a warrior like Ryder and the others and I would not be looking for love. Instead love would come looking for me.

Ayana brushed the Silverstone with the palm of her hand and the script sank beneath its surface.

'Then you no longer be Myana,' Vinton whispered in her ear. 'You become someone else. You become a patched up Being. Little piece of this, little piece of that! Not whole like now. And me, Vinton, will not be with you. That what you want?'

'Well, you're hardly ever there,' Ayana retorted.' Especially when I need you. I almost died the last time. It was Skylar who saved me. Where were you?'

'Maybe Apeno planned it,' Vinton said. 'Maybe Apeno no like reckless, always-asking-questions girl. No - Apeno no like that.'

'Then why's he made me this way in the first case?'

Vinton was silent for a long while. 'Sorry,' he said finally. 'Me, Vinton never thought about that. Earthbounds call that Feel-oo-sophy. Earthbound just like you — always ask questions. Too much! Then they get wrong answer. Wrong answer never right but every Earthbound think they right. So they fight. One destroy one. Many destroy many. Then Poof! All destroy all. World of Earthbound finish!'

'Feeling dramatic today, Vinton?' Ayana laughed.

But she realised that Vinton was serious. 'When Change come upon you,' he said. 'Maybe not for eyes to see. Maybe you change inside. It happen before. Maybe you got all the power but you don't know. You see, Myana, you not same like other Innovera Being.'

'That's the problem! I don't want to be different,' she cried 'These scars I sleep and wake with. I didn't ask for them. I don't want them. Do you know what it feels like having to hide half of your face from the rest of the world? Not knowing where they came from and who you are? And Apeno will not help me!'

Her eyes filled up with tears.

'I will tell you this much, Ayana Yé Maya.' Vinton's voice suddenly changed. It seemed to come from inside her head and the walls of her Pod at the same time. Ayana looked up and saw that Vinton looked more solid than she'd ever seen him before. And she knew that it was Odors Apeno talking to her through him because only He knew her by her full name. She was seized with mild panic and embarrassment.

'Odors Apeno, forgive me. I open my heart to your words,' she said quietly, respectfully and bowed her head.

'No one is of this world apart from Shay Osun - the wise one amongst you. Everyone has arrived. Soon you will have done your time here, Yé Maya. You grow pained and impatient with the silence that surrounds you, but there are things I will not tell you because you must discover them yourself. That way you understand them better because you have lived them. That is the way a Being grows – through experience. More than anyone else who resides here, you hunger to know your beginnings. I watch you endanger your life for answers that will come to you in time. Know that I have heard you and to protect you from yourself. I will unveil to you, your past.

You are a child of the Planet of Beginnings.'

'An Earthbound,' Ayana murmured sadly. 'So it is true after all.'

'Why such sadness? Love brought you here. Goodness brought you to Innovera Yakov. You are here after your first Passing.'

'I-I died?'

'Not as you understand it. You are hearing me now, aren't you? You are breathing. Do you call this death?'

'What caused my first, erm – Passing?'

'Close your eyes, Yé Maya. I will take you there.'

Ayana closed her eyes. The Pod grew warm. Her head hollowed out. Now she was sitting in the front seat of a car. Her heart was throbbing with excitement. A woman, her mother, was at the wheel beside her. Strapped in at the back was her ten-year-old brother, Aiden.

Aiden was sitting quietly, looking out at the city lights that were streaming past. On the other side of the bridge they were about to cross, there came the joyous sound of great festivity. The sky was lit up with fireworks. A cheer went up from the crowds on the banks of the great river that flowed through the city.

Her mother turned to her smiling, 'Happy New Year, sweetheart. Happy New Year, Aiden.'

Her mother had barely turned back to concentrate on the road when her eyes and mouth opened wide in horror. An oncoming truck was zigzagging across the bridge towards them.

The truck hit them full on. Ayana felt the bone-shaking impact followed by the tearing grate of metal, and then the sensation of being suspended in a void as the car left the bridge. The river was like a glittering sheet of steel rushing up to meet them. She heard herself screaming. She could not see her mother's face, or what was left of it as the car hit the water.

As soon as the vehicle struck the water, a calmness came over her. Her mother was a broken shape against the steering-wheel. Ayana was struggling to unstrap herself. The seatbelt gave way. She found that she could barely move. Her body was almost as mashed up as her mother's, yet she managed to pull herself over to the back of the car and unstrap her brother. He was still but he was breathing.

How she managed to extricate herself from the sinking car and rise to the surface with Aiden, she did not know. Many hands were there to drag them out. The body she lived in did not make it to the hospital. Aiden's did.

'Where's Aiden?' She asked.

'He too Passed.'

'He - died?'

'Passed.'

'To where? I beg of you, Apeno, please tell me: where is my brother now?'

'That,' Apeno said, 'Is what brought you here. The purest of all love - the kind that puts the life of another Being before itself.'

'Please,' she pleaded, 'tell me where my brother is.'

'In a place of waiting, Yé Maya. To get to him, there is one thing you have to learn: patience.'

The Pod grew cooler, and with it the fading away of Vinton and the voice.

Ayana covered her face with her hands and cried.

CHAPTER TWENTY-TWO

WHEN SHAY was not out in the Living Forest with Skylar, she hung around Ayana.

Ayana welcomed the friendship of this tall Innoveran girl who was the only Intuit she knew.

Many of the Students thought that Shay's powers were similar to hers because they both saw into others, but in reality they were quite different. Ayana could reach beyond the minds of others and access their life force which made it possible to heal. Shay on the other hand understood the language of their bodies. She picked up the emotions behind the almost invisible movements of their hands and eyes and faces. There was also a part of Shay that read the intentions of others just before they acted.

She told Ayana that she recently discovered a new ability when she was out in the Living Forest with Skylar. She could sense the presence of the unseen Beings that haunted the edges of the forest where the River of a Thousand Eyes reached the boundaries of Verheer.

She told Ayana of the Escapeet that attacked them when she and Skylar were resting in one of the clearings dotted throughout the forest. Shay's eyes darkened with the memory.

They were there for a while, she said, when she felt its presence directly over her. Whatever it was, she realised that it was trying to enter her. Her cries woke Skylar. He was puzzled and confused at first, but then he understood.

Skylar pulled her close to his chest and held her there. With the other hand he stirred the air so fast it created a small whirlwind that lifted the dust and leaves off the forest floor.

They saw the shape of the Escapeet outlined by the cloud of swirling dust.

Shay shook her head and laughed. 'A Verheeran! A little Escapeet, no doubt feeding on the creatures in the forest.'

'So close to Innovera Yakov?' Ayana asked.

'That's nothing,' Shay replied. Did she, Ayana, know that there was one that came amongst them from time to time?

'Its powers are great,' Shay said. She said she knew this because as soon as it entered Innovera Yakov she felt its presence. She also knew when it departed because there was something in the air that changed. Somehow everything felt much lighter and cleaner.

'I feel that same darkness in Blu Tara just after the Escapeet leaves,' Shay whispered.

'That's why you've been warning Gamma?'

Shay folded her robe across her knees and sat down. She took Ayana's hands and looked into her face. 'I have to tell you why I've been coming to see you, Ayana.'

Ayana eased her hand away. Shay reached out and took them again. 'Why do I feel this same darkness over you sometimes? I've been so afraid for you. Have you been...'

'Is that why you've been coming?' Ayana cut in quickly. 'I thought we were friends.'

'I am your friend!' Shay sounded almost hurt. 'Don't you

see? You're so full of feelings. So uncertain of everything, I-I can't help feeling for you.'

'Everybody has feelings,' Ayana said reproachfully.

'Not like you. Not like us, Ayana. Wanting love so desperately..'

'Who says that I am desperate, Shay! I'm definitely not desperate for anything.' Ayana got up to leave.

'But you are! Why don't you face yourself, my Sister. Truth is the only thing that can lead you to what you wish for.'

Ayana stopped abruptly. 'You-you called me *Sister*. You..'

'I did,' Shay said.

Ayana shook her head with disbelief. To be called Sister or Brother by another Being in Innovera Yakov was almost as personal as merging. With that one word, Shay was telling her that she would fight for her and die for her if ever the need arose.

'What have I done to deserve this, Shay?'

Shay lifted her shoulders and dropped them. It is how I feel Ayana, and that is good enough for me.

'Why?' Ayana asked again.

'Because you feel that way to me. Because there's nobody else like us.'

'I-I don't understand.'

'A time will come when you will, Little Healer. Trust me.' Shay got up to leave.

'Don't go, Shay.' Ayana held out her hand to the girl. She cloaked her thoughts, knowing that Shay would not need to access her mind in order to read her.

'Tell me what I feel,' Ayana said. 'I don't always know.'

Shay looked at her uncertainly. 'You're sure? I mean...'

'Go ahead,' Ayana insisted.

Shay took Ayana's hand and looked into her eyes. 'Okay – but don't be upset with me if..'

'Please,' Ayana insisted.

Shay looked earnestly at her. 'There's a great hunger inside you, Ayana. You want to be loved but you're afraid to love in return. So afraid, Ayana. Why?'

Ayana lowered her eyes.

'Is it because you do not love yourself? These hands of yours - they are telling me so many things. You choose to love the things you cannot have. To protect yourself. From what?' Shay closed her eyes. 'I see a divided heart. I see two Beings. One is light - Innoveran light. The other..' Shay dropped Ayana's hands. 'The other is that - that thing that visits us.'

Shay looked horrified and shaken. 'Are you the one that lets it in, Ayana?'

Ayana felt as if she had been struck by Shay. She was truly dumbfounded by Shay's way of knowing things. She didn't think it possible for anyone to reach so deeply into her without being allowed to access her mind.

'Escapeets,' Shay whispered. 'There are many ways that they can enter our world, Ayana. But the surest way is through someone's heart. You must stop it now or else it will destroy you.'

Shay got up briskly and hurried away from her without a backward glance.

She was so shocked by Shay's uncanny revelation, Ayana could barely move. She stood at the entrance of her Pod confused. The image of Ice sprang into her mind. Were Shay's words about her being afraid to love, true? Was that why she had never given a moment's thought to Ryder's advances? And why did she not feel the danger from Ice that Shay spoke about?

What she, Ayana, felt from Ice was a desperate search for love and for the kind of companionship that she herself had always longed for.

Why was she so sure of this? What was it that drew her to this stranger, despite the frightening darkness that he came from? And yes, Shay was right. She too had felt Ice's presence in the colony. But she was not the one that brought him here. She was very sure of that.

It had to be someone else, and whoever it was, that Being was a great danger to all of them.

CHAPTER TWENTY-THREE

THERE WERE many creatures that occupied the air in Innovera Yakov: the graceful white Lyanas with tails as delicate as feathered glass; the semi-transparent Airlins which were so fast in flight they were almost invisible. The Joybirds made music with their wings. They danced in circles and created tinkling sounds when they tapped their beaks against each other's. Starflies took to the air in multicoloured bursts. The students would scoop them up in silver nets, leap high into the air and release them so that it looked as if the skies of Innovera Yakov had released a great shower of stars.

But above all these flying creatures only one held every Innoveran in awe. They were the Aarvols. The rare times when they saw them, it was always from a great distance, riding the high drafts of the Ishu Mountains, their long shining tails whipping behind like bright metallic streamers. Each feather was a glinting blade. It was as if Odors Apeno had carved them out of molten copper - so bright were these creatures against the Ishu peaks.

Rumour had it that to gaze into the eyes of one of them was like staring into the portals of another world. Their beauty was matched only by the swiftness and ferocity with which they tore into their prey or anyone who dared to enter their territory.

The students were out in the open ground playing a game of Sky Fall. Ayana was covertly watching Ryder competing against Sizler. They rose side by side to just beneath the clouds, then allowed themselves to free-fall without using any of their powers, breaking their descent only at the very last Innobeat. The one who came closest to hitting the ground without actually touching it, three times in succession, was the winner. Ryder surprised them all with his balance and his daring. Before the Change happened to him, he was less than average. Now he was one of the very best she'd seen.

Ayana was laughing at the antics of a young student named Kino. He was pretending to be terrified of even leaving the grass to take to the skies when she felt a gentle throbbing in the air.

It was as if the atmosphere suddenly took on a small electric charge. The students must have felt it too because they all stopped what they were doing. They were looking at each other with puzzled expressions on their faces.

Everyone looked up at the same time because the sky was filled with a sound that was so unusual, they could not decide what it was.

Gamma and Blu Tara brought their fingers to their lens and kept them there. Side by side, legs slightly apart, the twins stood in fighting poses.

Ryder had his arms pulled back, his spear shimmering and ready. Shay's head was bowed. She was pressing her fingers against her temple.

Some of the students rushed into the Learning Dome.

Now they saw, rising above the highest peaks of the Ishu Mountains, eight golden shapes - Aarvols with wings spread wide, and whistling in the wind. The largest was in the middle making in a steady gliding arc towards them.

Ayana rushed to her feet. 'I sense no danger,' she shouted at Gamma and Blu Tara. 'Besides it is forbidden; we must not harm them.'

'No danger,' Shay agreed. 'Let them come.'

Blu Tara's hand tensed over her lens. Gamma's arm shot out and blocked it. 'Did you hear that, Blu! She said that we should let them come.'

Blu Tara obeyed her without protest.

It was a thrilling sight watching the Aarvols carving the air in a steady path towards their colony.

'What does it mean?' one Student asked.

'I believe it is an omen,' another answered.

'It is not,' Ayana replied. She sensed something so wonderful up there amongst the approaching creatures, she could barely breathe.

The Aarvols circled above them casting great light-flecked shadows on the Learning Dome and the nearby trees.

Then a figure - the largest amongst them - descended swiftly, joyously from the midst of the Aarvols, a stream of golden hair fluttering in the wind.

Skylar leapt into the air and shouted something. Shay stretched out her arms towards the skies and shrieked.

'It's Krave!' Blu Tara said, incredulously.

'Krave?' Gamma echoed. She stepped back, looked up again and fainted.

Krave landed in the middle of the field. He looked the same as before except that the colour of his eyes was now a bright sapphire. Silver streaks ran through the flowing gold of his locks. His legs were sturdier, his shoulders broader and his body was even more upright.

He was looking up at the seven Aarvols now circling in a perfect pattern above his head. Krave made a sound and the creatures broke rank. Their great metallic shrieks cut through the air in response.

It was then that they saw what Krave had become. The fabric at the side of his legs parted. Silver wings fanned out from each calf. A murmur of astonishment and adoration rose up from the small crowd as Krave took to the air again on his wings. He rose quickly and joined the Aarvols. They made room for him. Then they began a luminous dance together, first rising on the mountain drafts then descending in dizzying, swooping acrobatic swirls. They'd never seen such speed, such accuracy in flight. Krave and his Aarvols came within a hair's breadth of the rising rocks. They swerved away just when everyone believed it was too late for them to avoid a head-on collision with the forbidding rocks up there.

When Krave returned he was smiling. This time he greeted them all with a hug and a big wave of the hand.

He went to Gamma last. She'd recovered from her swoon and looked unsteady and confused as Krave approached. Krave was smiling broadly. He took both Gamma's and Blu Tara's hands and bowed slightly. 'And how are the two Sungirls?' He did not wait for their answer. Krave turned hugged Ayana warmly then went back to talk with Skylar.

'Has he forgotten me?' Gamma whispered. 'Has Apeno erased me from his mind?'

'He hasn't,' Shay assured her. 'If he had I would know.'

It was Shay and Skylar who explained what happened to Krave Sonar. They all knew that Skylar had taken his brother's body up to the caves of the Ishu Mountains. That was Shay's idea. It was the ancestral home of her people. Up there were special places that her people had always used to heal themselves.

At first they thought that the swelling at the side of Krave's legs was some unknown Verheeran infection that Skylar brought back from one of his trips with Shay out in the Living Forest. But as time passed they noticed the parting of his skin and the gradual appearance of silver feathers. With every phase of their moons the feathers grew and spread. When they were fully-grown, they folded in on themselves and went back in.

It was then that Krave regained consciousness. He was too weak even to talk. At first he'd forgotten everything including the accident with Gamma in the Circle of Knowing. He did not remember Skylar either.

The first time they sat him at the mouth of the cave a strange thing happened. The Aarvols descended from their nests high up amongst the peaks and perched on the outcrops of rocks facing the cave. They cocked their heads at him and made noises as if in conversation with each other.

Sometimes one left and returned with a yellow berry that it deposited at Krave's feet. For a long while Krave was too weak to pick it up. And whenever Skylar tried to help, the Aarvols made such a racket he was worried that they would attack him.

Finally Krave managed to pick up the fruits but he did not know what to do with them.

'They showed him what to do,' Shay said. 'I saw it with my own eyes. They showed him how to take it between his fingers, break it open and rest each half on his eyes. Have you seen his eyes? Have you seen when they become like theirs?

And as his eyes got better he began remembering. The way they look at him and walk around him when he sleeps, you would believe that they've been waiting for him all their lives. I saw them lift him in the air and carry him so high, I was afraid for him. There was always one of them above him, lifting him, two on either side and two directly below him. And then,' Shay's eyes widened with amazement. 'There was that time they dropped him. Krave was struggling and falling and the Aarvols were screaming at him as if they were trying to tell him something. I understood. I didn't know what they were saying but it hit me like a stroke of lightning that they wanted him to use those wings. They wanted him to fly!

At last he got the message. And,' Shay clasped her hands together. 'In the name of the great god of our people, I will never forget that first time I saw Krave unfold those wings to fly, especially when he began to rise and turn with them. Such joy! It was as if the Aarvols were laughing. Skylar kept rubbing his eyes. He could not believe what he was seeing. After that we knew that Krave was safe. We left him with them. Have you seen his arms?

Ayana nodded. They had all seen Krave's arm - the streaks of silver that ran all the way down from his shoulders to his fingers.

'We saw him use them once,' Shay said. 'A Skydog was harassing his friends. You do not want to see it. Ever seen a Skydog turn to ashes? And during all this time,' Shay laughed out loud. 'Every one of you believed that he was gone.'

'I never did,' Ayana said.

Gamma turned to her. 'You never did?' She looked vulnerable and tearful. Ayana felt sorry for her.

'Never,' Ayana insisted.

'How did you know?'

'Apeno didn't erase him from our memory. None of us forgot him.'

'Yes,' Gamma smiled. 'I should have known. He was all I thought about.' Gamma turned round suddenly and walked away.

'It's the Change,' Shay said, looking up towards the mountains. 'Another one of us ready for the Journey. I'm wondering who's next?'

'Gamma hasn't changed yet,' Ayana reminded her.

Shay hugged herself. 'And that terrible sister of hers. I have to say, I'm not looking forward to that.'

'It is the will of Apeno. What has to be must be.'

But even as Ayana said it, she felt a shiver of dread run through her at the thought of a more powerful Blu Tara.

CHAPTER TWENTY-FOUR

WHEN GAMMA opened her eyes she found Blu Tara leaning over her. She'd been so deeply shocked and elated by Krave's magnificent re-appearance that her core had cooled suddenly and unexpectedly and she momentarily lost consciousness.

She remembered vividly the way he looked at her. She couldn't believe that he saw her. His eyes barely rested on her face before he turned his back, hugged Ayana and walked over to Skylar. He gave a final wave to the crowd of adoring Males and Females and just like that, turned around and flew off.

He was even lovelier to look at now. Surely Apeno made Krave Sonar in His very own likeness, because she, Gamma, could not imagine a more splendid Being. Krave's shoulders were definitely broader and his eyes shifted between burning sapphire and molten lava. The few words that he spoke were considerate and gentle.

'He's the most attractive of all of us,' Gamma sighed.

'Well, a bit taller and shinier,' Blu Tara replied dryly. 'Me - I go for darker Males.'

Gamma looked up at her and frowned.

'Joking,' Blu Tara smiled. 'Yes, I think he's forgotten.

Maybe he's lost his mind. He even smiled at me. Can you believe that?' Blu Tara pulled back her hair and preened.

Gamma shot to her feet. 'I have to see him.'

'I wouldn't raise my hopes,' Blu Tara said. 'Like I said, I'm pretty sure he's lost his mind.'

Gamma rushed out of the Pod.

When Gamma arrived, Krave was standing in the grounds with his face towards the sky.

He seemed to be whispering to the Aarvols in the far distance. Their sharp cries came back on the wind in a bright chorus.

'Krave?' Gamma said looking up at him hesitantly.

'Yes?' He turned smiling towards her.

'I'm so-so...' She moved closer and looked into his eye. 'You've really changed. Now you're...' Gamma reached up to touch his face.

Krave took her hand and brought it back gently to her side.

Gamma lowered her eyes. 'You're still, er, angry at me? I'm sorry. I didn't mean to hurt you. I thought...'

'You didn't hurt me,' Krave said softly. 'As you can see, I'm healthy and alive. In fact,' he turned his face up towards the Aarvols. 'It was a good thing. You made my Change come sooner.'

Krave looked back at her and for a moment she thought he would bring his lips down on her hair as he used to do. But he stopped short, looked her in the eyes and smiled. 'You are truly lovely, Gamma Orion.'

'The Dimmer Zone,' she said, 'Can we go there, erm, again? Now if you want.'

'No more Dimmer Zone, remember, my friend?'

'Is that all I am now to you Krave Solan. A friend?'

'It's a good thing, don't you think, Gamma?'

Krave lifted her hand and pointed it towards the mountains and the Aarvols. 'Up there I had a dream. A pink bird – a sparkling Sunbird - appeared to me. It was walking in the light.

But it was not walking straight. It was limping. It was trying to get to a place where an Aarvol stood because it knew it would be safe there. There was something behind it: a bigger bird. It was cloaked in darkness. Yet in my dream I could still see it. It was coming after the amazing injured bird trying to...'

Krave stopped and looked down at her. 'That Solar Eagle realised that what was important was not being *with* that injured Sunbird.'

'What was?' Gamma asked. Her lips were trembling. She could not look at Krave.

'Protecting it. Saving it from the darkness.'

'Are you – are you saying that it's over, Krave. Is that what you're saying?'

'I'm not saying anything you haven't told me yourself. Now I see the sense of it, I'm saying I understand.'

'When did I ever say that, Krave? When did I ever say I didn't...' Gamma looked up sharply, as if she had been slapped. She pressed her palm against her head.

'Blu Tara,' she shouted, 'what are you doing in my head? I told you not to invade my thoughts. I told you!'

She turned fiercely burning eyes on Krave. 'I have to go now. Maybe we can talk about this another time?'

'Anytime,' Krave answered. 'Let Blu Tara know she has no more reason to be jealous.'

With a leap Krave was in the air, his silver wings fanned out.

Gamma watched him rise with a sinking heart.

CHAPTER TWENTY-FIVE

AYANA DID not like the way Ryder was looking at her. She felt his resentment so strongly she couldn't help turning her head to look at him. He was standing at the back of the Learning Dome with his spear leaning against his leg. He did not lower his eyes. If anything his expression grew fiercer.

The others did not notice his hostility; or if they did, they did not care. It made her nervous and self-conscious. The more he glared the more irritated she became.

As soon as the lesson was over, Ayana hurried out of the Learning Dome. She kept her eyes on the doorway so that she would not miss Ryder amongst the crowd.

He was about to step past her when she tapped him on his arm, 'What's the problem, Ryder?'

'That's a question you should ask yourself,' he retorted and turned to leave.

Ayana was incensed, 'If I've got a problem you certainly don't figure in it, Ryder. I just don't like the way you stare at me.'

'They're my eyes, I look at who and what I want, the way I want.'

'No you don't, Ryder! And certainly not at me!'

Ryder's whole manner was a shock to her. This was not the quiet, adoring Male that had been courting her.

'Do something about it then. Why don't you tell me...?' He suddenly became the old Ryder that she knew. His face softened and he looked down at his feet. What she sensed in him felt more like pain.

'Tell you what?' she said, softening her voice. Ayana tried to reach into him to get a better understanding of his feelings.

Ryder turned angrily on her. 'Don't even try it, stupid girl. I cannot abide you anymore. You're blind - that's what you are. Blind!'

'Ryder! I...'

'You're blind to everything except that silly freak who struts around as if he owns the place. What can he do that I can't do? Huh? What's he got that I don't have? At least I'm not stupid enough to climb a Golkan tree and get some silly healer to lay their hands on me. Or maybe I should do that to get myself some attention. I should throw myself off a tree. Or go grow some wings or something.'

Ayana shrunk back, overwhelmed by Ryder's bitterness. *Krave*, she thought, *he's jealous of Krave*. But Ryder's words had raised her temper. 'You're wasting your time,' she told him flatly.

'Fine!' Ryder snapped. 'And you're wasting mine. Go love your ghosts. That's what they are because you cannot have them. Is that what you call love?'

Ryder hoisted his spear and took to the air in anger.

Ayana ran to her Pod and sat there staring at her Sylva. Ryder's words to her were so ugly and insulting; they simply could not be true. And yet she could not dismiss them from her mind. Didn't Shay say something similar to her? Had those two been talking about her?

Ryder had turned into a monster with a spiked tongue.

Ayana wished she could have the same argument with him again, now that she knew the kind of person that he was. She would invade his thoughts and tell him things about himself that would make him squirm.

What did he mean by chasing after ghosts? Could he have found a way into her mind and found out about Ice?

The Changes had come upon him early. Was he hiding some extra power that allowed him to sneak into other people's mind? Still, she knew it could not be. No one could break through her mental defences without her knowing.

Ice, she thought, did he really have a hold on her? Was Ryder right?

At least she could prove to herself that it was not so. She could face Ice. She could look into his world whenever she wanted, as long as she wanted. And if he tried to grab hold of her again she would fight back. If that didn't work, she could close the portal of her Sylva the moment he turned to face her.

Ayana picked up her Sylva, ran her palm along its surface and concentrated.

It was a while before the underworld of restless water appeared. It looked slightly clearer than before. For some reason Verheer was teeming with activity. She watched the shapes of its citizens rushing past each other. They all appeared to be moving with a purpose. Everyone was heading eastwards to the great dark edifice that rose up like an underwater mountain from the very depths of their ocean world.

'Ice,' she whispered, *show him to me. Show me him right now.*

The Sylva dimmed. The image of the underworld began to zoom by in a rush, past what looked like dark-grey outcrops of rocks and canyons. They were so deep it was impossible to see the bottom.

The darkness lightened and the ocean disappeared and there were forests and a great wide river. Ayana leaned forward blinking. It was the Living Forest where it met The River of a Thousand Eyes. Innovera Yakov! It was near where she had fallen from her Sylva and Skylar came to her rescue.

Her Sylva brightened even more and then she saw him. Ice! She could make out that figure anywhere, with the robes flowing around his body like heavy water. His head was slightly tilted towards the sky. He seemed to be waiting.

The lower part of Ice's face was exposed: pale white skin, the finely moulded jaw line of a very handsome young Male. His hands were dark as the Verheeran rocks she'd seen through her Sylva. He had the longest and most delicate fingers that she had seen on any Being.

If it were at all possible, she would step into the mirror of her Sylva so that she could stand before him and see the rest of him close up. She so wished she could look into those terrible embracing eyes.

She was about to obey the sudden reckless impulse to let him know that she was looking at him when she saw movement to the left of her vision. It was a shadow at first which quickly turned into a shape. A tall, slim figure with shimmering blue hair appeared.

Blu Tara! Ayana almost dropped the Sylva.

Another figure appeared beside Blu Tara. Ayana recognised the boy. Kino – the gentle soft spoken student who everyone nicknamed Flicker because of the quick and nervous way he moved. In the Game of Dodge, everyone wanted Kino on their side. Once he had the crystal in his hands it was impossible to catch him.

Blu Tara said something to Ice. Ayana shook her Sylva. For some reason it was not transmitting their words.

Smiling, Blu Tara nudged Kino towards Ice. Ice nodded at Blu Tara and she nudged Kino even closer.

The boy held out his hand in greeting towards Ice.

Ice extended a long, pale arm as if about to greet Kino.

As soon as their fingers touched the boy's expression changed. With a movement so swift, it was barely noticeable, Ice's coat spread like a great black wing and folded around Kino.

Kino's scream was printed all over his disappearing face. In a moment the boy was no longer there. Little bubbles of his life force rose from Ice's mouth, blinking like a thousand fading eyes before they melted in the air.

Ayana felt the tears slipping down her face, stinging her peeling scars. She'd felt Kino's pain - his terrible dying agony before the dark figure consumed him.

It felt like a dream. It was too unreal to be true. It was as if this stranger, along with Blu Tara had pushed a hand into her guts and twisted it.

Ayana felt betrayed. Not only did Blu Tara know Ice, she clearly had a connection with him. Everything that Shay said about her was true. Shay's fear of Blu Tara made sense now. Her warning to Gamma about the danger she was in, was not at all unfounded.

Ayana felt a mixture of helplessness and anger overcome her.

Has Apeno seen this? How can He allow this?

Would anyone believe her if she told them? Now that Kino was dead, they would have already begun to forget him. If she mentioned his name to the students, they would look at her and ask her who he was. With Kino gone, Ice turned to

Blu Tara. She stepped into him in the same way Kino did a while ago. Blu Tara bowed her head and knelt before Ice.

Ice gestured for her to stand. With her head still lowered, Blu Tara said something to him. He nodded briefly before the long fingers reached up and pulled back the cowl that covered his head.

Now, for the first time, Ayana saw the full face of the stranger - pale as the underbelly of a Lilyfish. Large dark eyes and hair that rolled down his back like the waters of a black river. Ayana stared at him with fear and wonder at the same time. And as she watched, something in her stomach melted. Apart from Krave this was the most awesome Being she had ever laid her eyes on.

Blu Tara raised her hand to touch Ice's face. Ayana held her breath. She almost cried out in surprise when Blu Tara's hand went straight through him.

Trembling, Ayana closed the portal of the Sylva. Too dazed to move, she remained as she was. She stared at the blank Sylva in her hand, wondering what she should do to save the colony from Blu Tara.

Would anyone believe me if I tell?

If she told, wouldn't they want to know how she came to see all of this?

She could see the students surrounding her like a hive of Volcan bees, full of questions.

Why was she following a Verheeran through her mirror? Didn't she know that it was forbidden? How many times had she done this? Why would she want to defy the edicts of their world and do such a terrible thing? Did she not think of what could happen to them all if a Verheeran entered through her portal? Who was Kino? Was she making this all up just to bring attention to herself?

Ayana dragged herself off her Podseat, shed her robe and cleansed herself.

When she finished, she summoned her Sylva and left her Pod.

She was waiting outside the Learning Dome when Blu Tara appeared. Blu Tara looked happy. Her hair was now bright cobalt and her skin was glowing. Ayana invaded her thoughts immediately. Blu Tara froze with the shock. Then her hands reached up to her lens.

Ayana knew that Blu could easily destroy her. But how would she explain to the others why she, Ayana, who appeared to be doing nothing apart from watching her, was so brutally attacked?

She communicated these thoughts as viciously as she could to Blu Tara.

Blu Tara dropped her hand.

'I saw you feeding Kino - one of your own people - to that - that thing.' Ayana did not know how or why she remembered Kino's death. But the sight of the Innoveran being consumed by Ice remained imprinted in her consciousness. Maybe, for some reason, Apeno wanted her never to forget Kino.

Blu Tara's thought-words struck back at her. 'We saw you too. We knew that you were spying. You're a spy Scarface. Your nosiness will get you into trouble. Soon!'

'I don't believe you. You're a traitor and a liar. I will tell the others.'

'I would have dragged you in and fed you to him too. But he told me, no. You saw me whispering to him, didn't you? What do you think it was about?'

'Why, Blu Tara?'

'Why what?'

'Why do you like hurting and destroying so much?'

'I neither like it nor dislike it, Scarface. I do what I have to do. Blu Tara looked earnestly at her. What do you know about sacrifice, Scarface? Do you know what I gave up to be here?'

'No, you traitor, go ahead and tell me.'

'You wouldn't understand. You're too dense and stupid.'

'Try me, Blu Tara. Try me! You who feed a Verheeran with your own people.'

'My own people,' Blu Tara looked around her mockingly, 'where are they? I have no people in this empty shiny world. And seeing that you already know so much - what happens to a shadow when you feed it? Especially an Escapeet?'

Ayana looked away and shuddered. She knew the answer of course: it gained substance. You feed an Escapeet with the substances of a world; it becomes part of that world.

'So yes, Scarface. We both knew that you were there.'

'Liar!' Ayana shot back, and that makes you even worse than I believed.'

But Ayana wasn't so sure now.

'He's not ready for you yet. Ice told me that. A time will come - and those are his words, Scarface - when the Earthbound will be useful. That's what he called you - an Earthbound. And he should know. Do you want me to tell the others that you bleed? That the only thing that keeps you standing is some silly liquid flowing through some teeny weeny drains inside you? That is your weakness; isn't it? That is what Ice told me. So please go ahead and tell. Ayana I dare you.'

Ayana stiffened at the insult, but her anger was up and she would not let Blu Tara have the last word.

'You're nothing, Blu Tara. Strong as you are, you're still a slave. I know that now. You kneel before a Verheeran. You kiss his hand. You bow before him like a little Earthbound girl.'

Blu Tara's hand shot up to her lens.

Go ahead, Ayana said defiantly. 'Make this your best shot, Blu. One thing I can tell you; it is likely to be your last.'

Blu Tara's mind had been so locked into Ayana's she did not see the quiet gathering of students throughout the grounds.

Ayana's stillness and her stare and Blu Tara's rigid fighting posture had given them away. It was clear that this was a serious Mindfight. It was a clash of inner forces and it could turn out to be deadly.

Mind wars were rare in Innovera Yakov. The Voice had warned them against it since it made them all behave like Earthbounds. They would be tempted to take sides, pooling the powers of their minds with the person they wanted to win. Many would perish and become empty shells at the end of it. But it was a tempting risk.

Blu Tara looked around her quickly. Ayana did the same. She did not expect it to get this serious. But now, like Blu Tara, she needed to know who was likely to be on her side, and what her chances were of coming out of this alive. For she had no doubt that Blu Tara meant business.

She saw Shay standing in the doorway of the Learning Dome. Her friend was as still as a crystal pillar. All the life was in her eyes and she was looking straight at Blu Tara, her finger already pressed against her temple. Ryder appeared from nowhere. He stood a short distance away from them with his body slightly turned. He had his head down and his eyes closed, as if he were listening for the slightest movement from Blu Tara. And not far away was Skylar. He seemed to be unaware of the battle between them. But Ayana was not fooled and Blu Tara surely wouldn't be either. Skylar would be looking out for Shay and Krave.

There were those who - no doubt – had already decided to take Blu Tara's side. They feared the consequences if she won and found out afterwards that they sided against her. Ayana sensed who they were: Sizler and his crew of friends who admired the way Blu Tara commanded respect through fear. But Ayana also felt their doubt. Most of Sizler's crew were nervous about Shay. Whatever she had done to them had made them very afraid of her.

All this Ayana picked up while her eyes never left Blu Tara's hand. She did not know how she would handle Blu Tara's attack or from where she suddenly got this inner strength to override her fear. She surprised herself by being able to tune into the minds of everyone around her. Most of them, she realised, were on her side.

'Earthbound!' Blu Tara's thought words exploded in her head.

'Traitor!' Ayana shot back.

'Bleeder!' Blu Tara's hair was flaming.

'Spy!'

'Weeper!'

'Kneeler!'

'Earthslut!'

'Slave!'

Without being summoned, Ayana's Sylva dislodged itself from her breastbone and settled in her hand. It spread out and became a brightly burning mirror. It felt alive in her hand.

And as Ayana closed her hand around her Sylva, everything around her became amplified. She could hear every breath and heartbeat of the students. She felt the furnace of Blu Tara's core, could reach the furthest corners of her mind, and Blu Tara could no longer block her out.

Odors Apeno is on my side, she thought. *He is right here beside me.*

Ayana sensed Blu Tara's uncertainty. In fact, she could

read Blu Tara's thoughts. Apart from Krave Sonar, no one had ever stood up to her like this before. And there was no turning back now. She could not afford to lose face in front of this Earthbound who already knew too much.

And yet she - Blu Tara - could not ignore the bright mineral stare of Shay, or the needle tip of Ryder's spear aiming at her sternum where her core resided. And Skylar over there - a dark shape to the left of her, like a giant brooding rock.

She could take them all down, all at the same time, but her own fusion would destroy her too.

It was Gamma who saved them all.

They had not seen her standing in shadowy corner of the dome behind a Golkan tree until a blade of light exploded against the mound of rocks at the far end of the field.

The explosion shook the ground under them. Soon the air was filled with flaming, falling boulders and a rain of molten rock. It sent the students scattering for shelter. Those who took to the air came back down abruptly because the air had become a burning inferno.

And still Gamma wasn't finished. A gush of bright blue flames shot from her eyes and encircled Blu Tara.

Hands on hips, Blu Tara stood in the middle of it like a Flamebird in its very own nest of fire.

Gamma strolled towards Blu Tara and stood beside her sister.

'That's it then,' she said in a cheery voice. 'Show's over, right? Getting a little hot round here, isn't it? Come on Blu. We've got sooo much to talk about.'

The two sisters rose above the flames. Blu Tara threw Ayana a parting glare. 'Watch out, Scarface. Ice has his eyes on you.'

'Not before everyone here knows what you are. Slave!'

When Ayana turned around, Shay was standing beside her.

Many of the students gathered behind Shay, whispering amongst themselves.

'You're not the same,' Shay said. 'Now it is clear for all to see. The Change has come upon you.'

Really?' Ayana touched her face. The purple scars were still there. She felt like crying. 'Do I - do I look the same?'

'Not inside, you don't,' Shay smiled. 'And Ryder - do you see now that he will kill or die for you?'

Ayana lowered her head. 'Yes,' she said. 'I see that.'

'He will come to you Ayana. Soon. He can hardly hold it in anymore. His whole body tells me that. What will you tell him when he comes?'

'I do not know,' Ayana said. 'I honestly do not know.' She looked earnestly at Shay. 'What's wrong with me Shay? Why can't I just be satisfied?'

'Simple,' Shay hugged her and smiled. 'But it takes practice and conviction.' She blew on Ayana's tears. 'You know what that is?'

Ayana shook her head.

'Like I keep on telling you it's learning to love yourself. How many times have I told you this, Ayana? Nothing is more important than that, not even the new powers you are discovering.'

CHAPTER TWENTY-SIX

'AYANA'S NOT the same,' Gamma nudged Blu Tara jokingly.' I'm sure you felt her force when she was standing up to you. Little Healer is growing all the time.'

'What force!' Blu Tara grunted, shaking out her hair.

'Hah! Look at the way the others were prepared to fight for her. She stood up to you this time, didn't she?' You couldn't scare her; could you? Gamma laughed.

Blu Tara shrugged. 'I would have blown all of them away.'

'And then?'

'And then what? I don't worry about consequences, Gamma. I do what I have to do. You should know that by now.'

'And what do you have to do exactly?' Gamma was now looking at her with a deep frown. 'I'll be honest, Blu. I understand you less and less. And the less I understand you, the less I think I like you.'

'Gamma! You say such hurtful things.'

'It's true. And I'll tell you this too, Blu Tara. If you did hurt Little Healer. I would have hurt you too. She's the only one we have.'

'You couldn't. We're twins.'

'Don't count on that. You've been counting on that for

too long. I'll tell you what happened when Krave returned. I realised I'm not afraid to die.'

'You're saying you don't care about us? You're saying you don't give a damn about me?'

'I'm saying a lot of things have changed, Blu Tara. Inside me - that is. I'm no longer afraid for myself and that means I'm not afraid for you either. That's all.'

Blu Tara looked at her directly in the face. 'Gamma, a Being can always learn to be afraid again. Who knows. That might be something to behold.'

Gamma returned her look. Her eyes were like deep volcanic pools staring back at Blu Tara. 'Something to behold or something to enjoy, Blu Tara - which is it?'

Blu Tara looked away.

CHAPTER TWENTY-SEVEN

AN URGENT thought-summons broke into Ayana's Rest. It came from Skylar.

Ayana shot off her cot because she picked up a deep distress in his voice. She sent thought-words to him, wanting to know what the trouble was.

Skylar's response was choked and abrupt.' Now, Little Healer, come please.'

Ayana jumped onto her Sylva and sailed over to the Learning Dome.

A pale figure was lying on the grass in front of the building. Skylar was standing over it. Shay's green robe was unmistakable. Ayana landed quickly and touched the girl.

'What happened to her!' She screamed.

Ayana pressed her ear against Shay's chest then leaned back and lifted the girl's head onto her lap.

'I want to know what happened,' she demanded.

There was an unpleasant odour coming off Shay's garment. It was the smell of sodgrass.

Sodgrass only grew at the back of the Learning Dome which was why no one ever went there. Its smell was so pungent as soon as anyone touched it, it stuck to the skin for ages regardless of how thoroughly they cleansed themselves.

Ayana pressed her palms against Shay's face. Her friend was still breathing but her breath was coming in long elongated spurts.

'Talk to me, my Sister,' Ayana whispered. 'I'm here with you now. Who did this to you? Please tell me that you hear me Shay.'

For a moment, Shay's eyelids fluttered. She rested pale blue eyes on Ayana's face. Then she reached up and touched her.

'I'm leaving Ayana. I'm leaving Innovera Yakov.'

'Don't say that Shay; please don't say that.' *Ayana concentrated, drawing on the forces of her moons.* She felt Shay blocking her.

Shay shook her head. 'No, Ayana. You cannot save me now.'

'I can help you Shay. Why are you resisting me?' Again she felt her friend pushing her back. Shay's mind was powerful. Ayana could not reach the girl's life force.

She never had this experience before. No one had ever tried to block her from saving them. She'd never known that this was possible.

'They - they appeared from nowhere, Ayana. Cold - so cold, Ayana. I fought back. I said everything I knew. I said too much. And I gave them hell. Never knew I had it in me.'

'Who was it, Shay? Please tell me who it was.' Ayana whispered urgently.

She could see that Shay was struggling. 'Don't have much time, Ayana. It does not matter. You will find out anyway. I will not die Ayana. I will live in you. Take my powers; place your forehead against mine. Before it is too late.'

'I can heal you, Shay.' Ayana shook her gently. 'Don't fight me.'

'Hurry Yé Maya. Odors Apeno wills it.'

With a violent heave of her body Shay closed her hands around Ayana's neck and dragged her down towards her. Their foreheads collided. Ayana felt as if all the heat-waves and the mountain winds of Innovera Yakov had combined and rushed into her body.

Shay's dying agony made her gasp. Images scrolled through Ayana's head of strange green waterfalls, Beings with eyes as crystalline as Shay's. They were smiling at her, reaching out their hands to touch her. And somewhere deep inside her head a soft voice was whispered. *My powers are yours now Ayana. They will serve you well.* And then Shay melted away like mist before their eyes.

On the spot where the girl had lain, the earth began to stir. Something pale and translucent peeped out of the soil. It grew quickly. A Witloc Lily - white and delicate as air stood nodding in the breeze.

Ayana rose to her feet and walked over to Skylar. Throughout the time that she was with Shay, he was beating the air with his great hands and groaning like a Golkan Tree.

Ayana touched Skylar on his hip. She felt his pain. He grew quiet when she touched him again - this time on his shoulder.

'She's not gone,' she whispered. 'Her power resides in me now. And because she lives in me, we will remember her. Let me prove it to you, Skylar that I carry Shay inside me.'

Ayana projected thought words to Skylar. 'In that place, where the River of a Thousand Eyes enters the Living Forest, she gave you a string of beads. She said that you should wear it the day you begin to love her back. No one else knows this apart from you and her.'

Skylar looked at her with deep and sorrow-laden eyes and nodded.

'How would I know this if she did not live within me now?'

Ayana lifted her head. A new force had arisen within her. She looked at every face around her in turn and spoke, her voice ringing in the bright air.

'Whoever did this, or made it happen does not deserve to be amongst us. Shay had no enemies apart from those of you who made yourselves believe she was your enemy.

But you know as well I do that a true Witloc does not die.' Ayana pointed at the flower. 'This is a reminder from Odors Apeno that Shay will come again. And when she returns whoever destroyed her in this world will pay for it with their own existence. Whoever you are! From now on you are cursed. Shay taught me something important. Ayana turned to face Blu Tara. It is easy to be bad. True courage comes from being good. But the most important thing I learned from her is this,' Ayana shook her head and threw back her hair. Now all of her face was exposed. No one teased her; no one turned their eyes away. 'She taught me to accept and value the person that I am.'

Sizler laughed. Ayana swung her eyes at him. He laughed again more forcefully.

'If you don't shut up, I'll shut you up,' she told him calmly. A murmur of surprise rose up from the small crowd.

Sizler turned his back on her.

Ayana touched her forehead and pointed her finger at him.

She invaded his thoughts so brutally, he stumbled backwards.

'Come to me,' she snapped.

Sizler tried to fight her, his body twisting every which way. Ayana held him in her mind-vice. This new courage and power she realised was not hers but Shay's. Shay had only just left their world. Yet it felt as if the new powers that she had now were a missing part of herself. She suddenly felt complete.

Sizler stumbled towards her, his knees half-bent, his mouth half-open.

When he finally stood before her, his eyes were glazed and he was breathing heavily.

Ayana stretched out a hand and pressed her thumbs against his eyeballs. She stared into his face.

'It was not you or one of your friends who killed her,' she said. 'I know that now. You and those who follow you like fools, do not have the strength to vanquish her.'

Ayana released him. Sizler's knees buckled under him and he rolled onto the grass.

She turned again to the crowd. 'Be certain of this. In my Sister's name I'll find the one who thought that they could destroy her. And I will make you pay.'

CHAPTER TWENTY-EIGHT

WHEN GAMMA returned to her Pod, Blu Tara was nowhere to be found. She searched everywhere, asking all the students whether they had seen her anywhere. None of them had.

She projected her thoughts towards Blu but received no sign of life from her. It was as if her sister had left Innovera Yakov altogether.

Gamma returned to her Pod and threw herself on her cot. Krave confused her. His manner with her contradicted his words. He almost kissed her, didn't he? He wasn't angry with her. In fact he was gentler with his words than she had ever heard him.

She saw the adulation in the eyes of the other females and even the males. They were all willing to surrender themselves to him and to his wishes. All he had to do was look in their direction.

Now she knew that she would abandon herself to Krave without argument or resistance. She felt she desired him more than she ever desired any other Being before. She thought of her earlier doubts about Krave Solan when he had so wanted to merge. It was stupid of her to fight against something that she so badly desired for herself. She wondered what was wrong with her.

She saw all this clearly now and it left her feeling depressed and disappointed with herself.

If there was one thing she was certain of now, it was that Blu Tara cared only for herself.

Her twin sister's cruelty never ceased to astonish her. If Blu Tara were in her shoes, she would not have hesitated to merge with Krave.

She believed that Odors Apeno was close to approving their union. At the Circle of Knowing, wasn't the crystal changing from that dreadful green to red? It was already pink when that nasty accident happened and the crystal shot out of her hands.

She did not want to think about it. It was too upsetting.

Exhausted, she sank back to rest. It was then that she sensed a presence in the room. She looked around her, expecting Blu Tara. The Pod hummed in its own soft way as usual, dimming to accommodate her period of rest.

She was aware that she wasn't asleep; and yet she wasn't awake. A strange feeling of lightness and emptiness spread throughout her body.

A deep voice filled her head. It said the name she so often heard in her dreams, *Itania.*

She heard herself answering, *I'm listening; I'm here.*

Your heart is leaving me. You must come to me now.

The voice was so full of emptiness and longing, it reached into her core. *My world awaits you, Itania, I am waiting. I want to see your face before me.*

An image appeared in her mind of a young woman with flowing red hair, lying on an old stone floor and staring into a mirror. The pale face of a young man appeared with eyes so large and dark and embracing, she wanted to walk into them and drown.

Itania it is time. I will guide you home.

A soft cry escaped Gamma. She tried to resist. But the call was stronger.

She felt herself rising, her mind now emptied of everything but that voice and the image of a face she could not remember seeing. Yet it was so familiar she recognised every expression that passed across it.

She rose from her cot and began a dream-walk to the exit.

Gamma stepped out and took to the air.

CHAPTER TWENTY-NINE

FROM HIS cave in the Ishu Mountains Krave Solan noticed the pink streak of light lifting from the colony below. He knew immediately that it was Gamma. He thought nothing of it at first but then he noticed the erratic pattern of her flight and the direction she was heading. His sight had sharpened so dramatically, that even from this distance he could make out every strand of her flowing red hair.

He watched her for a while, wondering what was up with her. They were all due for an important lesson at the Learning Dome quite soon. It was an odd time to be leaving to go anywhere else.

One of the Aarvols whose name he knew as Ki descended at his side and nudged him.

'What's the bother?' he said. 'I'm not supposed to follow her. I told you my dream; didn't I?'

Ilo - Ki's sister - leapt off the ledge above them and made a tight, noisy circle in front of him. Then she settled at his feet. The golden eyes of the creature had darkened. It leapt into the air again and circled, its cry echoing through the canyons down below.

'Don't think so,' Krave said. 'I'm happy sitting here.'

The others became agitated too. Esh, Si and Hanu threw

themselves off their perches and joined in the noisy screeching and wing-beating.

'As you wish,' Krave sighed, taking to the air. 'Like I told you, I'm not supposed to go near her.'

Soon they were in the clouds, not drifting on the wind this time but cutting a fast path eastwards.

Gamma was a pinprick of light ahead of them. Krave climbed higher with his companions, narrowing his eyes against the gathering darkness.

Ki was right. Gamma was heading for Verheer.

Past The Dimmer Zone the sound of thrashing water rose up and reached Krave and his friends.

'What's she doing?' Krave queried. 'What could she be thinking?'

The Aarvols did not respond.

The world below them darkened further. Some way ahead, Krave glimpsed the heaving ocean. Dripping rocks rose out of it like jagged teeth. The little light that spilled over from The Dimmer Zone touched the edges of the waves. They glinted like grey sheets of metal.

'It stinks,' he said. 'Everything here stinks.'

Again the Aarvols did not respond. They were making little throaty sounds, communicating with each other in a language that Krave had never heard them use before.

Ki had lowered his feet slightly, his talons were half spread and glinting wickedly.

Gamma was now directly ahead of them. She slowed down and dropped onto a dark shore strewn with broken rocks and boulders.

Krave knew that once Gamma touched the water, she would have entered the world of Verheer. The currents of those waters would suck her in and take her down towards the darkness.

Gamma was walking towards the edge of the water slowly. He sensed the fear in her. Innoverans had a natural fear of darkness and perhaps this was what was holding her back.

Krave tried to reach Gamma's mind but all he met was emptiness. He tried a second time. It felt as if part of Gamma wasn't there. There were just half-formed thoughts and the image of some dark, pale-faced figure.

It struck him that Gamma was dream-walking. He'd heard of it many times before. Young and vulnerable Innoverans were prey to the demons of Verheer. They were lured there by Escapeets who entered them and took over their minds. What could have happened to Gamma to bring her to this state? Had he, by being made to change his mind about her, harmed her in some way?

Krave called each Aarvol by name: 'Ki, Esh, Ilo, Hanu, Si - let's get her out of here.'

Ki shot ahead of them, his talons outstretched towards Gamma. Krave shouted her name over and over but Gamma did not hear him.

Ki swooped down. Something seemed to strike him, throwing him back with a force so great he somersaulted in the air and screamed.

Out of the ocean rose a shape - the figure of a Male, cloaked it appeared, in robes of flowing water. Krave recognised it as the face she was carrying in her mind.

The figure lifted an arm into the air and a wave rose up at his bidding. It swelled and crested then shot forward in a thunderous roar, lifting Gamma off the shore. And yet it appeared as if the water was not touching her. Gamma seemed to be walking on a cushion of air above it.

Gamma moved towards the stranger. Her arms were outstretched. Her steps were slow and dreamlike.

Ki had recovered and was so angry now it was all Krave could do to calm him.

'Careful, Ki, we have one shot at this. Don't let your temper spoil it.'

The stranger's hands lifted again. Krave felt the force of an energy that knocked the breath completely out of him. He regained his balance quickly. He rode high and circled, the Aarvols following his every move.

'Come on, friends. Now! And don't let that water touch you.'

They swooped down together; Krave in a rolling twisting dive, the others knifing the air with angled bodies. The stranger's hands rose again. A blast of light struck Krave in the eyes. His vision blurred and darkened. What felt like hands began to reach into him. He grunted with the pain, so weakened now, he could barely hold his flight.

'Blank your thoughts,' Si shouted. 'Merge your mind with ours.'

'Become one of us,' said Esh. 'Then he cannot enter you.'

Krave obeyed immediately.

Now he felt his body lifting. He opened his eyes and saw the world as he had never seen it before. Ahead of him there was the great dark rock-edifices rising out of the ocean. The restless world of Beings underneath the water was looking up with curious eyes. And on either side, directly ahead, the vast stretch of the ocean filled with dripping rocks.

Now that his mind was merged with the Aarvols, Krave used only thought-words.

When the water brightens, we begin the Dance of the Ishu Winds.

Krave felt the delight of his companions. He hoped that it would work. They had nothing else to fall back on to save

Gamma and themselves. This was their only chance.

'Fools!' A voice filled the air. 'You are nothing here. You are less than dust. You dare come here to battle me. You will not return.'

'Be that as it may, but I will not let you have her.'

With that Krave rolled over, a jagged white light uncoiling from his arms. It hit the water in a sizzling dancing burst and ran along the surface towards the Verheeran. A wall of water rose up and blocked the path of the white-hot light. The brightness spread in a giddy mesh as Krave rose higher and rolled again. This time his whole body ignited, lighting up the dipping circling Aarvols below. A bolt of lightning shot from him and carved the water open, sending it rolling backwards on itself.

It surrounded the Verheeran in a web of electricity.

'Okay friends, your turn! Now!'

Talons outstretched, the Aarvols came down in a rush over the trapped Verheeran, circling him with such speed and awful cries, he looked confused.

Ki, who'd been circling the outer edges of the battle, swooped in on Gamma, bringing both of his outstretched legs under Gamma's armpits. Ki lifted her, rising high and fast with a triumphant shriek.

'Go!' Krave shouted. 'Go!'

But Ki was already just a golden fleck of brightness in the air, racing for the distant light of Innovera Yakov.

The energy around the Verheeran was weakening. Soon he would break loose and Krave knew that the full powers he sensed in him would be let loose.

'Done!' Krave shouted. 'Let's get out of here. Fast!'

Krave rose with the Aarvols, angling westwards with them on a fast wind, all of them like golden ghosts surrounding Ki and Gamma.

CHAPTER THIRTY

INNOVERANS CALLED the Season of Alignment, The Great Blossoming. It was the period when students grew into their full powers. Their bodies changed dramatically, so that many of them were so different from their former selves, they were hardly recognisable. Some grew tall and willowy; others became wide and squat as boulders. A few remained the same, especially those whose growth happened only in their minds.

Sizler and his crew sprouted wings. They were not as magnificent as Krave's but they could swoop and dodge with the speed and grace of Starflies.

In fact, every one of them could now travel in the air at speed.

They knew that this was basic preparation for The Journey. Taqua was the only real surprise. She was a quiet, black-skinned girl who made amazing sculptures with her bare hands, and whose laughter tinkled in the air like bells. Odors Apeno made her in a way that she could stretch and wrap herself around anything, like rope. And once she did this, it was impossible to detach her.

No one would have known that the Change had come to her if Iguy - one of Sizler's followers – hadn't challenged her.

In his usual mocking way, he claimed that he could break loose from any grip she had on him.

Taqua accepted the challenge. They sized each other up. Before Iguy could move she'd wrapped her limbs around him. Iguy was stronger now than he had ever been before and so he began the struggle to unwrap himself. But it soon became clear that his intention was to hurt Taqua. He dug his fingers hard into her body and, with her hanging onto him, he dashed himself against a rock. Taqua held on despite the obvious pain that twisted her face into a mask.

Then Iguy closed his hands around her throat and began to choke her. Taqua held on for as long as she could. Then she released a piercing sound. Suddenly she was no longer in Iguy's grip. A pool of water swirled around his feet. It began to flow rapidly up his legs and body. Soon all of Iguy was covered in what looked like living water and he began to scream.

After a while, the water flowed off him and formed a puddle at his feet. Iguy opened wide terrified eyes at it then turned and ran. The water rose again, took on Taqua's lovely shape and she was herself again.

'Right!' She said, staring at the others while swinging her hips at Sizler's crew. 'Anybody else wants to try me?'

No answer came from them.

'Good!' Taqua dusted her hands and strolled off while the whole colony fell about with laughter.

They were all waiting for Gamma and Blu Tara to change. Some hoped that it would never happen to the two sisters. They dreaded the idea of a more powerful and dangerous pair of Innoverans. Yet, they did not want to miss it when it happened.

When the Change did come upon the two girls it took a while before anyone realised it.

They were in the middle of a lesson when Gamma's lens dropped off. It barely made a sound.

Ayana was the only one who looked up from her meditation because she sensed a sudden change in the atmosphere of the room. Gamma retrieved it quietly and hid it in her hands.

A small sound involuntarily escaped Ayana. Gamma without her lens was something to behold. It was as if those glittering eyes were the portals to two great suns.

The students swung around and saw it too. They stampeded towards the exit, expecting everything to go up in flames.

But nothing happened. Gamma came out after them with Blu Tara at her side. Blu Tara's lens was still fused over her eyes.

Now they saw bright fire-trails patterning the twins' arms. Gamma lifted her head towards a bank of dark clouds piled up in the far east of Innovera Yakov. Two needle points of red light shot from her eyes. In an instant the clouds ignited into a flaming ball; then they disappeared, leaving behind a clear sky.

Blu Tara turned towards another bank of clouds, this time to the north. She touched the corner of her lens. The clouds flamed for a second and then disappeared.

'Why does Blu Tara still have her lens on?' Taqua wondered aloud.

'Apeno is no fool,' Ayana answered. 'When she lifts that arm to shoot, at least you can see what's coming and try to save yourself.'

Taqua laughed.

Ayana looked curiously at Taqua. 'What did you do to Iguy?'

Taqua laughed again. 'I gave him a bit of an itch - that's all. Now if it was Sizler, well I would've turned to acid and really give him something to think about. Down there!'

Ayana looked at the girl and giggled.

'They're hot!' Taqua said, looking admiringly at Gamma and Blu Tara. 'And you know what's funny, Little Healer? They burn, I itch.'

Now that the Blossoming had happened to all of them, everyone was in a state of waiting. The time was drawing near when they would be summoned to the Learning Dome for the last time.

They would be told the rules of their departure and the many challenges ahead. And at the end of it all, their leader would be revealed.

The one chosen to lead them out of Innovera Yakov and into the many hazards of The Journey would not be of their choosing. And they could not contest it.

Already there were wagers amongst the students of who the chosen one would be. Most thought it would be the magnificent Krave Solan. Others believed that the power and the forcefulness of Blu Tara would qualify her as the ideal choice. If not Blu Tara, then it would be Gamma for her patience and her judgment.

Skylar was not to be dismissed either. He was the strongest Being anyone had ever seen this side of Innovera Yakov and he was not afraid of anything.

And Ryder, wasn't he in the running too? He had to be. They had barely seen what he could do with that magic spear of his. And what they had already seen was enough to convince them that he was not to be messed with.

Ayana's vote was on Krave. He had flight and speed and courage. Besides, he was magnificent. If they met enemies on the way, his beauty alone would be enough to knock them out.

Vinton appeared before her, laughing.

'Silly girl,' he said and promptly disappeared again.

CHAPTER THIRTY-ONE

INNOVERANS INHABITED the great Ishu Valley where the sun was brightest and the shadows of the Ishu Mountains did not fall on them.

Although most of them had never gone beyond it, they knew that the Ishu Mountains stood like a great wall between them and the dark and scary world of Verheer. Once in their lifetime, nearing the end of their stay in Innovera Yakov, the five moons of Innovera entered into a strange conjunction and the colours of their world were reduced to a deep blue.

They could hear the waves of the Verheeran ocean battering against the mountain walls on the other side more clearly. The tops of the rising crests caught the light of the five moons and made their frothing tops glint like jagged metal.

The whole colony was on alert for the single wave that would eventually break through. There was always one that did. And when it happened, there was no other sound in the universe like it. It was as if all of Eden Gobad was folding in on them. The waters would fill the valleys bringing a sickening stink with it along with the carcasses of creatures they had never seen before.

Many creatures and plants perished. Other living things had built up their own defenses. They sank deep into the soil and stayed there until the rains that followed, cleansed the land and restored it.

It was the only time an Innoveran could be killed by illness brought in by the ocean, especially if the water touched them.

Shay's ancestors, the natives of Innovera Yakov, learned to predict this time by the behaviour of the Aarvols and the great Golkan trees in the plains below them.

As if they knew of the coming of the terrible waters, the Golkan Trees began to secrete rivulets of acid down their trunks. They had already begun to do so.

Even the Golkans were not always prepared, the Voice said. Once a Great Flood happened so suddenly and unexpectedly, there was no time to prepare for it. Those who survived were so sick and broken that Odors Apeno took pity on them and sent a Solarwave across the land to rid it of everything so that their world could be renewed and life could start all over again.

Ayana could smell the rising ocean. When it grew so strong upon her senses, she broke into the monologue of the Voice to warn the students to be prepared. A few told her to shut up. Who was she to interrupt the Voice and start spreading false alarms? Who was she trying to impress?

Blu Tara threw a malicious smile at her and turned her back.

Ayana left the Learning Dome upset and humiliated.

The moon was less than halfway through its cycle when the rest of the Students began to smell it. Then they heard the roaring. The Voice summoned them and told them what that meant.

Their duty was to save everything they could. The more of the flora and fauna of Innovera Yakov they rescued from the Great Flood, the less work it would require to restore everything to the way it was before.

They could not just take to the air and let it happen down below. If they did, then what would they return to?

Finally, it was their only chance to test the new powers they had acquired. It was their greatest test before The Journey. This, said the Voice, was their final test: The Game of Minds.

And at the end of it, every Innoveran had to be accounted for. No one should be left behind.

It happened immediately after the Voice spoke to them. The Great wave broke through the mountains and all of Innovera panicked.

Ayana looked at the confusion around her. She turned her eyes up at her moons. They were hidden behind a thick shawl of clouds.

She could feel the fear and anticipation in the air. She sent out her thought voice to the colony.

'We cannot just stand here and wait for it to come upon us. We should all work in pairs and let each person be responsible for the other in that pair.'

'I'm already a pair,' Blu Tara snorted. 'Why not three or four, or each Being on their own for that matter?'

'I cannot tell you how I know. I can only say what I feel. It is for the best.'

'So when does our Little Healer become clairvoyant?'

'Like she said,' Ryder cut in, 'we cannot stay here and do nothing. I'll take to the air. I'll be able to see what's happening from up there.'

'No,' Skylar said. 'My brother flies with the Aarvols. The things he sees with his eyes, we cannot. Let him go instead.'

Krave took off without a word. They watched him cut a fast, bright path towards the mountains.

'A vantage point is what we need,' Blu Tara told them,

pointing at the low-lying hills beyond. 'At least we will see it coming.'

'And what good will that serve?' Ayana retorted. 'You heard the Voice; it is our duty to protect the colony.'

Krave returned in a rush. 'Big! Big beyond words my friends and it drives a great wind ahead of it. We'll have to take to the air. We'll have to abandon the colony.'

'It is not Apeno's wishes,' Ayana said. We have to find a way.'

'Then stay and get washed away, Scarface. The rest of us are off.'

'Apeno will not give us these restrictions if there wasn't a way around them.'

'Now she claims to be the voice of the Great Apeno himself.' Blu Tara laughed. 'Would somebody talk some sense into her? I say we get out of here right now.'

Ayana dropped her Sylva. She spoke slowly letting her voice resound across the grounds of the Learning Dome. 'I believe the solution lies with us. This is meant to be a test. If we run away that means we failed without even trying. I say, let the brave amongst us stay and face it.'

'I say we leave,' Blu Tara shouted. 'We have no choice.'

'There is always a choice,' Ayana countered: 'to run away like Stardogs or to find a way to counter it.'

'So be it,' Blu Tara flung back her head contemptuously. 'You choose your fate. The worst death is a stupid one. Who's coming with me?'

The winds were gathering around them. In the far-off distance they saw approaching water like a moving mountain.

'Ayana's right, I'll stay.' Gamma's musical voice drifted in the air.

Taqua pointed a finger at herself, 'If I don't stay I will miss it. And I certainly don't want that.'

Ryder stuck his spear in the soil. 'If Ayana stays, I stay with her.'

It was only after their agreement that it suddenly became clear to Ayana what they all needed to do.

Blu Tara alighted beside Gamma in a raging ball of fire.

'We need you, Blu,' Ayana told her calmly. 'We cannot do this without you.'

Blu Tara looked at her mistrustfully.

'We have to go to meet The Flood, Ayana told them, 'as far up the Ishu Valley as possible. It has to be just before we meet the Golkan forest.'

'I will not follow a fool to my destruction,' Blu Tara said.

'Shut up,' Gamma snapped. 'Where's your guts, Blu Tara?'

'What's the plan! There is no plan,' Sizler blared. 'Blu Tara is the only one here making sense.'

'Then climb your little hill and die there,' Ryder growled. 'Like Taqua said, I'm heading for the action. Let's go citizens!'

They took to the air with Sizler and his followers reluctantly trailing after them. They headed north towards the oncoming Verheeran tsunami.

'Shay, Sister, Friend,' Ayana whispered. 'Stay with me. I'm not sure I know what I'm doing.'

They were still some way from the great forest when Ayana asked them all to stop. Ahead of them the trees stood like a dark fortress with their branches almost brushing the clouds.

Ayana knew she could not go back now. She could not tell them that she was guided by the voice of a girl who died to save them all.

'First we have to slow it down. We have to break the force behind that wave.' Ayana's voice was filled with urgency because the great swell was drawing nearer. The ground was quivering under the driving force that was heading towards them.

172

She looked up at the solitary soaring figure of Krave directly above them. He had been silent for a long while. She felt his worry for them.

'How long before it hits the forest, Krave?'

'Eight hundred Innobeats. I think.'

'Not long,' Ayana said. 'Not long at all. It's as long as it took us to get here.'

She turned to Skylar, aware that all eyes were on her now. 'Skylar, you who know the language of the trees; you whose voice they listen to, will you have them slow the waters?'

Skylar turned soft amber eyes on her. 'Don't understand, Little Healer. I don't understand what you're asking.'

Ayana clasped her hands and bowed. 'Have them fall Skylar. Have them fall for us. Have them make a great dam. It is the only way.'

Skylar shook his head. His shoulders heaved. It looked as if he were in great pain.

'They will rise again,' she pleaded. 'You know that, Skylar. They will hurt for us but they will rise again. Have them fall for us.'

Again Skylar shook his head.

'I saved you once. I gave you back your life. Do this not just for me but for all of us. I beg of you.'

Krave's voice reached down to them. 'It's hit the forest Little Healer. It just hit. Whoooo! I'm coming down.'

'You'll be of no use down here, Krave. Please stay.'

Krave went silent.

'If not for us, Skylar, then please do it for Shay.'

Skylar's great shoulders heaved. He raised his head and roared. The sound broke like thunder from his lips. It felt as if his voice filled up the world. And then they heard the rising heartbeat of the trees, the drawn-out droning of their trunks.

They waited and when they thought that it was all for nothing, the wall of trees ahead of them swayed.

Skylar raised his voice again - a cry that seemed to erupt from the very ground on which he stood. The Golkans groaned and tossed. Then came the falling as they pulled up their roots and crashed to the earth in waves.

Krave was up whistling in wonder, while below them the world rocked under the great weight of the dying trees.

From up there, Krave ordered them to move back. The forest had broken the force of the tide but they had not completely tamed it. It was still a raging, storming thing as it swept on towards them.

They obeyed Krave, moving further backwards along the valley, waiting now for the flood to break through the wall of fallen forest.

'Now what?' Gamma asked. Her voice was small and strained.

'We wait,' Ayana told her.

'For what,' Blu Tara wanted to know.

'For it to break through.'

'Then what?' Blu Tara swung around to face her.

'Then,' Ayana looked her directly in the face. 'Then Blu Tara, we will be in you and your sister's hands.'

Gamma understood straight away. 'Ah!' She pulled Blu Tara towards her and whispered in her ear. A small smile creased Blu Tara's face. 'Not bad,' she said. 'Not bad at all.'

Gamma raised her voice. 'Move back, Innoverans, we need some serious distance between us.'

'And that,' Blu Tara added gravely, 'is a warning.'

Ayana and her companions left them there and move further down the valley.

They stood on a hillock and watched the sisters prepare.

Gamma and Blu Tara were shoulder to shoulder in the near distance, like two bright torches - one an eye-searing blue, the other red-hot pulsing metal. Together they were amazing. They were two pillars of fire ready to take on a raging flood that was coming to drown their world. Ayana's heart felt so full she wanted to cry.

'There will be rain.' she said. 'We cannot allow it to touch us. My shield will cover everyone. But you will have to use your inner force to help me. I am not strong enough.'

'And those two?' Taqua pointed at Gamma and Blu Tara.

'Water won't go near them,' Ryder grinned. The others laughed with him.

The water broke through in mountains of white spume. Gamma and Blu Tara were tiny specks of light below.

'Now!' Ayana whispered and called upon her moons. She felt the cooling winds surround them.

From their invisible tent they watched Gamma and Blu Tara let loose. Rolls up rolls of flame erupted from their bodies in bright succession. The students crouched down, wincing with every spreading ball of fire. And then the two girls merged and rose into the air, flames fanning out in an arc so wide it seemed to reach the other end of their world, scorching the land beneath them dry. Billows of steam rolled away from the advancing twins, as if terrified of their presence.

A light drizzle began to fall. Ayana was shaking with the strain of keeping their shield intact.

She realised that she had asked too much of her companions. Ryder sensed the problem.

'I'm stepping out,' he said.

'You can't,' Ayana gasped.

'I am!' He closed his mind and stepped out of the bubble.

'It's contaminated,' someone shouted.

'Not if this works,' Ryder grunted, spinning his spear above his head so fast it became a blur. The rotating weapon created a powerful wind, pushing back the rain.

Ayana watched in admiration. Taqua laughed, 'That Male can spin me anytime.'

Soon the rains faded altogether. Ayana dropped her shield and stood up. The world spun. She could barely stand. Taqua's voice sounded faint and far away.

'It's over. We've done it. We beat the flood.'

'Tired,' Ayana said, 'Sooo tired.'

A pair of hands scooped her up. Azure eyes stared down at Ayana. 'Want a ride?'

'If she don't want it, I do,' Taqua giggled wickedly.

'Thanks, Ryder. I definitely need one.' Ayana closed her eyes and smiled.

CHAPTER THIRTY-TWO

THERE WAS little evidence of the disaster that came close to sweeping away all life in the Ishu Valley not so long ago.

The only sign of the sweeping flood was the traces of ashes along the valley floor where Blu Tara and Gamma scorched the earth and purified it.

Innovera Yakov buzzed with laughter and conversation not only because of the relief of being saved so spectacularly, but also because there were no more lessons. The Voice was silent. Now, they were all waiting for it to summon them for the choosing of the one to lead them out of Innovera Yakov.

In the meantime, they chatted and laughed and celebrated. They could not get over the spectacle of Gamma and Blu Tara driving back a wall of water with the sun-searing heat that emanated from their bodies.

Skylar fell into a foul mood whenever he looked north towards the fallen Golkan forest. They would rise again in all their magnificence but it would be many seasons before their branches swept the clouds again, and by that time he would be well on his way on the Journey. While the young males trailed adoringly behind Gamma and Blu Tara, Skylar mourned the loss of his great tree-friends.

Krave made himself scarce. He spent his time with the Aarvols, returning only for his lessons. By some mysterious means, news reached the colony of an epic battle between Krave and a great Verheern warrior prince. It was said that Krave fought the warrior single-handed after entering Verheer just for the fun of it. And did they know what? Krave Solan won hands down - all on his own!

Ryder had his followers too. Males and Females sought him out, vying with each other to be volunteers for his dangerous spear tricks. Some even considered it an honour to die at his hands, if he miscalculated his throw. Many Males and Females invited him to merge. Ryder declined politely.

CHAPTER THIRTY-THREE

WITH SHAY no longer there to talk to, Ayana spent most of her time meditating in her Pod. Vinton told her that it was what Apeno wanted. Ayana asked no more questions. Much to her shame, Apeno knew of all of her journeys to Verheer. Did she dare think for one moment that he was not aware? She could swear she heard Apeno laugh.

'Then you saw what Blu Tara did to Kino?'

'It is a single life,' Apeno answered.' What is one life to many? Even evil has a purpose; you will see.'

Now, he bid her to focus more on Verheer. She must enter it, not only with the part of herself that saw and heard, but she must also feel its coldness. She must drift with the tides that flow beneath its oceans and allow those tides to take her to its deepest and most dreadful parts.

Ayana did as she was told, travelling to such depths sometimes that the darkness felt as solid as a wall. Sometimes she thought her spirit would die there - or that she would never be able to return to her body. She squirmed at the scaly creatures that brushed past her. She floated past eyes that bored right through her head. She walked on shifting, slimy rocks. And at the end of each of those mental journeys, she found herself pale and shivering on her cot.

'Why?' she kept on asking, 'Why me? Am I being punished?'

When Odors Apeno chose to answer her, it was only to give a more demanding task.

'Next time, Yé Maya, You go further down. There the world is even more forbidding.'

At the end of it, she would lay back weak and feverish, until Apeno summoned her again.

It was after her twelfth journey, when she believed that she could not survive another trip that the natural brightness of Innovera Yakov dimmed and their world was filled with a dense and watery blue light.

Ayana left her Pod to watch the five moons draw together and align. They were surrounded by a spreading halo of ultraviolet rays. Behind the moons the twin suns of Innovera Yakov hung like two golden pendulums, growing visibly dimmer as she watched them.

Already weakened by her mind-travels to the underworld, and now that her moons were cloaking the light of their suns, she felt as if all her life-force had been scooped out of her.

She was in this state when the Voice finally summoned and she entered the Learning Dome.

Students pushed past her roughly, eager for the announcement of the one that would be chosen to lead them on The Journey.

Krave was in the middle of the hall and for the first time he wasn't smiling. Gamma stood erect beside Blu Tara and was doing nothing to hide her nervousness. Skylar leaned with folded arms, against the walls, his long green hair falling down his shoulders like rope. And even now, Taqua was busy looking sexy. Every movement she made was a pose, although she didn't seem aware of it. Ayana squeezed herself through the crowd until she found a quiet corner at the back.

The Voice began to speak and they fell silent.

Innoverans! You are gathered here for *The Choosing.*

During all the seasons that you have been here, many of you emerged as worthy. Some of you hate Innovera Yakov. You were plagued by dreams. You asked questions. You received no answers. You discovered powers that you did not know exist within yourselves. In these last moon-cycles you have gone through The Changes.

Why these changes? What brought you here in the first place?

Many amongst you wish to live in no other world but this one. But you must move on. It is the great law that governs every world there is: all life must move on and be replaced by other lives.

Now it is your turn to travel to another life. And in leaving you cannot return. Innovera Yakov can no longer contain you.

There is a place prepared for those of you who survive. Many of you will not, for you will ignore the most important lesson you have learned here.

On your journey through Verheer.

A murmur of surprise and terror filled the hall. The Voice went silent. Quiet descended on the room once more.

That world will fight you back. It will block every attempt you make to cross it. It will do everything to consume you.

But know this Innoverans, Apeno would not release you from this world if all that lay before you was certain death. There is a path, and that path is mapped out in all of you. It is for you to find it.

Which one amongst you will lead? What is it that quali-fies you? Is it the fearsome powers that some of you possess? Is it the unbreakable strength and courage of those who stand amongst you? Is it your great speed and nimbleness; the accuracy of your eyes or arms? Or is it -

At this point The Voice dropped almost to a murmur.

Is it the one with a heart so big, it can embrace you all?

Every breath, every shiver in the room was amplified as they waited. These, they knew, were not questions. They dared not answer them.

The voice grew terrible and strong. It filled up the Learning Dome.

Innoverans! Prepare yourself for flight! You will follow the River Of A Thousand Eyes to where it ends at the great swamps of Verheer. The Verheeran ocean awaits you there. Ayana Yé Maya - the one you believe least perfect amongst you will lead you there.

She will take you east, always east until you arrive to the new world that awaits you.

The hall exploded into a buzz of consternation.

Struck dumb by the announcement, Ayana could barely gather her thoughts.

'Why me,' she whispered tearfully. 'Haven't I been through enough?'

The arguments were coming mostly from the younger students. A scuffle broke out in one corner of the room.

It was Blu Tara who broke them up, her voice shattering against the walls of the hall like glass.

'Shut up!' She snarled. 'There's nothing that you can do about it. You can't change anything, so stop your bickering. We make do with what we've got. And if what we've got won't do The Journey itself will sort that out. Real leaders are not chosen. They emerge!

'Who stopped the flood?' a young voice asked indignantly. 'Wasn't it you and Gamma? So how come...'

Taqua's voice rose high. It sliced through the Student's words.

'Use your mind! You were ready to run away before Ayana stopped you and told you there was a way. Who made you stand up and defend? I'm not saying that Blu Tara and Gamma didn't make a world of difference; but it wasn't their idea. It wasn't their good sense that saw us through this. I'm not saying we didn't need the help of every Male and Female here. I'm saying it was Little Healer that we have to thank above everyone else. So take your pick of whoever you want to lead you. But I know who I'm going with.' Taqua glared at them and marched out of the Learning Dome.

CHAPTER THIRTY-FOUR

WHEN AYANA rose from her Rest, the scars on her face were worse than ever before. She took her Pad and tried to speak her dream into it but all that came from her were a few hoarse syllables.

She shook her head in confusion. The vision of her brother, Aiden, appeared to her. The dream was so vivid it felt as if Aiden was actually with her in the flesh. He was stuck in a deep pool, and was reaching out to her, shouting her name and begging her to help him. But even though he was very close to her, she could not reach him with her hands. She screamed so much she lost her voice.

Ayana stumbled out of her Pod and mounted her Sylva. Instead of rushing over to the Learning Dome, she headed for The River of a Thousand Eyes. She wanted to die. She was going to throw herself from its bank and let its sleepy waters swallow her.

She was halfway across the Grounds when Vinton's glowing figure appeared in front of her.

'What you prefer, Myana? Perfect face but empty head, or face like yours, but full with the wisdom of Apeno?' Vinton's ghostly face was bright red.

'Vinton - I..'

'When River take your life, what use you be to Innovera Yakov? You no call that selfish?'

'I'm tired, Vinton. I've had enough.'

'Enough is nothing. What about all the wonderful things you no see yet? What about the lovely, lovely place you go to after Innovera Yakov? You no want to see that?'

'How do I know we'll ever get there?'

'How you know you never get there?' Vinton retorted.

Ayana shook her head and frowned at him. 'What do you think awaits us there, Vinton? How many Students can I lead safely to the other side?'

'Myana will never know that if she jump inside Big River. Okay?'

Despite herself, Ayana chuckled. Vinton's little red face was funny. The colour didn't suit him. It made him look like a constipated Starfly.

'You laugh at me? I no see the joke.'

'No you wouldn't,' Ayana glanced at him again and chuckled.

'Why you laugh, Myana? You no go kill yourself no more?'

'Who said I was going to kill myself?'

'You!'

'Did I?'

The truth was, Vinton had lifted her mood. She felt much better with her little friend beside her.

Vinton returned to his usual twinkly green. 'You not forgetting something?'

'What?' Ayana narrowed her eyes and frowned at him.

'Important appointment over there.' Vinton raised a finger at the Learning Dome. 'Everybody inside, Myana. They listen to last instruction. Only foolish Myana outside trying to die right now.'

Ayana shot off with Vinton's whispery chuckle trailing after her.

The atmosphere in the Learning Dome was still, although it was packed with Students. There was barely enough space to move. As soon as Ayana stepped inside, she was surrounded by the low fluttering of heartbeats and the anxious breathing of her companions as the Voice filled every corner of the room.

...and so, you will rise above The River Of A Thousand Eyes. You will travel east; past the Dimmer Zone until you arrive at the Rocks of Oron. You will know that you are there, when you see Rising Islands. You will rest there. But not for long.

'And if we do rest there for long?' Blu Tara asked.

You will never leave.

'Why never?'

The Voice ignored her and pressed on.

You must remain there until...

'Until what,' Skylar boomed.

Until you find what awaits you there.

'And what awaits us there?' Skylar's shoulder's shook with his impatience.

You will know this when you get there.

A wave of frustrated sighs greeted the announcement.

Those who were afraid of the unknown or simply preferred to remain secure in the world they were accustomed to, began protesting loudly.

'No one can make us go if we don't want to.'

You will have no choice, The Voice replied.

'We do. We can choose to stay here.'

For a while the Voice said nothing. When it spoke again it was to leave them even more perplexed.

Innoverans, these are my final words to you. Before you leave this world, you must drink of the River of a Thousands eyes. You can only enter those waters freely and together, when you drink of it. It is the gateway to itself.

The students shook their heads incredulously. 'But we were told that it will kill us if we drink of it. Or it will steal our memories.'

'Forgive me for insisting,' Gamma pleaded. 'But we do not understand. Wouldn't we lose our memory? How often have you told us that? I only ask because...'

Go drink! The Voice was loud and reprimanding.

Stunned, they wandered out of the Dome and headed for the river.

Most of them hung back. Gamma looked distressed. Krave's and Skylar's head were close together whispering to each other.

Ayana felt Ryder's presence. She looked up to see him standing a little way behind her. It felt as if he wanted to consume her with his glittering eyes.

'I'll drink with you,' he said. 'Whatever you do I'll do, Ayana.'

'Sorry, Ryder, you do this for yourself, not for me,' she answered.

Ayana turned her head away. Her eyes fell on Krave in the distance, still whispering to Skylar and she felt her heart flip over. Their whispering was pointless. She could hear everything they were saying to each other. They were both agreeing to drink together.

Krave, she thought, how much I would love to drink with him. I would give up everything - for that.

She turned around to repeat her refusal to Ryder but he was no longer beside her.

The arguments amongst the students were loud and heated. They did not understand, they said.

It was a riddle. It had to be a riddle. What was all this stuff about entering the river by drinking it! Did they really have to drink, or was the riddle about something else? Wasn't that how riddles worked? Riddles always meant something different, didn't they? No one wanted to lose what little memory they had.

'It is the will of Apeno,' Ayana said.

'Will of Apeno...Will of Apeno - that's all she says,' Blu Tara jeered. 'Are we meant to do everything your Apeno tells you without question?'

Ayana pretended she did not hear Blu Tara.

Gradually the crowd became quiet. They were worried about what would happen to them when they drank, but more fearful of the consequences of ignoring the instructions of the Voice.

Ayana knelt with the others, cupped her hands, dipped them in the water filled her mouth and swallowed. The bitterness made her body shiver. She retched but clenched her throat and held it in. All around her the others were coughing and twisting their faces with disgust. The two friends Manis and Oria, both dark russet in colour - beautiful and slender like Innoveran Stickbirds - were the first to stand and walk away.

Sizler and twelve of his closest friends stood a long way back from the drinking Students. He was pointing at them and laughing. 'She'll have you jumping in and drowning yourselves next. I'm not putting that filth in my mouth. I don't care who orders it.'

Ignoring Sizler, Ayana rushed to her Pod, threw herself on her cot, so feverish and sick in her stomach she could barely move.

Chapter Thirty-Five

THE BLARING horns from the Learning Dome brought Ayana back to consciousness. She blinked and shook her head. She had been visited by the oddest of all her dreams so far. She found herself alone in the Learning Dome. Everything outside was in flames. She was the only life in Innovera Yakov. She wanted something from the Voice. It was the answer to a question that she could not remember asking.

The only thing she remembered now was the answer the voice gave her.

Only your favoured five must breach that entrance for one, from which is no returning. You shall be the last to enter, then it will begin by ninety.

Ayana grabbed her Sylva and hastily left her Pod, shocked to find that all of Innovera Yakov was covered by a murky darkness. There was no glitter to the trees, the gemstones and the clouds anymore. Everything seemed to be swimming in a thick, grey light.

The Alignment was happening and, as far as she could see, every Student knew that their time for leaving Innovera Yakov had finally arrived.

They were all spread out on the Playing Grounds with

their heads turned up towards the sky. Standing together like this - even in the semi-darkness with the soft glow of Gamma and Blu reflecting off their bodies - the five hundred or so Innoveran Students looked awesome.

The Playing Grounds were alive with the rustle of their feathers, the soft rattle of horns, the ripple of multi-coloured skins, the glint of crystalline eyes; and hair fluttering in the warm wind like rainbow-colored flames.

'They're amazing,' Ayana whispered as she hurried across the Grounds to join them.

Taqua drew beside Ayana. 'Hear that?'

Ayana looked at the tall, wiry girl and nodded.

The hot, dry air around them hummed and they could clearly hear the distant bellow of the ocean of Verheer. Ayana could smell it too — a choking, sulphurous stench — much worse than the River of a Thousand Eyes.

As they watched the five great Moons of Innovera moving to block out their sun, Ayana felt the fear rising like a slow chill in her body. She felt the increasing pulse rate of every one of her companions. Even the great slow heart of Skylar was beating louder. Krave's nervousness filled the air with an uncomfortable electricity and Gamma's and Blu Tara's hair were smouldering.

Bit by bit, their world was covered in a glow that was so thick and purple, the Ishu Mountains were no more than a faint outline against the deepening sky.

A hard wind rose up from nowhere and created little swirling dust storms in the fields.

Ayana straightened up and stepped on her Sylva. It lifted her slightly above the ground and as it drifted towards the front with her, she felt something stirring in herself. The feeling was new and strange and strong and it blocked out the fear that she was feeling earlier.

'It is almost time,' she said, raising her voice so that everyone could hear her. That means complete darkness. But we must not be afraid. This world will be reborn but we will not be here to see it rise again. We will be in the New World that Odors Apeno promised us. And I believe that as we stand here watching the darkness come, the world that we are going to is being remade. That New World is waiting for those of us who survive The Journey.'

From the corner of her eye, Ayana saw Skylar straighten up, then stiffen. He left Krave's side and began pushing his way through the crowd towards her. When he reached Ayana, he looked up at her with his large, glowing amber eyes.

'That voice - that, that's not you,' he rumbled softly. 'That is the voice of Shay!'

Ayana did not speak to him. Instead, she sent him gentle thought-words. *Shay lives in me, Skylar. I have already told you so. That's why none of us can forget her. And now...* Ayana leaned over her Sylva and touched Skylar's puzzled face. *Now, dear Skylar, I know how much you loved her. But you never told her. Why?*

Skylar lowered his head and returned to his brother's side.

Once again, Ayana faced the Students, 'Not long now. We must hold on.'

'And if we do not hold on?'

'I do not know the answer to that, Blu Tara.' Ayana answered truthfully. 'I only tell you what I have been told.'

She looked up at the skies. Her most powerful moon, the Blue Moon of Innovera was the biggest. There was a thread of light around its edges, getting fainter and fainter even as she stared. It will be total darkness soon. And then what? What were they to do, exactly, when all the light above them died?

Where was she to take the Students, after they got to The Rocks of Oron?

Throughout The Darkening, Sizler stood apart whispering fiercely to his companions. Eight of his friends formed a loose circle around him. Now he spoke up angrily.

'It's a fool's run. When this is over,' Sizler pointed at the sky, 'there will be light again and you'll be destroyed and gone before you know what fools you are. We're not going anywhere. '

'We must,' Ayana insisted, 'the Voice told us so.'

Iglo — Sizler's most aggressive disciple - glared at her. 'Who says this isn't one of your little tricks to fool us? This Voice! Why haven't we ever seen the face behind it? A voice that belongs to no one; that never shows its face tells you to go kill yourselves and what do you do? You jump at the chance.'

'And look who's leading you,' Sizler cut in contemptuously. 'A scarfaced Earthbound! If any of you wants to stay with us, you'd better join us now.'

Two girls promptly detached themselves from the back of the crowd and walked over to Sizler's group.

Ayana sensed the weakening resolve of the others. Many of them were unsettled by Sizler's words. Skylar realised this too.

'Shut up,' he grumbled menacingly. 'Or I will shut you up. Both of you!'

Sizler and Iglo backed away, putting a safe distance between themselves and Skylar.

'You don't want to come, I'll make you!' Skylar bellowed at their retreating backs. He rose to his full height and began walking towards them.

Ayana shot urgent thought-words at Skylar. 'Leave them Skylar. Their minds are already set. There is nothing we can do.'

Skylar shrugged and rejoined the Students.

'Stupid Males,' Blu Tara hissed.

'Dumb Female,' Sizler retorted from the distance before disappearing with his group into the Learning Dome.

Suddenly the ground beneath them quaked. The Golkan trees closest to the learning Dome convulsed and groaned as if in the grip of a terrible fever. Their heartbeats began thundering.

The sky lit up in the Far East – a bright explosion that ran like a red-hot blade across the edges of their world. Then everything went black.

Gamma and Blu Tara ignited.

'Now!' Ayana said. 'We lift ourselves! We lift!'

They took to the air in a rush: some quiet as a whisper, others raising themselves with a great flapping of arms and wings. Gamma and Blu Tara shot ahead of them in two flaming streaks.

They rose high and fast over Innovera Yakov, turning East - like the Voice instructed them - towards a giant curtain of clouds that hung there.

Krave turned west, breaking away from the group. They sensed his change of direction immediately. Gamma swung away to join him, but then she slowed down and rejoined the group.

He'd broken off to bid farewell to his friends. More Aarvols than they had ever seen in Innovera Yakov were circling in the sky. The air vibrated with their soft cries. Krave joined them for a moment. The same sounds came from him. They rose together, dipped and circled in an intricate weave of gold and bronze and silver. The sounds they made and the whistling of the wind in their wings created a music that was so wonderful and sad, it quietened the Students.

At last Krave left them, turning back from time to watch the Aarvols rise higher and higher into the air till they were like a sprinkling of starlight against the purple backdrop of the sky.

Not long after they set off again, Krave Solan - who always preferred to fly highest - shouted down at them. 'Look! Look down there! Look back!'

What they saw behind them made them turn and hover, horrified, over the world they had just risen from.

A raging fire was spreading across the Grounds. Below them, Innovera Yakov rocked and shuddered. The Ishu Mountains had disappeared from sight completely and every Golkan tree lay flat, drowning in a twisting river of flames.

Where The Learning Dome had been there was nothing. The vast spread of rocks and grass on which their Pods stood had become a carpet of dancing fire.

Ayana thought of Sizler and his friends, trapped down there, consumed by the fire that now covered their world. She felt sorry for them. She knew that the others would not be rejoicing at their destruction. Like her, these Students she was travelling with, would all realise, that this was what the Voice meant when it told them they had no choice. When the time came they all had to leave.

And as she, Ayana, told the Students earlier, Innovera Yakov will rise again as if it was never touched by the fiery hands of Odors Apeno. It will be filled with other students who will arrive from other worlds; and eventually, after many moons of preparation and training, will also make this own frightening journey.

She remembered what Shay once told her:

In Eden Gobad - our universe - nothing truly dies or disappears, Ayana. Every life renews itself and returns - sometimes different, sometimes the same. But nothing truly dies.

Ayana and her companions hung in the air and watched Innovera Yakov burn.

'East!' Ayana said at last to the stunned Students. They obeyed her without question. They dipped and swerved in a giant scintillating flock towards the red patch of light in the east where their journey and the dreaded world of Verheer began.

CHAPTER THIRTY-SIX

THEY WERE just flying past the darkened Moon of Dotan when a group of Izus drew up beside Ayana in a noisy swarm. At the best of times — these guardians of the Garden of Knowing - were bothersome little Beings. They complained at the slightest opportunity because they were never satisfied. But even if the Izus were the dwarfs of Innovera Yakov nothing much frightened them. The rare times that they were, they glowed an intense red and launched themselves at whatever it was that scared them. Then they exploded causing terrible destruction, only to reconstitute themselves.

'Where exactly are we going?' They wanted to know. 'And why not go West instead of East?'

West sounded better, they protested. *East* sounded like a place no Being ought to go to. And where exactly in the East were they meant to go? Nobody knew anything about the Rocks of Oron, they complained. How were they meant to find it in this big and wide and ugly place? And how was she, Ayana, meant to guide them if she didn't know where it was herself?

The racket grew so loud that Ayana could barely think straight. Skylar tried to shut them up but they just became even more agitated. Now they were surrounding her and she could feel their heated breaths on her face. Ryder came to her rescue but as soon as the Izus saw him, they began to glow red. Ryder moved back quickly.

'Get back!' Ayana shouted.

'Or else?' One of them snapped back.

'Or else,' Blu Tara said, 'I'll fry every one of you.'

It was the wrong thing to say. Blu Tara must have known this. Their eyes and faces became a flaming red. Anything could have happened if Vinton hadn't popped up directly in front of Ayana, glowing just as red as the Izus.

The shock of Vinton's appearance halted the angry Izus and silenced them.

'Back! All you! Everyone! You touch her, you blow up. Then what happen? You die! Or maybe you don't die, then what happen? Nothing! Because still you don't know where you go. No more Innovera Yakov, so where you go? Verheer? Oh-no, they eat you down there. You stay up here? Oh-no! You go weak, then you fall and die.'

Vinton waved his little hands at the astonished Innoverans. 'Everyone! You follow me. Everyone, you hear? I show you something. Everyone – if you don't come with me, you die.'

Soon, they were over the Dimmer Zone. Vinton plummeted downwards. They Izus followed him, the air buzzing with their questions once again.

'Who are you?'

'Where did you come from?'

'Why we never saw you before?'

'Are you real? How do we know you're not a fraud? Maybe Silly Healer made you up to save her skin and fool us.'

'Shut, uuuup!' Vinton snarled and again they all fell silent.

Ayana's mysterious little friend took them down to a valley of dripping rocks. They landed in a huddle on a ledge overlooking a great valley, which was in such deep shadow it appeared to be bottomless. They listened to the beating of the waves just beyond and turned their faces away from the biting wind that rose up from the valley floor.

Vinton rose in the air and hovered above their heads. He was now a soft transparent green. 'Now I show you why Myana boss,' Vinton swooped down and with a flick of his hand he drew back Ayana's hair revealing the terrible scars on her face. Ayana screamed and pulled away. She covered her face with her hands.

'This I must do now, Myana.' Vinton's voice was soft and comforting in her ear. 'If me, Vinton, don't do this then everything fail. Everybody lost. Understand?'

Vinton eased Ayana's hands away. With bright green fingers he traced her scars, following the winding purple lines that had disfigured and shamed her from as far back as she could remember.

'All of you! You want to know where you go. This,' he shouted, tracing a long curling mark down Ayana's cheek. 'This, the River full of Thousand Eyes. See how it turn?' Vinton's finger followed another scar. 'This tell you where we go now, after Dimmer Zone. Oron Rock. You see?' Vinton said, caressing Ayana's face. 'All this is map. Right here! And, you know, map change every time. Not whole journey straight away, but stage by stage. Scar change, make different map for every stage. So!' Vinton raised his boyish voice; 'If Myana lost, everybody lost too. That's why she boss. You no keep her safe; then you die. You understand?'

There were gasps of incredulity. Even Blu Tara's mocking expression changed to disbelief.

Ayana looked at Vinton, speechless. She touched her face. 'You never told me. You never...' She touched her face again. 'All this pain! All my life I thought it was for nothing. Just there to shame me.'

'When right time come I tell you. Right time is now. I tell you once before, long time. Remember? But you think Vinton talking nonsense.'

Ayana saw the new respect in the eyes of her companions.

'Where did that come from?' Blu Tara pointed at Vinton.

'He's always here,' Ayana answered, smiling wickedly at her. 'You just couldn't see him, Blu Tara. Where now, Vinton?' Ayana whispered.

'Oron Rock,' he whispered back. 'Says so on your lovely face.'

'And then?'

'Then Big Journey begin,' he answered grimly. Vinton's lips were no longer moving and yet Ayana heard his voice deep inside her head. 'Much dark where you go, Little Healer. Many perish, I think. And if Myana perish too, me, Vinton follow you. We very careful. Big danger from the blue one.'

Vinton turned away from her and waved his little arms at the crowd of Innoverans. 'We go East now. And no more noise from big-mouth Izus.'

This time they rose together in complete silence. Beneath them an unbelievable world unfolded. A world without end of heaving water and strange thunderous sounds that trembled the very air around them. What looked like dark columns of rocks pushed themselves out of the ocean striving to pierce the sky.

These were the first signs of the civilisation of Escapeets they heard so much about. Warriors and monsters lived down there. Those were not really rock columns. They were the tips of Verheeran citadels and fortresses that broke the surface. They looked dead and silent, but Ayana was not fooled.

The Voice told them that Verheer was a world as complete as Innovera Yakov was. There were Beings down there that were stranger than anything they had ever seen before.

Riding high above the Verheeran coastline, Ayana continued to lead the Students eastwards over deeply shadowed beaches crowded with boulders, mysterious buttes and promontories, which crouched above the shoreline like an army of multi-headed beasts.

It was getting colder too - the kind of coldness that Ayana never felt before. The chill was creeping through her skin down to her very bones. Sometimes they saw movement down below: an explosion of spray; a sudden foaming of the water; or streaks of bright blue light that flickered on before shutting off again.

Ayana's mind was buzzing with questions. It felt as if a whole hive of Izus had taken residence in her head.

Why was it called The Rocks of Oron?

Why had no one ever heard about it until the Voice told them of its existence?

Why couldn't they rest there for too long?

And if it is dangerous, like the Voice suggests, why do we have to land there in the first case?

Perhaps, she guessed, it was the highest point from which they were going to lift off for the Journey across the ocean of Verheer; or maybe they would be able to get a glimpse of the new world they were heading for.

CHAPTER THIRTY-SEVEN

ALTHOUGH THEY had never seen it before, they recognised The Rocks of Oron as soon as it emerged against the murky skyline. They were still a great distance from the Rocks of Oron, and yet it stood out like a black claw above the water. The talons on the claw were spread wide. Eight of them pointed westward except the smallest on the right. That one curled downwards, aiming directly at the water. Ahead of it were islands that pushed out of the water like the teeth of giant monsters.

'We here,' Vinton whispered. Despite her friend's attempt at cheerfulness, Ayana could hear the worry in his voice. The sight of rocks was frightening enough. But there was also the smell - a choking mix of burnt flesh and rotting vegetation. Yet there were no trees; and there certainly was no sign of fire. If anything, the place looked wet and desolate.

They hovered, looking for the best place to land. Ayana glanced over at the islands in the water. They rose and sank with every heave of the tossing ocean, and yet they did not drift.

'That's why they're called The Rising Islands,' she muttered.

'Terrible place,' Gamma folded her arms around her shoulders and shuddered.

A voice came from somewhere in the back. 'Can't we stay in the air? This place stinks.'

Crell pushed his way through the tightly bunched group. He was one of those Students that no one really noticed. When the changes came upon him, he sprouted an impressive plume of feathers. Crell was the only one amongst them with a tail and a red fleshy crest where his hair should be. They saw him use that tail once when a Stardog appeared from nowhere and tried to consume him. He flicked it out with such speed and viciousness it impaled the creature and killed it instantly.

As if in direct response to Crell's question the sky lit up. A blade of light cut a bright path across the rocks. Some of the students, their imaginations already filled with the many horrors of Verheer, broke away in panic.

'Stay together,' Ayana ordered.

'I'll take a closer look,' Krave said. And he shot off.

Gamma followed Krave.

'The rest of us will wait here.' Ayana said. Her Sylva was shuddering under her. A deep unease crept into her chest. 'We'll wait until they tell us it is safe. I think...' Ayana kept her eyes focused on the rocks. 'Something awaits us there.'

Blu Tara pretended not to hear her and shot off to join her sister and Krave.

Gamma landed first, then Blu Tara. Krave hovered over them. With his wings spread out like that, Krave Solan looked magnificent.

So..so beautiful, Ayana thought, touching the scarred side of her face. She quickly looked away.

'How much longer do we have to remain here, Ayana?' Crell's voice broke through Ayana's thoughts.

Skylar glared at him. 'As long as we have to, Birdface.'

Skylar then drew up beside Ayana. 'We can't stay here forever. Blu Tara says its fine down there.'

Ayana waved the Students forward. They landed in a rush. Most of the younger Innoverans formed tight groups, whispering amongst themselves.

Ayana studied the rocks around them.

'What we do now?' Crell demanded.

Strangely, the Izus were saying nothing. In fact, they were more interested in Vinton who flitted amongst them making signs with his hands that only they understood.

'Why isn't she telling us anything?'

'Because she is as lost as we are,' Blu Tara said to Crell. 'There's no map on her face now. Just that horrible pink line.'

Crell curled his tail around his waist and stormed off.

'You sure we have to stop here, Vinton?' Ayana sent urgent thought-words to her friend.

Even Ryder was looking at her with doubtful eyes.

It was not long before Crell's distressed cries came from somewhere in the near distance. They realised that he'd wandered off and fallen into one of the many rock pools dotting the jagged landscape. In an instant Krave was over the pool, his right arm sizzling with electricity.

Crell's tail was thrashing wildly but they could not see what he was struggling against.

'Whatever it is, I'll...' Krave lifted his arm and aimed.

Ayana stopped him, 'Do you want to kill him?'

Krave dropped his arm and shrugged. 'There's nothing there anyway. Just a shallow pool.'

'Then why is he sinking?' Blu Tara folded her arms and grinned. 'Looks like he's giving up. Shouldn't somebody help him?'

Taqua leaned over and stared hard into the water. She leapt on a ledge above the pool. 'There's something there that's got him! I'm sure of it! Don't know what it is though.' They watched Taqua's body collapse and liquefy and then flow in a bright green stream into the pool.

Nothing happened for a while, then the water erupted. Crell's tail came alive again and thrashed; his hands emerged and closed around a rock ledge. Skylar reached down and dragged him out.

'What was it?' they asked.

'Dunno,' Crell croaked. 'It pulled me in.'

'What pulled you in?'

'Something,' he was shivering with fear. 'Couldn't see it. I just felt it.'

They turned their attention back to the water.

'Taqua!' Ayana gasped. 'Where is she?'

As if in response to her question, a stream of water flowed backwards form the pool and formed a shimmering puddle at their feet. It solidified and a smiling Taqua stood before them.

'That's not a pool,' she said. 'It's a creature. Not water either. That's its digestive juices. Some sort of acid. Would've made a slow meal out of Crell. Anyway, she shrugged. 'I neutralised it.'

'You neutralised it! How?'

Before they had time to find out more from Taqua, the rocks behind them moved. The whole face of the cliff was convulsing. One of the Izus shouted and took off. Panicked, the others followed. Ayana's Sylva shot her in the air.

'It's alive!' someone shouted. 'The whole place is alive.'

They looked down just in time to see a section of the rocks they had just been standing on, opening up like a great mouth. It closed around two of their companions. Just as

Crell's outcry broke through the air, Ayana thought she heard Blu Tara laugh.

The last they saw of Crell was the end of his tail flailing desperately as he was swallowed up.

Skylar was also trapped.

He had tried to save the two young Innoverans and now his feet were pinned down by the grasping rocks. A terrible roar exploded from his chest. He was fighting back, his shoulders hunched, his fists battering the rocks that bound him.

'Not Skylar!' Ayana wailed. 'Not Skylar. We have to get him back.' A rush of anger swelled up in her chest. She swung her Sylva in a tight, angry curve towards her struggling friend, projecting her mind at the writhing rock-face as she swooped.

'Your weakness,' she hissed, 'I will find your weakness.'

Ayana concentrated hard scanning every crack and furrow on the rock-face, until she felt a different energy emanating from a narrow opening that was almost hidden from their view.

'There!' Ayana pointed a trembling finger at the tiny opening. 'There! We must strike it there!'

She projected a stream of thought-words at the rock-wall. 'You will not have him. We will take him back.'

Krave moved in first with a blast of electricity that made a bright net around the crevice. Gamma and Blu Tara merged. The air hummed with their energy as they directed a blinding blade of fire into the crevasse that Krave had just marked out. The whole of the outcrop shook. Something deep within it groaned. A terrifying rumble rose up from the very belly of the monster. But Skylar was still trapped and the struggle against the clenching rocks was weakening him.

Ayana had little time left to save him. Her mind had suddenly expanded. She knew the capabilities of each Innoveran in her charge. And while Blu Tara and Gamma poured their heat into the rocky opening, she summoned Taqua with thought-words.

See what you can do, she told her urgently.

The strange girl that Ayana had come to love and admire so much, dropped down beside Skylar. The rocks reached up to grab her but closed themselves around nothing. A swirl of smoking liquid formed around Skylar's feet. The smell of burning filled the air. The rock around Skylar's feet dissolved and solidified instantly.

'We will take him back from you,' Ayana screamed. 'Gamma, Blu! Pull back!'

Gamma and Blu Tara rose into the air.

'Ryder,' she called. 'Send your spear in there.'

'Yep!' Ryder hollered drawing back his arm and rising as he did so.

Ryder's long body rode the air in a awesome swinging curve. The weapon left his hand and buried itself in the crevice, raising sprays of molten rock.

The mountain shuddered. Another groan rose up from deep within it and Skylar broke free with Taqua close behind him.

The two took to the air with a bound followed by the sky-splitting cheer of the Students.

'Vinton, send in your friends.' Ayana hollered.

The air shook with the sound of shattering rocks and the thunderous snarl of the life force that lived inside it as the Izus threw themselves at it.

When it was over and the Rocks of Oron were reduced to rubble, Ayana looked around. She thought of Crell and Nissi – the other Innoveran that had been taken - and it was all she could do to hold back the tears.

She turned to face her companions. 'In Innovera Yakov how many of us remember the lives that have been lost? None! We do not know why that is. But on this journey we must find a way to remember everyone that does not make it. Even if it means burning a picture of their faces on our skins. We must remember. It is our only way of valuing the lives we lost. That's why, she wiped her eyes. That's why we must teach ourselves to remember.'

'Now you know why we stop there,' Vinton told her, gravely.

'No. Why?' Ayana frowned at him.

'Now Myana know for sure that she lead very powerful army.' Vinton spread his arms as if to embrace them all. 'Apeno show you that.' Vinton pointed at the destroyed rocks. 'Apeno teach you new lesson. He show that Myana know to fight.'

'Where now?' Gamma asked. Her voice was gentle and respectful.

Ayana looked down at the roaring water-world of Verheer then up at the wall of mist in the distance, past which she could not project her mind.

They hung in the air waiting for her word. Ryder was looking anxiously at her. Blu Tara was strangely quiet. She remained beside Gamma whose head was lifted in the direction of the wall of mist.

Krave drifted down beside Ayana's Sylva. 'Where now, Little Healer?' Ayana stared into his golden eyes and felt the warmth creeping through her body. She looked away quickly.

'I do not know, Krave, she replied, touching the single scar that now ran down her face. 'The map is gone. Just...'

When she turned back to face Krave, he was staring thoughtfully in the distance.

'There is always a way,' he said. 'I know that now. We only have to find it. We have to work it out.'

'True,' came Gamma's musical voice. 'We know now that it's never obvious. And yet it always is.'

At least, Ayana thought, they are no longer fighting me.

She touched her face again, traced the single scar, then dropped her hand in defeat.

'Where now,' she turned to Vinton, hoping that somehow Odors Apeno would speak to her through him. But Vinton looked even more lost than she felt.

'Is me Vinton to ask you, Myana; "Where now." Not Myana asking Vinton. I done tell you: where you go, me, Vinton, go with you. Okay?'

Ayana looked out at the ocean and saw nothing but dirty restless water. Angrily, she raised her voice. 'We have come this far. We have done our best. Apeno promised us a way. But now that he's brought us here, I can't believe He's abandoned us.'

It made no sense. If Apeno took them out of Innovera Yakov and made it impossible for them to return, it was because there *was* a way to get to the new world.

Ayana scolded herself for doubting. *I should believe. I should have more faith.*

Faith - the Voice told them something about it once.

Sometimes all a Being is left with to see them through the worst of times is faith. Faith is the greatest of all powers.

But what was the use of faith if there were no directions out of here?

She remembered that long, dark time of suffering in her Pod when Apeno Himself entered her mind and led her through the terrible, freezing world of Verheer. Was it all for nothing? Were she and her fellow Students brought here only to be abandoned, with no hope of returning to Innovera Yakov?

At least He should grant me one last wish, shouldn't he? He should let me see what I look like without these nasty scars.

She looked down bitterly at her face reflected in the Sylva. A hard wind came off the ocean and pushed back her wing of hair. The scar was still there, of course. *Like a punishment, like...*Ayana caught her breath. She looked up quickly. Her eyes locked on to Ryder - not his face but the spear he sat astride. *Like... the head of Ryder's spear!*

Ayana looked again at the shape of her scar and she cried out, *It cannot be. It cannot be....*

The others rushed over and surrounded her.

'What is it?' Gamma shook her by the shoulders.

Ayana pointed at her exposed face.

'You just discovered that?' Blu Tara chuckled. Gamma pushed her sister back.

Krave and Skylar drew closer.

'What does it look like?' Ayana could hear the trembling in her voice.

She said nothing more, she opened her mind so that they could all access it.

Everyone went silent. Even Blu Tara's hair had paled. But she recovered quickly and pretended not to care.

'That,' Blu Tara pointed a finger at Ayana's face, 'could mean anything. It could be exactly what it looks like: a scar. No more, no less.'

'Nonsense! It was Ayana's marks that brought us here,' Skylar said. 'It led us to those Rocks, where the Voice said we must go. Now it has changed to this.'

Skylar turned to face the group while pointing at Ayana's

face, his big voice rolled out loud and clear so that everyone could hear him. 'Innoverans! This is the head of an arrow and it is pointing down.'

'What does it mean?' one of the Izus asked.

'It means,' Ayana hesitated. 'It-it means we have to go down. We have to enter the ocean.'

'You asking us to drown ourselves?' Blu Tara snapped.

'What's the matter now, Blu Tara? Scared of a little water?' Ryder teased. But he too sounded nervous.

The more Ayana thought about this next challenge, the more terrified she became and the more convinced she felt that this was what the scar meant.

'We have to believe,' she protested. 'It is our biggest test so far. Besides we were told this in a riddle. Remember the last words of the voice?'

Drink of the River of A Thousand Eyes for you cannot enter those waters freely and together unless you drink of it. It is the doorway to itself...

'We were afraid but we drank and we didn't die. Don't you see? "Those waters" did not mean the water of The River of a Thousand Eyes. It meant this ocean which is the doorway to Verheer.'

'But we're already in Verheer,' Gamma protested.

'Above it, not inside it,' Ayana replied.

'Then you go first,' Blu Tara challenged.

'I would if that is what it takes to convince you; but I cannot,' Ayana replied. 'We must all go in together.'

Taqua approached her puzzled. 'Why?'

'I do not know. Those were the instructions from the Voice. *"You can only enter these waters freely and together."* Ayana addressed the others. 'Those of us who drank have nothing to fear.'

'Then why am I afraid?' A small voice at the back replied.

'You have to believe, Izami. It - it is an act of faith.'

'Faith, my eyes! You are the leader, then lead.' Blu Tara threw Ayana a taunting smile.

Ayana shot an angry finger at Blu Tara. In the thick air, her voice rose strong and clear. 'You! You challenge me at every turn. But I tell you this right now: it is not you that speak, it is the ugliness inside you. You think you know better? You believe that it is *your* strength that makes you smarter? Then I'll step aside and let you lead. Go on! I hand it over to you. Come on, get us out of here!'

Blu Tara paled. She drifted backwards as if Ayana slapped her. The air grew so hot it crackled.

'What do you mean by that?' She grated. 'Say that again, just..'

'Shut up!' Gamma flamed. 'She's right! And you're proving it right now. Now give me your hand. Little Healer says, together! So, come on! Everyone of us will hold hands.'

They came together and formed a great circle above the tossing water.

'What's up with them?' Gamma was staring behind her. The two Students Manis and Oria who were friends from the time they arrived in Innovera Yakov had pulled themselves out of the ring. Their faces were tight with fear.

Krave broke the circle and went over to them. 'What's the matter?'

'We - we cannot go,' Oria said.

Ayana pulled up beside Krave. 'Manis, Oria? Come, it's alright to be afraid; we're all afraid.' Ayana touched Oria's arm.

'Is not that. We... we didn't drink. We didn't believe. We... Can...can you help us?' She wailed.

Ayana looked into Oria's amber eyes. 'But, I - I saw you drinking from the river.'

'We pretended. We did not believe. We thought....' Oria looked away.

'We cannot leave them here,' Ayana said.

'Nothing you can do, Myana. They no believe; they disobey. To go we have to, soon. See down there? Ocean changing. Bad water rising bigger. Soon, maybe, is not possible to go.'

Ayana followed Vinton's finger. Indeed the water below was being whipped up by a high wind.

'Now we go. They no believe; they pay!'

Ayana wiped her eyes and returned to group. She joined hands with Taqua and Ryder and turned her head towards the boiling surface of the sea.

'On my word,' Skylar said.

All around them there were great intakes of breath.

Ayana gave one last look at the weeping friends. *They have no place to go to. They cannot return. Apeno, why are you so cruel?*

She bowed her head and tightened her grip on Taqua's and Ryder's hand.

'Okay Innoverans, let's go.' Skylar commanded.

With his voice still ringing in their heads, they plummeted from the dark air into the thrashing water.

CHAPTER THIRTY-EIGHT

As THEY plunged towards the waters, Ayana projected comforting thoughts at the distressed friends.

How terrifying it must be to be left alone up there in semi-darkness, with no place to go back to and no hope of coming along with them. She wanted to cry. What would Manis and Oria do now? Even as Ayana asked herself the question, she already knew the answer. They would hang above the raging water until they became exhausted. Finally the ocean of Verheer would claim them.

They felt themselves pulled downwards into a whirlpool of thick and dirty water. Ayana held fast to her Sylva. Her companions were dim and twisting shapes around her. She projected her thoughts but found she could reach no one. All her powers had left her. And she could not breathe.

Was this what dying felt like? Was this Apeno's way of getting rid of all of them at the same time?

Just when she thought that there was no end to this terrible spinning descent, when it was impossible to hold her breath any longer, something changed around them. They were still falling, still in the clutches of some terrible dragging force, still in the grip of a chilling coldness that penetrated their very core when they realised that there was no more water.

They were sailing down through another sky towards a landscape so rugged and strange, it felt more like a nightmare.

Even Blu Tara gasped when they saw what lay below them.

They found themselves on the top of a high rocky plateau.

They looked up barely believing their eyes. The ocean was above them. It was like a ceiling over their heads. The ocean was the roof of the Verheeran world.

Although it was still not bright here, it was less dark than above the water. Everything was covered in a faint and watery dimness. They realised the source of that strange glow were five phosphorescent lights somewhere in the water-sky above them. And yet there was no sun or moon in Verheer.

Dark rolling hills spread out beneath them. They could see no trees, or if there were, they were so strange the Students could not recognise them.

Just beneath them were rising formations of saw-toothed rocks that pushed their summits into the seething water overhead.

Streams of lava gushed out from the foot of nearby edifices like fiery tongues. They formed bubbling red pools at their base.

They watched hooded figures hustling amongst the rocks, gathering objects from the ground and dropping them into containers. They all appeared to be in a rush, pausing every now and then to lift their heads and stare into the distance then turning back to each other with quick movements of their covered heads before resuming what they were doing.

The Innoverans watched them intently. This was the first sign of Verheeran life they had seen. Silent and watchful, they dimmed the glow of their skins and eyes to avoid detection.

Suddenly, as if they something had unnerved them, the Verheerans lifted their containers and with an odd sideways hop, took to the air together. They skimmed just above the rocky surface with their load held close against their bodies and disappeared amongst the gloom.

'They fly like us,' Taqua whispered.

'What are they?' Gamma wanted to know.

Skylar drew closer to Ayana. His amber eyes glowed softly as he looked into the distance as if he were trying to see what lay beyond the walls of rocks that rose up on either side of them. Skylar sniffed the air and turned grimly to Ayana.

'You smell that Little Healer?'

It was the same odour she noticed in the air just as they arrived at the Rocks of Oron, above the water.

'Living Rocks,' Ayana confirmed.

Ayana projected her thoughts towards the others in an attempt to draw this to their attention. No one responded to her thought-words. She concentrated hard and tried again. For some reason she could no longer reach them with her mind.

'Skylar,' she said. 'can you contact Krave. Without words, I mean.'

Skylar concentrated for a moment. He angled his head at her and frowned.

'Not from here,' he said touching his forehead.

Taqua pulled up beside them. 'I was trying to reach you, Ayana.'

Ayana shifted on her Sylva. 'There is something here that's blocking us.'

It is a different world, Taqua. Very different from our own. It has different laws.

'How are we to manage then?'

'We will,' Ayana answered. 'So far we have, haven't we?'

Taqua looked at the darkness before them. Ayana realised how much she liked this girl who was not afraid of anything.

'Go tell the others if they haven't realised it already.' Ayana told her.

As soon as Taqua left, Ayana turned to Skylar. 'Maybe it's a good thing, Skylar.' She dropped her voice further. 'There is something I must tell you.'

Skylar listened while Ayana told him everything she knew about Blu Tara and her secret meetings with the stranger from Verheer. She told him of her suspicions about Shay's untimely death. When she described how Ice devoured Kino, Skylar grunted in disbelief. He threw a long stare at Blu Tara who was hovering beside Gamma.

'Why didn't you tell us this before?'

Ayana could not answer truthfully so she preferred to remain silent.

'I'll be watching her,' he said, after a long pause. 'And her sister.'

Ayana looked across at the pink girl. She was leaning against Krave and looking tenderly into his face. Ayana noticed how much she was drawn to him now. Gamma never strayed far from him. And Blu Tara no longer seemed to mind. In fact the tall Innoveran was strangely quiet. Ayana watched her through narrowed eyes.

'Gamma doesn't know,' Ayana said. 'I'm very sure of that.'

This was Ice's world. Maybe Blu Tara already warned him and he was somewhere out there in all that darkness waiting. But, she decided, that was not possible. Blu Tara did not know that they were meant to *enter* Verheer. To be actually inside it. Not even she, Ayana, did. Most of the students did not know of Ice's existence not to mention the great destructive powers he possessed.

When Krave boasted about defeating him, he did not tell them that his adversary was Ice - although Ayana realised it from the moment she heard of Krave's fight. Only she and Shay knew of Blu Tara's connection with the Escapeet. Shay paid for that knowledge with her life.

Ayana looked around at the mass of Students gathered round her. They were still recovering from the discovery of this new world that they heard so many frightening things about. They huddled together closely, afraid to lift an eyebrow lest they betray their presence to the Verheerans.

From the time they saw the Verheerans at the edge of the lava stream, they knew they couldn't remain where they were for long without being detected. They had to press on.

'There is only one possible way to go.' Ayana pointed at the canyon directly ahead. 'Down there, then straight ahead. As fast and quietly as we can.'

Chapter Thirty-nine

As soon as Blu Tara entered Ice's world she began wondering where he was.

She was impatient for him to come and take her away from these empty Innoverans. During all those seasons of waiting for him to finally transport her to his domain, her time in Innovera Yakov felt like an eternity.

When the ache of missing Ice became unbearable, she imagined herself travelling through the Abyss beside him - his princess and companion. She, Blu Tara — the one Ice had chosen above his own kind would offer up her own powers so he could become even more powerful. So that they could walk amongst the Beings of his world unchallenged.

With him and his army, she would invade the world of the Earthbounds and Innovera Yakov. She would trap and feed him every living Being he wanted to consume.

The last time they met was when she followed Shay into the Living Forest and directed Ice towards the girl. He had no appetite for her. He said something strange: she was not of Innovera Yakov or of any other world he knew. He sensed this by her energy and the fact that she showed no fear of him. He preferred the ones who feared him.

After that she could not let Shay live, of course. Besides, Shay hated her. Unlike Scarface, she had no hold on Shay. Shay would not think twice about reporting her to the others. She could have reduced her to a puff of smoke, but she preferred to destroy her another way. More painfully, more slowly by embedding one of those darts that Ice left her as a gift. He said it grew inside the bodies of his fighters. Once it entered an enemy, the pain alone was enough to kill them.

Ice – Prince of the Abyss. *Her Ice!* The only Being she would kneel down and bow her head to. Yet, it frightened her when she saw how frustrated he became as he reached out to embrace her and his arms went through her body as if she were made of air.

Being with him in his world would make her solid in his arms. However cold his wide embrace she was warm enough to withstand it. Whatever the price of being with him, however horrible the world was that Ice lived in, she, Blu Tara, was determined to be with him.

The first thing she did when she arrived was to try to warn him of their presence in his domain. But something about this place made it impossible to send thought messages through to him. She had to be careful. She could not do anything to rouse the suspicions of her companions. Least of all Gamma. Even Gamma would turn on her if she knew the truth; and if they fought, Ice would never forgive her for the destruction they visited on his world.

So, like the others, she watched the Beings below collecting the rocks. Ice told her they were full of poisons for their weapons. She knew what they were - Ice told her many things about his world -

The creatures were Ikapeets, the lowest of the worker-servants. They built and mended the great fortifications that separated the two regions that made up Verheer.

According to Ice, the upper region of their world was named, The Shallow. It was less important to Verheerans than The Abyss.

'More ancient than your bright and silly world,' he sneered. 'Verheerans have no need for suns. Our eyes provide the light. They go out only when we sleep.'

'What happens if you're attacked?'

'We are protected by the Ikapeets; they never sleep. They have no eyes. They do not think. They are there to kill. They know us by the energy that flows through every Being in our world. No living Being enters our world without them knowing.'

If Ice was right, the Ikapeets and he already knew that they were there. Perhaps he was biding his time. Drawing these Innoverans deeper into Verheer. Blu Tara narrowed her eyes at the canyon ahead; perhaps Ice was at the end of it waiting for them to emerge.

Blu Tara looked up to find Skylar's eyes on her. She flicked her hair and sneered at him. The giant did not look away. He did not smile back either. *Stardog*, she thought, knowing that he could not read her mind. *I could turn you to ashes any time. In fact I'll make Ice make a meal of you.*

Blu Tara turned her back on him.

CHAPTER FORTY

GAMMA DID not understand the mix of the dread and nervousness that filled her as soon as she entered Verheer. The more anxious she became, the more she clung to Krave.

Hard as she tried, she simply could not see him only as a trusted friend. Over the many seasons of not communicating with him, her feelings had not changed. If anything they had become stronger. The distance between only served to make him appear more desirable in her eyes.

She missed the tingle of his skin against hers. She wanted to have that time again with him when they laughed together at the same things. Most of all, she could not forget his hands - those hands that held her in the Dimmer Zone, threw her far up in the air and caught her fall with such tenderness and love.

She looked out at the Verheeran darkness, hugged herself and shivered. This place looked new and strange to the others but to her, it felt familiar. Had she seen it in one of her many confusing dreams? There was not much that frightened or surprised her but she did not understand her jumpiness, and the feeling that there was something more frightening out there than all the other dangers of The Journey.

It looked as if Blu Tara felt the same way too. Gamma had never seen her sister so nervous and distracted. Blu Tara hardly noticed anyone around her. And for the first time she did not have a sarcastic reply to whatever the others said.

Gamma rushed over to Krave.

'Krave,' she whispered.

Krave leaned towards her.

'There is something I must tell you, before...before..'

'Before what?'

'There is something I must say, Krave. I...'

'Then say it, Gamma. Tell me..'

'I don't know how to start.' Gamma pressed her lips against his ear. 'Promise me you won't let me out of your sight.'

'What's the matter, Gamma; what's bothering you?'

'You promise?'

Krave looked at her and frowned. 'What's wrong?'

'I-I don't know, Krave. I don't know how to say it. You promise?'

'Of course I do. That's easy. Is that all?'

Gamma placed a nervous hand on his. She looked over her shoulder and edged even closer to him. 'That will do for now. That will have to do.'

CHAPTER FORTY-ONE

THEY SET off along the canyon hugging the rocky sides. They knew that it was not a question of whether they would be discovered. It was simply a matter of time. The floor of the canyon changed abruptly. It began slanting downwards. From that point on, it was covered in a carpet of small plants. Their bony branches were intertwined in a thick, dark mesh around each other. At the centre of each one there was a soft phosphorescent glow.

Something about the glow emanating from those plants excited the Flitters. Ayana had wondered what use they would be in the new world. Would they remain cleaners of their Pods? Or would they be given a higher role? Once or twice when their agitation became too much, Skylar growled at them and they fell silent, but not for long. Their chattering soon filled the air again. It made the Students nervous.

One of the Flitters, more adventurous than the others, suddenly broke away and dived towards the little glowing forest. The others followed immediately.

They had no time to land. The tangled branches shot open, stiffening like spears and impaling every one of them.

Horrified they watched as the branches folded themselves

around the little squirming bodies. In a moment they were gone, pulled into the greenish glowing core.

Oddly, the only one who moved to save them was Blu Tara. She ignited in a bedazzling incandescence and dipped downwards.

Before she could touch her lens Gamma leapt in front of her.

'You create a firestorm now, then it's as good as telling every Verheeran that we're here. Is that what you want to do?'

Blu Tara did not reply. Still burning blue, she pulled away from Gamma.

'Dim! Dim yourself!' Gamma hissed at her.

Blu Tara kept her glow defiantly for a while, then gradually dimmed.

Shaken by what just happened to their companions, the rest of the Flitters floated high. They rose above the others, their wings shimmering dimly in the gloom.

'Stay close!' Ryder commanded. But their fear made them ignore him.

Ayana kept a nervous eye on them as they became tiny specks against the moving water-sky.

No one knew what happened next but they heard a high-flying Flitter scream. The cry was cut off abruptly. It was followed by more and more snipped-off cries.

The Flitters had pierced the water-roof or were being sucked up into it. The water-sky grew black with swimming shapes. Large creatures with fins as wide as wings circled the flailing Flitters.

Ayana and the Students watched the last of their small companions disappear into the bodies of the creatures, which floated away with ponderous movements of their wing-fins, leaving only silence.

'Is that the way?' They heard Krave mutter bitterly. 'Is that how it goes?'

'What do you mean, Krave?' Gamma queried.

Krave said nothing for a while. When he spoke again, he sounded almost tearful. 'That every lesson of survival that we learn here, we pay for it with our lives.'

'We must be silent,' Gamma told him gently. 'We should speak only when we must. I-I do not like it here.'

Krave came down and hovered beside Gamma. She took his hand and rose with him above the group.

She stared into his eyes.

'Krave,' she whispered urgently. 'Look me in the face and tell me what you told me when you decided to be only friends. Tell me to my face you do not love me.'

'What do you think?'

'I'm not asking you to ask me what I think. I want to hear you say it.'

'I do. Gamma - you already know that.'

'Then let's merge!' Gamma stood shivering in front of him.

'It cannot be in a world that does not belong to us. You know that.'

'Sorry,' she said after a long silence. 'Sometimes I think I cannot bear it...watching you...knowing...'

Gamma looked out into the distance. 'Like I said before, I cannot tell you how I know this. I don't know why I am so certain that I have seen this place before. This - this darkness. It's like a dream, only it is not a dream because we are all here. The Flitters screamed and we all heard them; we watched them die - which means that this is real. All my life - what I can remember of it - nothing frightened me. And yet,' Gamma pushed back her hair to stare at Krave again. 'There is something here that scares me. That makes me know that if you do not have me now. If we do not merge, then maybe we'll never do. I-I don't know how else to say it.'

Krave touched her face and rustled. 'It was not a dream, Gamma. You came here before. Or in the world above this. I promise you, Gamma; when we get to the new place that awaits us we will. Your sister will have to live with it. Or die. Do you see how strangely she is acting?'

Gamma smiled at him, unhappily. 'Yes, I cannot read her now, Krave. I don't know what she's thinking. Maybe it's all connected, I mean all this and me and her.'

Krave pulled her close to him. He traced a finger along her ear. 'At least, we have each other to look forward to. Go to your sister now, she's watching us and looking very, very jumpy.'

Chapter Forty-two

THE VALLEY was deceptive. The crossing was not as level as it first appeared.

They found themselves descending further and further into a narrowing canyon. The tops of the mountains on either side of them came together and formed a high-vaulted tunnel.

The further down they went the hotter it became and the more signs of life they glimpsed. Shadowy creatures with wings drifted above their heads, ignoring them completely. Finally from the rocky outcrops behind which they hid themselves they saw small groups of Verheerans - Females with dark glowing hair, taller than the tallest Innoveran with pale faces and glistening eyes. Some of them were so pretty and slender it took their breath away.

By this time Blu Tara and Gamma were the only ones not bothered by the heat.

Just when they thought there was no end to their descent, they emerged into a place so different from the one above, some of the Students thought that they had finally arrived.

It was as if they had just stepped out of a furnace into a world of freezing air and ice. The water-sky was no longer above them. The ceiling of this world was rock. It went on and on way beyond their vision.

They found themselves at a crossroads. Two pale paths ran on either side of them. And directly ahead was a dark, wide road at the end of which they saw what looked like rows upon rows of Pods.

Just past that there were taller structures crowding against each other with openings at their sides. Verheerans floated in and out of them in streams. Somehow Ayana knew that they were in the heart of Verheer.

'Their city,' Ayana said to no one in particular.

'Looks like,' Skylar's thought-voice echoed in her head.

Ayana gasped. Their powers had returned.

'Where now?' one of the students asked.

Ayana knelt and brought her face down close to the mirror of her Sylva. Sure enough her scars were different. The crossroads was outlined there. A dark peeling patch of grey was just under her temple. Past the patchy scar on her face there was a pale circle on her jawbone.

Ayana lifted her head and scanned the distance. Beyond the city, on a rise directly over it there was something pale and circular, almost like a cloud. It stood out because it seemed to have no place in this dim domain.

'There,' she said, pointing past the city. 'That is where we have to get to. And then...' She could find no more words to speak for she was struck with terror.

'How do we get there?'

'There's just two ways,' Ayana answered. She hesitated briefly. 'Over it or through it.'

In the silence, Ayana closed her eyes. 'Which is the best way, Vinton?'

Vinton who had disappeared once they entered Verheer, did not answer her.

Ayana turned to the others. 'We make our way above it.'

'What are waiting for?' Skylar urged. 'Let's go!'

Skylar turned to the rest of the group. 'Speed,' he said. 'We fly as fast as we can. But we leave no one behind. Now is not the time for caution. Speed is what will save us! You hear me? Little Healer's shield won't protect us either. It will only slow us down. On my word! Let's go!'

They took off in a rush, gliding fast beneath the rocky roof but not half as fast as they wished. There was something in the nature of the air that slowed them down.

They were directly above the city when what looked like black rain rose up from below and cut through a group of Students that flew underneath the others. No sound came from them. They simply tumbled from the air stiff as rocks and hit the ground.

Krave shot ahead with Gamma beside him. They followed his fast zigzag pattern over the city.

But now at the edges of their vision, rising from the city below in waves they saw a sea of fast-approaching lights, and knew that Verheer had been roused and was after them.

Ayana sensed that the students who had been knocked down would be food for these strange Beings who, for some reason, gained something extra from the life-force of Innoverans.

They hurried on, but with the Verheerans closing in on them so quickly it felt as if they were moving at a crawl.

They arrived with little time to spare. What they saw in front of them was a pale sharply rising rock-face with a transparent arch carved into it, like the entrance to the Learning Dome.

But there was no doorway. There was no opening that they could see that would let them in. It was smooth except for five small holes that occupied its centre. Besides they had so little time. They could hear the rush of wind against the wings of the approaching Verheerans. In panic and desperation, Skylar threw himself against it. Nothing happened.

'Maybe it does not open from outside,' Krave said breathlessly. 'It makes sense; doesn't it? Else the Verheerans would get through. That means someone's got to get inside to open it for us.'

Taqua stepped forward.

Gamma shook her head. 'No! Taqua, I do not think.'

'Why not!' Taqua replied.

'Something's not right about this, Taqua, you've been taking all the risks so far. It's always you Ayana sends in first.'

'She does not send me in, I choose to go!' Taqua retorted. 'Can anyone else here do it?'

'We have no time.' Krave was looking anxiously behind him. 'Either we do this now or we get out of here, fast.'

Ayana's Sylva was humming nervously under her. 'It is the place,' she said. 'It has to be.'

Taqua ran up to the door and began to liquefy. They had never seen her move this fast. Before they knew it she was pouring herself into the lowest hole.

Nothing happened. Ryder peered in. He turned round to face them with a puzzled expression on his face.

'Where is she?' Gamma tremored. The mysterious girl had not appeared on the other side.

Gamma raised her hand against her temple. Krave grabbed her wrist and pulled her back.

'If you bust it open, it will stay open for anything else to get in.' he said.

Ryder's voice cut through the confusion. 'Innoverans! They're almost on us. We can't stay here. We have to move.'

Ryder's cry shot through them like a jolt of electricity. They streamed away from the rock-face, again, following every one of Krave's evasive turns.

The Verheerans slowed down briefly turning sharply away from the pale rocks before resuming the chase.

Now they were bathed in the cold light of the chasing Verheeran eyes.

Krave urged them on. 'Stay together,' he commanded. 'Only spread out if I tell you to.'

A wave of screaming reached Ayana. She did not have to look back. It was the sound of her companions at the tail-end of the group, being systematically cut down.

'We have to turn around and face them,' Gamma screamed..' Blu Tara! Where's Blu Tara! We have to face them and fight back! Blu!'

'We cannot do it here; they'll surround us. There!' Krave was already heading for a rising wall of rocks directly to the right. 'We hit back with our backs against that.'

Once there, they turned to face the oncoming legion and as they spun around Ayana felt something in the students change. It was the same feeling she experienced when they retaliated against the Living Rock of Oron. Already, many of them had perished on this short flight to this wall of rock against which they were now defending themselves. These creatures with pale faces, streaming hair and burning eyes had sucked the bodies of their companions into their own as if they were made of water. Those who stood their ground with her now, were no longer afraid.

Gamma placed herself in front. On the way she called for Blu Tara many times, but her sister was nowhere to be found. The tall, fiery Innoveran planted her hands on her hips and stood in the midst of her own swirling inferno.

'Come!' She raged at the tumultuous army. 'You've got to get through me first!'

She swung her arms in a wide arc. Loops of fire rolled out of her, cutting a devastating path amongst the Verheerans. But still they came.

Krave leapt forward throwing himself at the dark army, his golden body weaving amongst them like a crazy Starfly. He was no longer a lovely rainbow-colour gold but a murderous blue-white pillar of pure energy, scattering the oncoming warriors. Frying to a frizzle those who dared to lay their hands on him.

And still they kept on coming.

Skylar stepped directly into the path of the oncoming Verheerans, as casually as if he were taking a stroll through the Living Forest. The Verheerans flocked him, their coat-wings outstretched to engulf him. It was a mistake.

His hair came alive, the great green strands wrapped around the bodies of the enemy followed by horrible tearing sound. They fell away from him like rags.

The younger students called upon gifts they barely knew they possessed until this moment. Some made walls of solidified air in front of them; feathers became flaming darts and shot from them in volleys. The Izus threw themselves in, allowed their rock-hard bodies to be enfolded then exploded, taking dozens of Verheerans with them as they died.

It dawned on Ayana right there, in the middle of it all, that this was what Odors Apeno had been preparing them for.

All the games and play-fights, the Sky-Roll contests, the tournaments of Catch and Dodge, the Game of Blades, the races to and from the Ishu Mountains; all the new powers they acquired just before the Alignment were preparation for this one moment in their existence when it meant fighting for the one thing that was more precious to them than their own lives. Hope - Hope for a purer, higher form of Being.

Ryder made a propeller of his spear and sent it off. The sound of the spinning weapon filled up Verheer. It created a crashing whirlwind that spun the enemy away in droves.

And yet they kept on coming – a numberless army rising out of the Abyss determined to crush and consume them.

To the right of Ayana a different type of Verheeran appeared. They were like those she first saw at the lava stream. A volley of black darts shot out of their bodies. One struck a student in the face and she fell rigid like a stone to the depths below.

When the second volley came Ayana was prepared. She focused, raised her hand. The objects froze mid-air. Ayana raised the other hand and sent them back. They ploughed into the enemy and threw them backward in a twisting shrieking heap.

Yet the battling Innoverans were having little effect on the attacking hordes. The more Innoverans they destroyed, the more they seemed to multiply. It was only a matter of time before they were swamped.

Ayana sent desperate thought-words to her companions 'We have to break away. We have to get back to the entrance.'

'There is no entrance.' A desperate voice replied.

'There is. We just have to know how to get in.'

Ryder's thought-words cut through. 'We need to stop them or stall them. We have to combine.'

After his first attack, Ryder had pulled back. A couple of times, Ayana felt his whole attention focused on her. He was protecting her and, she thought, ignoring the plight of the others. Did he feel she would be grateful to him for that? And there was Krave out there risking his life for the others. Did Ryder really think that he could win her over with that attitude?

'What do you mean – "combine"?' she said.

'Make a mind-wall around us, Ayana. Leave us an opening right there.' Ryder pointed directly ahead of her. 'Everyone get behind Little Healer. Ayana, can you do that?'

'I'll try,' she said.

'No time for trying,' he replied, 'You have to do it.'

Ayana focused and concentrated as the Students gathered hastily behind her while Gamma kept the enemy at bay with floods of raging fire.

'Krave!' Ryder's voice was hard and chilly. 'Throw everything you've got at them when I give the word. Skylar, you guard that opening for us. Let no one in or out.'

'Gamma,' he called, 'throw them a sheet of flame as wide and hot as you can make it. Krave you combine with her.'

Ryder looked at their mystified faces. 'Trust me,' he said. 'Ready?'

Ayana steeled herself and reached into the minds of all the Students. She tapped into their life forces. As she did so, her heart sank. She left Innovera Yakov with five hundred of them behind her. Now there were only eighty.

She made the mind-wall, deciding that she'd rather die than allow it to break or weaken. She knew this was their last chance. She hoped that Ryder knew what he was doing.

She looked out at the Verheerans beating against her shield. She caught glimpses of these ferocious Beings: toothless mouths, fluorescent eyes, finned feet. And that cloak she thought was a garment was an appendage that grew from their bodies. Ice! Where was he? And where in the name of Odors Apeno was Blu Tara?

'Now!' Ryder's command sliced the air.

A flattened swathe of fire shot from Gamma's eyes, flaring ever outward until nothing could be seen beyond it. A jagged web of bright blue light exploded from Krave's arm. It danced like liquid in the air and was swept forward in the tide of Gamma's flames.

There was not a Student who did not thrill when it was Ryder's turn. His was always a dance - a sparkling whirling spin before he released his spear. It left his hands in a bright streak. It hit the path of light and fire that Krave and Gamma just let loose, and then the weapon began its deadly stirring whirl. For a moment the brightness lit up everything around them. The world shook, and then there was nothing but emptiness and silence in front of them.

'Quick,' Ayana urged. 'Follow me.'

Their progress back was slow. They were exhausted and they knew they were not strong enough to resist another attack. They soon caught sight of the structure in the distance – standing in a pale, slightly glowing mist.

Gamma flew as high as she dared and calling after Blu Tara, hoping to catch sight of the blue glow of her twin.

Krave followed just behind her, trying his best to hurry her on.

It was clear to everyone now that these two were together. And in the New World - if they managed to get there - they would merge.

Ayana could not prevent the flush of envy that filled her heart. The image of what they might become dazzled her mind. She could see them now – an amazing new fire-creature with golden wings so powerful, every living Being in their new world would bow down to them.

Ayana's thoughts turned to Taqua. What happened to her? Why did she disappear so strangely? And that door...it looked so much like that of the Learning Dome.

Something was nudging her, somewhere in the back of her

mind. It persisted even when she tried to dismiss it. It had something to do with an entrance, the breaching of it, the number three and her being the last to enter.

Then suddenly it all came flooding back: that last dream she had before leaving Innovera Yakov.

Only your favoured five must breach that entrance for one, from which is no returning. You shall be the last to enter, then it will begin by ninety and by ninety you'll begin.

One of what? Five of what? What five things did she possess that she, Ayana, favoured? Ayana stroked her face and then looked down at the surface of her Sylva. She parted her hair. Her heart somersaulted. Her face was clean and smooth. She had no more scars.

It shocked her that she was not flushed with joy. Now that she had what she always wanted; what she would have given everything she had for, she realised how lost she was. There were no more marks on her face to guide her.

My favoured five? What do I possess that numbers five? She touched her face again and froze.

'My fingers,' she whispered, incredulous. 'The hand I favour most – is my left hand. Of course!' Now it all made sense. The portal had only five holes. She visualised them as she saw them earlier, and Ayana smiled.

She sent urgent thought-words to the others. 'I think I know the way in now.

CHAPTER FORTY-THREE

THEY ARRIVED at the clearing with a shout of jubilation and relief. Ayana did not feel the same joy as the others. Taqua was not there.

'Taqua, where are you,'she whispered. And then, accusingly, 'Odors Apeno, is this the way it has to be? Must every Being I cherish disappears or die? What reason is there to go on? Is this a punishment? What have I done?'

Ryder touched her arm. 'We must hurry, Little Healer.'

Ayana raised her hand and reached for the holes in the rock. Just then, a sensation of coldness descended upon her. She looked around quickly and saw the Students half crouched, hugging themselves and shivering. A bright blue light fell on them from overhead. Then came the humming.

With a racing heart Ayana swung around to pinpoint its source. *Blu Tara*! Or rather the monstrous shape rising from the Abyss behind her – a monster of some sort with widespread wings and eyes as large and glowing as twin moons.

She barely registered the monster. Her heard jerked away from the burning eyes to the figure that sat astride its neck. Ice! He looked more even beautiful and forbidding.

Even in the semi-darkness of his world, his pale face glowed. Beside the stranger, Blu Tara glided.

They were flanked by Verheerans - a different kind. They were as tall as Ice, with eyes of burning amber. Ayana stretched her arm again to slide her fingers into the holes but something closed around her heart like a fist and she fell backwards off her Sylva. As she fell, she glimpsed Ryder just about to lift his spear.

Before he could throw his weapon a great spurt of smoke emanated from Ice's chest and struck Ryder. It lifted the tall spearman and dashed him against the rocks. Skylar leapt at them with whirling fists. He too was caught up in the air and dashed against the rocks. Krave dived high and fast. A few of Ice's soldiers rose with him, wrapped their wings around his feet and he plummeted to the ground. He hit the rocks so hard Ayana felt the vibrations through her body.

In an instant Ice's army formed a ring around them while he hovered above them all.

Gamma stood petrified, looking up at the stranger and her sister. At Ice's side, Blu Tara looked a perfect match - her face as grim as his, her eyes a dark crystalline blue.

'Tara,' Gamma called. Her voice was small and puzzled.' Blu Tara, why?'

Ice turned his head. Even the creature on which he stood turned its eyes on Gamma. When Ice looked back to Blu Tara, his eyes were like floodlights on her face.

Still he said nothing. He opened his coat and raised his head towards the rock-roof.

'Itania,' he said. Ice's voice was a whisper and yet its echo filled their heads.

From the moment Ice said 'Itania' something about Gamma changed. She became paler. She began to sway. Her voice was different when she spoke. It sounded younger, dreamier.

'That is my name. Why do you call me by that name?'

Ice leapt from his mount and stood in front of Gamma. His hand shot out and touched her face. Gamma was still swaying and talking to herself. It looked as if she was about to faint and yet she did not fall.

Ice said the name again. Gamma stooped with shaking head, her face towards the ground. She struggled to stand but she could not manage it.

'Is it you?' Ice said. 'Itania? Your voice lives in me. I touch, I feel, and I know.'

Blu Tara appeared suddenly beside Gamma.

Ice's voice rose above their heads and cut through the air like a blade. 'Who is this ghost that wants so much to take your place?'

Blu Tara dropped to her knees. 'Ice – all this I did for you. Haven't I fed you? Haven't I proved myself enough? Haven't I been loyal? Haven't I done all your bidding? Look! Look!' Blu Tara bowed her head and hunched shoulders exactly as Gamma. She became a pale gemstone pink. Now it was impossible to tell the difference between the two girls.

'Look at me, Ice.' Blu Tara turned up her face to the Verheeran, 'I can be her if you want.' Her voice was sharp and edgy and she sounded breathless. 'I am her, and she is me. Don't you see? We are of the same flame. Take me! Not her. I am already yours. She's forgotten you. She does not want to be with you. I do! I've done everything you asked. I've killed for you and I will die for you. Ice!'

Blu Tara turned to Gamma. Her voice was low and pleading. 'I've been to the Abyss with him. I've sat beside him in his domain. I know this now, Gamma. You - daughter of our Sun-world - will not survive this darkness. You'll be consumed by the cold. I do this for you.'

Ice raised his arm. The great creature turned burning eyes on Blu Tara. She immediately fell silent.

'Love does not forget.' His voice rang through the Verheeran air as if they were in a vaulted room. Like the creature, his eyes had brightened to a searing white. 'What are you! So many seasons of my time you wasted. Who are you?'

Blu Tara squirmed and shook her head, defiantly.

Pinned down under Ice's glare, something was clearly happening to her. She was shivering and squirming. She screamed as a pulsing blade of light from Ice's eyes struck her. She pulled herself to her feet. Another pulse of light brought her to her knees. It was clear that she was struggling to break loose. With a scream that pierced Ayana's very heart Blu Tara ignited. And that frightening destructive rage that every Innoveran recognised and feared was printed on her face. 'I will destroy...everything...I...'

'Impossible!' Ice shot into the air. A blue stream shot out of his eyes and hit her. Blu Tara's flame went out as if she had been doused. She turned pale white under Ice's bright blue gaze. Blu Tara began clutching at her chest.

'You're killing me,' she gasped. 'Release me – please. I did everything for you.'

Blu Tara's voice rose to such a pitch, even Gamma – still trapped in her dream-state – winced.

With half closed eyes, Ayana lay where she fell and observed the stranger who she used to follow in his world and desire with a swelling heart.

Now that she could see Ice in the flesh; now that she saw his cruel powers, Ayana wondered what, in the name of Odors Apeno, could have made her long so much for this pale, destructive creature.

Even from the distance where she was lying, she felt the

chill emanating from his body. *How could anything so beautiful be so evil?* She began edging her way towards the portal.

Krave exploded from his captors in a rage of beating wings. Ice touched his cheek and blew. Krave's body spun in the air and struck the portal. He lay still.

Once again Ice turned his attention to Gamma.

The moment he did so, with a cry that cut through Ayana's heart, Blu Tara broke away. She took to the air in a blinding leap. Everything about them lit up. A wave of blistering heat washed over them.

She is going to…

Before Ayana could complete the thought, Ice had taken to the air, his massive wing-coat spread out like an avenging Aarvol. He was spinning as he rose. Stirring up the air into a freezing whirlwind, he drew up beside Blu Tara and his eyes became a pulsing green. The light that came from him ran along her like a liquid. She screamed again as she cartwheeled in the air, her body flung downwards in a brutal arc. She hit the rocks beside the portal, bounced and remained unmoving.

Ice hovered in the air. 'You who are nothing but a thieving ghost. You dare deceive me!'

The Verheeran soldiers had broken their ring around them from the time Blu Tara broke away. Their eyes were all turned towards Ice and strange sounds were coming from their mouths.

Ayana knew that this might be their only chance. She crawled towards the portal stumbling over Krave. She had no time to heal him and yet she was tempted to risk everything and do it now.

She touched Krave briefly and he stirred. 'Get up, Krave. You have to get up now.'

Every part of her was hurting but she ignored the pain. She lifted herself to her feet and slotted her fingers into the rock. The rock-face shimmered and warm air brushed her face.

Ayana made urgent, secretive gestures to those who were nearest to her, and were partly hidden by those in front. A couple of them rushed for the door but were immediately thrown back.

'Single file,' She whispered. 'We can only enter one-by-one. It has to be single file.'

She crouched at the entrance of the portal, her heart beating so hard she felt that it would choke her.

There was no way their escape wouldn't be noticed as their numbers began to dwindle. The younger Students had already managed to drag in a barely conscious Skylar, along with Ryder who still looked stunned. In their haste to rescue him they had left his spear outside. They completely ignored Blu Tara.

All the younger Students had slipped in when a fluttering of wings made Ayana turn her head. Krave had risen to his feet. He'd somehow made his way to Gamma and was standing over her. Gamma was still rocking her body and muttering to herself.

Krave was bending to lift her when Ice's green light fell on him. Ayana expected Krave to fall screaming the way Blu Tara had done earlier. Krave did not even waver.

Something was happening to him. His wings seemed to be unfolding forever. They were twice as large as she had ever seen them and had become a blinding silver. His body swelled. His eyes were now a pulsing indigo and his golden hair was covered in a web of writhing energy.

Each of his hands had changed into the talons of his Aarvol friends and on his right shoulder was a bright curve of metal that shimmered like Ayana's Silva.

Ayana sensed a new energy in Krave Solan. It had suddenly come upon him, and she recognised it as the force that the Voice had so often spoken of at The Learning Dome. The power came from placing the life of another Being above one's own; that special power which only came from love.

A sound of metal scraping on rock came from Ice. It had a strange effect on the Verheerans. They, along with the great beast backed away from Krave and Gamma, leaving an open space between them.

'You!' Ice said, 'Innoveran Stardog, you die right here.'

'You will not have her,' Krave growled. 'Over my dead body.'

'So be it!' Ice hissed. 'You ran away last time. You have nowhere to run to now. I will have her. Then I will watch you die'

Another metallic sound from Ice and a flock of Verheerans rushed Krave. Krave stepped forward to meet them. And as the last of the students filed into the portal Ayana stood at the entrance and watched Krave tear into the Verheerans, scattering them like dried Golkan leaves, his shimmering wings remained spread out like a silver barricade between his attackers and Gamma. The last one came at him from above. Krave did not even look up. He dropped to his knees and shot an arm straight into the air, impaling his last attacker on his talons. When they were all spread out before him in an untidy heap of broken limbs and writhing bodies Krave shrieked like an Aarvol and rose to his feet.

From inside the portal, Ayana could hear Skylar raging. But she knew he could not come out again to fight with him. *that entrance for one, from which is no returning.*

Krave took to the air. Gamma was out there on her own now, with the other Innoverans keeping one eye on her and another on the battle.

A rain of darts streamed from Ice's open coat. A dancing, blistering ball of energy peeled off Krave's arms and reduced them to ashes. Ice spun fast, creating a chilling whirlwind. The Escapeet brought his hands together in a violent thunder-clap. Krave reeled back. Ice moved in quickly and folded his coat around him. From Krave came the long and musical Aarvol cry. The blade at his shoulders curved down swiftly. Ice blocked it with an arm and as he did so, the Aarvol cry came from Krave again. His wings shot out, thrusting Ice in a dizzying spin. The Verheeran recovered instantly, sending threads of smoke towards Krave. Krave dived. Ice thunder-clapped his hands and Krave reeled back struck again by that invisible force. He fell like dead-weight towards the rocks.

Ayana reacted so quickly, she barely realised it. She hurled a thought shield under Krave. It cushioned him and set him upright in the air. He spread his wings and began to climb.

'You will not have her.' He shouted. A salvo of white energy rolled off his body wrapped around Ice and sent him spinning towards the rocks. Again Ice recovered in that magical way of his. That strange metallic sound again. This time something dislodged from the high rock-ceiling above them and fell on Krave.

Krave was stunned. Ice moved in again and enfolded him in his coat. Ayana turned her head away. She could not watch him die; and yet, she could not prevent herself from looking up.

Krave's bright curved blade appeared, flashed once – lighting up everything around them and Ice spiralled away.

Now that Ice had backed away Ayana picked up Krave's life force. He was weakening. Some kind of poison moved inside him.

And yet, when Ice moved in for the kill, Krave held his ground. There was a burst of the green liquid light from Ice again. Ayana gritted her teeth, dug deep into her own life force and encircled Krave with her mind shield. The effort brought her to her knees. But she held it even as she felt the full force of Ice's murderous attack.

Krave dropped from the air like a stone and hit the ground near her feet. His body touched her, Ayana felt his life force fade.

With what little remaining strength she had Ayana held onto Krave and began to drag him towards the portal.

In that moment Gamma screamed. Ice lifted one hand and his soldiers surrounded her. Gamma screamed again and ignited briefly. Ice's gaze swung towards her.

Ayana called upon her powers and with all the strength she had, pushed Krave's body through the portal.

'Now,' the Students shouted, 'We go now!'

'We cannot leave Blu Tara,' Ayana said and reached down to lift the girl.

'We must,' Skylar growled from inside. He had recovered enough to speak. He was bending over his brother with his hands cupped around his face.

'She is the cause of all this.'

Deep down Ayana agreed. Why should she save Blu Tara? This Female who scorned her, undermined her leadership before they even began this journey; who made the life of every Innoveran miserable. Struck fear in their hearts and would destroy anything to serve her selfish desires – why should she save Blu Tara?

Apeno's words came back to mind. *Even evil has a purpose; you will see.*

'I must,' she said finally, 'It is Apeno's bidding.'

She had Blu Tara in her arms when Ice's cold white light fell on her. Sobbing with the effort, she looked up. He was hanging in the air looking down on her.

'You, Being of two faces,' he said. 'I have puzzled over you too many times. Inside, you are an Earthbound. Outside, you are a Being of a world or worlds I do not know of. It is why I must consume you. So that I can better understand.'

Ayana looked up at the stranger. A great calm came over her. She no longer felt afraid. She had done her best. Most of the others were safe. Like Apeno himself said. *What is one life to many?*

'You,' she said, looking up at Ice. 'You cannot love; you have no heart. There is something about you that puzzles me too. How could a Being this beautiful be so full of ugliness?'

Ice's eyes dimmed. She felt something tighten in her stomach. She remembered the sensation. It was the same as that last time in her Pod when he had taken control of her body.

'Come to me.' His voice echoed in her head. She struggled to shut him out of her mind but she found she could not do it. 'Come. I promise you this: it is a far better death than the one that faces you.'

She tried to move back but her feet would not obey her. She cried out but no words came from her.

As Ayana took the first step, a green face popped up in front of her.

'Wake up, Myana. You no wake up now. Paleface make food of you. Go!'

Vinton's voice had exploded in her head so loudly it jolted her out of her trance. Ayana spun around and shoved Blu Tara towards the portal throwing herself after her. Strong hands dragged them in.

As her body hit the floor she saw the doorway shimmering. And Gamma! Gamma was still out there! As the portal closed, all Ayana saw was Gamma's outstretched hand, her desperate screaming face as Ice alighted beside her and lifted her onto his mount.

The portal shimmered once then they found themselves in complete darkness.

Skylar dragged Ayana towards Krave. 'Save him,' he said. 'I can hardly feel him. He – he is almost gone.' Skylar's voice broke in her ears.

Ayana doubted she could save Krave as she'd done once before. In the darkness of this portal, she had no moons to call on and after shielding Krave then dragging him and Blu Tara in, her inner energies were spent. It would take some time to renew – time she did not have.

But she had an idea. It fact it was something she had just learned from Krave.

She lay down beside him on the cold rock-floor, took his hand and rested it against her heart. She placed her lips close to his ear and whispered. 'O Golden One, love gave you the power and strength to fight Ice. Let it make you strong again. Let it make you live – for Gamma; for the promise I heard you make to her at the beginning of this journey. You cannot die Krave, while Gamma is out there waiting for you to reclaim her. And if this love I have for you is real, then I give it all so that it may strengthen you and have you return to us.

And may the arms of Apeno embrace you now.'

Ayana kept her eyes closed with Krave's hand still pressed against her heart. She knew that however softly she had spoken, everyone would have heard her. She did not care. And gradually, from somewhere deep inside Krave she felt the stirrings of his life force - faint at first, but growing stronger with every breath.

She touched his face and sent caressing thought-words into him, realising that this great golden Male was not for her; that Krave Solan would never been for anyone but Gamma.

It was a while before he sat up. The vault that they were standing in echoed with the Students' cheers.

Ayana slowly rose. Skylar pulled Krave to his feet and held him close. And all she could hear was the distressed muttering from Krave's throat: Gamma! Gamma!

'I tried,' Blu Tara said suddenly. 'I-I tried to save her.' The girl lowered her flaming head and knelt shaking on the floor. Everyone ignored her.

CHAPTER FORTY-FOUR

THEY WERE in a cavern. The nature of the room in which they stood had changed suddenly. The walls were dripping and the sand under their feet kept shifting. The light that surrounded them when they entered was no longer there. Ayana looked at the narrow grey path ahead and felt uneasy. It was not at all what she had imagined. Not like the pathway to the New World that Odors Apeno promised them.

They were hemmed in on either side by steep walls that disappeared into complete darkness overhead. They were forced to walk in single file. Ayana walked ahead, while Ryder chose to be the last one in the line. He kept looking back as if he expected his lost spear to appear at anytime.

As they progressed, the smell of burning reached them. Soon rumbles and sighs and groans surrounded them.

'Is this it?' came a Flitter's distressed voice.

'It is the only way,' Ayana replied.

'That smell,' whispered Skylar leaning close to Ayana. 'Doesn't it remind you of something?'

'Yes,' Ayana whispered back. She sent him private thought-words. 'Living Rocks. And we're right inside. Don't tell the others, please.'

Where have you sent us now, Apeno? What more do you want of us? Haven't we done enough?

She recalled the last words of the Voice; they were engraved on her mind. She mulled over the riddle.

Only your favoured five – my left hand, that's done - *must breach that entrance for one* – only one of us entered at a time, done - *from which is no returning* – once inside we could not go back, also done - *You shall be the last to enter* - I was - *then it will begin by ninety...*Ninety what? It had to be a count – a count of what? It was surely not about the number of Innoverans that remained - only fifty of them were left now.

Then it struck her. As with the Living Rocks over the ocean of Verheer, they were given a limited amount of time before they sensed their presence and came to life. It was a countdown and they must already be at least seventy Innobeats inside these Living Rocks. At the most, they had twenty Innobeats to get out.

Ayana sent urgent thought-words to the students. 'Innoverans, it is not over yet. We must move as fast and quietly as we can. Walk softly; do not speak. Please trust my words. In fact, I think we have to run. We're inside Living Rocks!'

As if sensing their fear and urgency the ground began to shift. Fear gave them speed, although they could barely see ahead. They forged forward, with Ayana in the lead. A few of the Students used the glow of their skins to light the way. The rocks vibrated violently. The path began to close in.

Then suddenly there was no longer slipping sand beneath their feet, but gravel and a yellow glow ahead. The rocks around them heaved more violently this time and the sound that came from some deep place inside them was like the roar of a toppling mountain.

But they were there – almost. Just when they tumbled out into the open space, they heard a Flitter scream. It had just managed to escape but one of its wings had been snapped off completely. Deep within the belly of edifice there came another rumble, then a shout. Then silence.

'Ryder!' Ayana screamed. 'Ryder has been taken.' She sank to the ground and held her face in her hands.

Skylar held her arm and pulled her to her feet.

'Little Healer,' he said his voice dropping to a croak. 'Ryder's gone but...look at what lies ahead of us.'

Ayana followed his outstretched arm with her eyes.

From where they stood she looked out on a more frightening world than she could ever have imagined. Many of her companions were weeping as they too realised what lay ahead. They were on a bare mountain. Many mountains retreated into the distance. They pushed their flaming summits into fiery boiling clouds. Great rivers of melted rock flowed down their sides and made gigantic lakes of lava at their feet.

There were creatures too - the largest they had ever seen, with tails as thick as Golkan trees. Some were double-headed. Many were locked in battle, or feeding on their vanquished prey. From the mouths of those that flew in vast flocks above the smoking land, streams of smoke and fire spouted in huge bright columns.

There was no horizon either - just a wall of blackness against which there was a single bluish glow.

Ayana remembered Ice's words: *it is a far better death than the one that faces you.* This, she realised, was what he meant.

The last words of the voice, *... it will begin by ninety,* came to her again. It all made sense now. Everything made sense.

Stunned, she turned around to face her companions. They were too defeated and tired to protest. But on this high peak above that horrible boiling valley with flying monsters feeding on each other, every Student looked betrayed.

It was Krave who spoke at last. 'Apeno has deceived us. Taken away everything. Who wants to believe in a Being like that – one whose words cannot be trusted?'

With a trembling voice Ayana answered him, 'If we believe we're lost, then we're all defeated. Apeno may be cruel, but He cannot lie. Verheer was a distraction. It was just a passage to the portal.'

Ayana raised her voice in anger and defiance, 'Innoverans, we have not been deceived; we simply did not understand. It is from here that The Journey really begins. And there,' she pointed at the only patch of brightness against the distant wall of darkness. 'There is the world that awaits us.'

'And how do we get there?' Skylar growled. 'We cannot run; we cannot fly; it is impossible to walk. Tell us, Little Healer – tell us how we get there!'

'We will,' Ayana said. 'If we don't believe, Skylar, then all our struggles, all our losses will have been for nothing. If we don't believe, we're as good as dead.' Ayana looked around her nervously. 'We cannot remain here any longer. We have to move on. We have to find a way.'

'How?' Skylar demanded.

'I do not know,' Ayana answered. 'I honestly do not know.'

It was then they heard Blu Tara's voice. It was tired and subdued. 'It is like the world I come from, when our universe was born,' she said. 'I-I think I know a way out of here.'

Skylar drew himself up to his full height and glared at her. 'How can we trust you now, Blu Tara? After all you've done?'

'You have no choice,' she told him quietly. 'You can come with me, or remain here and die.'

Lightning Source UK Ltd.
Milton Keynes UK
UKOW042159260313

208228UK00001B/1/P

9 780957 531406